A TASTE OF TH

"My work is to discover why the food from this garden affects what people feel," Adair said, stepping a little closer.

"Why is that so important? It is what it is. It does what it does. It harms no one."

"It harms you."

"Nay, it—"

"It harms you. It causes talk, dangerous talk. Dark whispers of magic."

"Not everyone thinks such things."

"I want the whispers stopped. I dislike the thought that I might be dragged from my bed some night because some fools have gotten themselves all asweat with fear and are determined to root out the evil at Rose Cottage."

Rose took a deep breath to steady herself only to feel her breasts brush against Adair's broad chest. She knew he had drawn close to her, but not that close. That nearness made it difficult for her to think clearly. She was far too aware of his strength, his size, and her own deep attraction to the man.

"Lass, ye must openly deny there is magic here. Ye must show people that there are reasons why your food tastes better, why your garden stays healthy nay matter what afflicts the others."

Adair closely watched her face. He fixed his gaze upon her mouth. For now he would help himself to a little of what he wanted. Adair almost smiled when her eyes slowly widened as he lowered his mouth to hers. . . .

—From "The Magic Garden" by Hannah Howell

<u>BOOK YOUR PLACE ON OUR WEBSITE</u> <u>AND MAKE THE</u> <u>READING CONNECTION!</u>

We've created a customized website just for our very special readers, where you can get the inside scoop on everything that's going on with Zebra, Pinnacle and Kensington books.

When you come online, you'll have the exciting opportunity to:

- View covers of upcoming books
- Read sample chapters
- Learn about our future publishing schedule (listed by publication month *and author*)
- Find out when your favorite authors will be visiting a city near you
- Search for and order backlist books from our online catalog
- Check out author-bios and background information
- Send e-mail to your favorite authors
- Meet the Kensington staff online
- Join us in weekly chats with authors, readers and other guests
- Get writing guidelines
- AND MUCH MORE!

Visit our website at
http://www.kensingtonbooks.com

MAGICALLY DELICIOUS KISSES

Jo Goodman
Hannah Howell
Linda Madl

ZEBRA BOOKS
KENSINGTON PUBLISHING CORP.

http://www.kensingtonbooks.com

ZEBRA BOOKS are published by

Kensington Publishing Corp.
850 Third Avenue
New York, NY 10022

All Kensington titles, imprints and distributed lines are available
at special quantity discounts for bulk purchases for sales promotion,
premiums, fund-raising, educational or institutional use.

Special book excerpts or customized printings can also be created
to fit specific needs. For details, write or phone the office of the
Kensington Special Sales Manager: Kensington Publishing Corp.,
850 Third Avenue, New York, NY 10022. Attn. Special Sales
Department. Phone: 1-800-221-2647.

Zebra and the Z logo Reg. U.S. Pat. & TM Off.

First Printing: November 2002
10 9 8 7 6 5 4 3 2 1

Printed in the United States of America

CONTENTS

A BASKET OF MAGIC

Jo Goodman

Chapter One

January 1867
Dover Falls, Virginia

No one knew him. Not really. In some places this might have been a deterrent to gossip, but not in Dover Falls, where the townsfolk improved upon their ignorance by simply making things up. The tales they told about him were essentially harmless, though early on there had been a rumor that he had murdered his wife up North. It had circulated once, then abruptly died because there seemed nowhere to go from there.

He might not have occasioned tales at all if he had been less standoffish. His unpardonable sin was that he kept to himself, didn't bother anyone and didn't make a bother of himself. Unlike other people who lived on the outskirts of town or farther afield, he was not sociable when he journeyed in for his supplies. He did not inquire after Mrs. Fitch's health when all everyone else was talking about was whether she would survive the delivery of twins. He did not ask about Mr. Kinsey's recovery from the gout, or make a single inquiry as to the progress of the fund-raising for the new parsonage. If it occurred to anyone that he might not know Mrs. Fitch or Mr. Kinsey, or even that there was an effort afoot to build a parsonage, it would have only offered further proof that he was not one of them. Indeed, it underscored the generally held opinion that he had not made an effort to be included.

They had tried, of course. The preacher made the journey to Sperry Gap to introduce the stranger in their midst to God. He was turned away before he reached the cabin by a creature he swore was more wolf than dog. The fact that he made this oath on his own Bible lent the story sufficient veracity for those few skeptics still dwelling in the town. Miss Florence Henry, Dover Falls's schoolteacher since before the war, also took the trail into the foothills of the Blue Ridge to discover whether the newcomer might have children in want of learning. She met the same wolf-dog as the preacher and returned to town without an answer to the question of children or, more importantly, whether their neighbor was attached or spoken for. The last person to attempt a trek to the cabin was Mr. Imans. As the owner of the town's sole bank, he announced that he had a duty to secure and protect the stranger's assets, assuming there were any. He got farther than Reverend Pritchard and Miss Henry, making it all the way to the flagstone path that led to the cabin's front door. When he saw that door open he was in expectation of a warm welcome becoming of his status, not the leaping, snarling beast that was released.

The facts were these: His name was Kincannon and he was a Yankee.

The townsfolk learned his surname right off from Mr. Winslow, who owned the mercantile store where Kincannon was extended a line of credit, the same as if he had lived in Dover Falls all his life instead of only the last six months. It was Mrs. Winslow who apprised her friends of Kincannon's north-of-the-Mason-Dixon origins. Boston, she suspected, because of his peculiar drawl when he asked for lard and barley flour. She'd heard the likes of it before, when the Bluecoats tore through Dover Falls on their way to Port Republic in June of '62. That accent did not endear Mr. Kincannon to her, though she allowed that his money was as good as—and sometimes better than—anyone else's.

Abby Winslow knew something more about him, but unlike her aunt and uncle, she kept the particulars close. It was not terribly difficult to embrace these secrets. No one suspected she was privy to things they weren't.

She knew, for instance, that his Christian name was Dylan. She'd seen the letters DK stamped on the leather satchel he carried into her uncle's mercantile. People in Dover Falls would have been surprised that she'd had the temerity to inquire about them. In truth, she had surprised herself. She did not have a forward bone in her body. If there had been someone else in the store she would not have put the question so baldly, but she had been left alone with him while her uncle was filling a sack in the back room, and for once the silence was discomforting.

"Is it Douglas?" she'd asked.

He had blinked then. For a moment his dark lashes shuttered gray-green eyes, and when they lifted the expression in them was not unwelcoming, but rather mildly amused. "Douglas?"

Abby remembered she had pointed to his satchel. It was soft brown leather, scarred, worn, and faded to butter yellow on the rounded corners. The long strap that hung from his shoulder was in better condition and hinted at what the leather had looked like when it was new. The underbelly of the satchel bulged a bit, but the shape gave no hint of the contents. "Dee Kay."

"Aaah," he'd said. "Is it D for Douglas? No, it's not."

"Oh." She had turned to go. From the upstairs kitchen the warm fragrance of baking bread had caught her attention, and anyway, he had answered the question she'd put to him.

"Fey creature."

She'd never been called that before, or at least that description was not one she had ever overheard. Peculiar was the adjective most often used. Sometimes they whispered that she was an odd little thing. Those who were given to plainer speaking said she was not quite right, though they stopped short of pronouncing her daft. While these descriptions were not a kindness, neither were they cruelly meant. The intention was only to set her apart in some way, to comfort those repeating the words that whatever it was that made her different could not be visited upon them.

She had a timid smile, and on this occasion it was a trifle uncertain. It was not that she didn't know what fey meant, but that she wasn't clear if his purpose was to condemn or compliment. She could not get the sense of it from his expression, for the amusement she'd glimpsed earlier had vanished and he was studying her features with a certain intensity about his own, as though he were committing the shape of her raised face to memory. She'd stared back at him, too, giving as good as she got, though she was hardly aware of it at the time. If she'd known the thrust of her chin was almost childishly defiant she would have dropped it a fraction and concentrated on narrowing her eyes to add strength to her scrutiny.

What she did, though, was sniff the air. "My bread!" Lifting her calico skirts, she'd started for the back of the store on a run.

"Dylan."

Abby didn't stop to acknowledge that she'd heard him, but later when she returned and presented him with two warm loaves of anadama bread, the truth of it was in her shy glance.

He had looked from her upturned face to the bread she held out to him. He could smell the cornmeal and molasses and breathed deeply of the fragrance that reminded him of his mother's kitchen. "This is New England bread," he'd said.

"Yes."

"And you made it for me."

She nodded.

"But you didn't know I would be here today."

She had known, but she didn't want him to think she was peculiar right off so she merely smiled.

He took the loaves from her outstretched hands, raised them closer to his nose, then set them on the counter with the rest of his supplies. "Anadama. Did you know I'm from Massachusetts?"

"I've heard it, yes. Boston, they say."

"Framingham."

Abby's smile touched her eyes this time, though her thick lashes hid it from him. Framingham. It would tickle her lips to say it aloud. It was musical, just like his name was musical. Dylan Kincannon. Dylan Kincannon of Framingham.

She decided then and there that the wolf she'd heard about was not this man's familiar.

"I don't think he's coming," Georgia Winslow said. She ran her hand briskly over the red-and-green-plaid gingham lying on the table, smoothing the ripples in the fabric so she could make a clean cut. She picked up her shears, examined them for sharpness, then looked for her mark on the material. Without raising her eyes, she added, "You may as well take that bread back to the kitchen. We can have it with our stew."

Abby glanced at the rounds of potato bread she had prepared only that afternoon in anticipation of Mr. Kincannon's arrival. Golden brown and still faintly warm, they spilled over the top of the willow basket. She unfolded a blue-and-white-checked towel and tucked it carefully over the cornstarch-glazed crusts. "I thought I might take them out to Sperry Gap."

Georgia almost cut the tip of her index finger with the point of the shears. She looked up sharply, her brow furrowed. Clearly her niece had been struck by another peculiar notion. "To Sperry Gap? Tucker's cabin is what you mean."

"That is where Mr. Kincannon lives, isn't it?"

"You know it is." Georgia's mouth puckered, then twisted to one side. The expression might have been comical if it had not been so severe. "A Yankee in Tucker Maddox's cabin." She shook her head as though not able to grasp the truth of it. "He must be rollin' in his grave. Your uncle won't allow it, Abby. It's not safe. Not now."

"Because of the weather?" It had been raining since yesterday morning and at the elevation of Sperry Gap there was likely to be snow. A lot of it.

"No. Not because of the weather." Georgia spoke with a slight pause between each of her words, as though Abby might not understand her if she strung them tightly together. It was the cadence one might use with a child—or a slow wit—and though Georgia understood her niece was neither of these things, she erred on the side of caution, wanting to make certain she was being clear. "Because of the wolf."

Abby said nothing for a moment. She drew in her lower lip instead and worried it gently between her teeth. "I don't think there really is a wolf," she said at last.

"Nonsense. Miss Henry saw it. And Mr. Imans. Reverend Pritchard, too. You believe the preacher, don't you?" Georgia did not wait for a reply because it did not occur to her that Abby would find fault with her logic. "There's some that say Mr. Kincannon *is* the wolf."

There were still some in Dover Falls who said the world was flat. Abby wisely refrained from pointing this out. She'd heard the stories about the shapeshifting but thought they were meant to frighten the children from going where they ought not to. Sperry Gap was a narrow pass, given to rock slides and avalanches depending on nature's whims, and presented a considerable and dangerous obstacle to all but the most intrepid. Abby had already considered that Mr. Kincannon had got himself trapped on the wrong side of such a thing. There would be no delivering his potato rounds if that were the case. Until the weather changed to something drier and considerably warmer, the Yankee could be assured no one would come trespassing.

Abby picked up the willow basket and slid the handle over her forearm. "I'd like to go anyway."

"Oh, do be sensible. Take the bread to Mr. Malley. He'll be grateful for it and will pay you right away."

Abby shook her head. "I didn't make this bread for Mr. Malley. It wouldn't suit him. I made it for Mr. Kincannon."

Georgia sighed. This idea that Abby had, that the bread she baked was somehow intrinsically suited to the person for whom she made it, was easily her most peculiar notion. "Just for me?" people would ask when they received a loaf of cinnamon or pecan date or black bread from her. And when Abby said yes, that she'd made it just for them, she meant it in the most literal sense. There was no one in Dover Falls who did not appreciate Abby's bread, even if the presentation of it was often a trifle odd. Some people, in fact, encouraged her to open a shop next to her uncle's mercantile so she could sell her bread and pastries and turn a profit, instead of being content only to recover her costs. Abby always listened politely to their suggestions, just as she always declined to act on them. It would never work, she explained patiently, because someone might choose the wrong loaf.

When Georgia heard her niece talk that way, she invariably set her mouth in a tolerant smile and rolled her eyes ever so slightly. In this manner Georgia let everyone know she was in no way responsible for Abby's out-of-the-ordinary opinions. Having made her position clear, she could then comfortably return to whatever bit of gossip was occupying them. Lately it had been strange wolves and stranger Yankees.

"I suppose you're telling me that we cannot have the potato rounds either," Georgia said. "You know your uncle likes them."

"He wouldn't like these," Abby told her. "I put caraway seeds in them. Seeds don't sit well with him."

That was certainly true. Her husband would be up the better part of the night with indigestion. Georgia did not want that, but neither did she like the idea of the bread going to waste. She was not running a charity, even if Mr. Winslow did extend credit to his customers. "Very well. Ask your uncle if you can go." Abby was hurrying off before Georgia finished her sentence. She called after her. "And fix your hair. You know I can't abide . . ."

She didn't bother with the rest. Abby was already out of earshot.

It was dusk when Abby set out for Sperry Gap. Her uncle was not entirely in favor of her trek, but neither was he willing to say no. Abby could tell he did a lot of thinking before he finally gave her his nod. It was followed by a considerable number of cautions that Abby patiently listened to out of a deep respect for her uncle. Edward Winslow was her father's brother, now her only living blood relative, and he had not hesitated to send for her when he learned his brother and his brother's wife were dead. The last influenza outbreak before the war had taken them both, and once Abby was removed from quarantine, he traveled to Richmond himself to get her. There had been some misgivings among the townspeople about bringing her back, but her uncle had threatened to collect on their credit, then move his mercantile. That had been eight years ago, when Abby was only twelve, and it marked the last time anyone in Dover Falls had seriously taken issue with Edward Winslow. Three months after Abby's arrival he'd been elected mayor and had served in that position ever since.

At her uncle's insistence, Abby wore a wool-lined slicker over her gingham dress and a pair of his black leather knee-high boots over her more delicate shoes. She did not have to make the trip on foot, but had the use of the buckboard wagon and the dappled mare. Her uncle helped her load the back with the supplies Mr. Kincannon typically asked for on his twice-monthly sojourns to town.

It was at the point he was helping her climb onto the buckboard that he asked again if she was certain she should go. Even before she spoke he knew what the answer would be. It was there in the gravity of her expression, in the solemn and searching violet eyes and the way she pressed her lips together so the curve of them disappeared. There was little about his niece that reminded him of his brother because in so many ways she was her mother's child.

Rosalie had known things. Little things. Sometimes important things. It was her gift and her curse, and she'd run away to Richmond with his brother to escape it. It was Rosalie who wrote to him and told him she and Samuel would be dead by the time he read her letter. Abigail would survive, she'd written, and she was trusting him to come for his niece and raise her as if she was his daughter, not hers.

He'd learned later that Rosalie had penned her letter before either she or Sam had had the first signs of the illness. He did try to make sense of it but eventually accepted that there was no accounting for some things. Rosalie had simply known the truth and had acted on it. Abby, he had long suspected, was not so different, and Rosalie's attempt to shield her daughter in his care changed nothing.

From the porch of the mercantile Edward Winslow watched his niece release the brake on the buckboard and snap the reins once. He stood close to the steps as Georgia hovered behind him in the doorway. Rain spattered the toes of his boots and occasionally pelted his canvas apron. He stepped back when Abby disappeared into the fog that was slowly rolling into the far end of muddy Main Street.

Abby had not left the town proper before she supposed her uncle was regretting that he had let her go. It was because she was special to him, not peculiar or odd. He never once rolled his eyes at the things she said or suggested that she should open her own shop. When she said she *had* to go, he didn't ask her what she meant. What he wanted to know was if she would return safely, and she had been able to answer that with an unequivocal yes.

"Are you worried about the wolf?" she had asked him. "There isn't one, you know. Aunt Georgia and the others are wrong."

Edward Winslow had not seemed as certain about that as she was. "There're wolves," he'd told her a shade gruffly, remembering Kincannon's narrow-eyed interest in Abby. "And then there're wolves. See that you know the difference."

Leaving Dover Falls behind her, Abby wondered if she did.

Dylan Kincannon looked up from his reading, his head cocked slightly to one side. He cupped his ear, trying to get a better sense of where the sound was coming from and, more importantly, what precisely the sound was.

He put down his journal and pushed himself out

of the rocker, almost tipping forward when he set too much of his weight on his right foot. Grasping the table beside him for support, Dylan steadied himself on his left foot, then reached for the walking stick he'd fashioned from a good piece of black cherry. The satiny, reddish-brown wood was warm and smooth under his palm and he relied on its strength to help him get to the window.

The moon was full, but the curtain of steadily falling snow made it difficult to see much farther than ten yards beyond the cabin's porch. The ground cover also muffled the approach of his visitor, though the regular rhythm suggested it was something mechanical he was hearing and therefore of human origin.

Dylan leaned his walking stick against the wall and shrugged into his leather coat. He didn't take the time to button it, but turned up the fur-trimmed collar so it protected the damp, curling ends of his ebony hair. After removing the maple stock Winchester rifle from the wall rack, Dylan opened the door and gingerly stepped onto the porch. He did not go far. There was no purpose in allowing anyone to see that he was limping.

In the distance he could make out the arc of a swinging lantern. It seemed to wink at him as it moved back and forth between the trees. At first he thought someone must be holding it, then realized it was too high off the ground. That was when he identified the sound he heard as the intermittent but unvarying staccato of a squeaky wheel.

A wagon? The notion was astounding. That anyone would come within two hundred yards of Tucker Maddox's old cabin after the banker had been run off was surprising. That it would be attempted after nightfall was even more unexpected. First it was the parson, then the schoolteacher, and finally the banker. Dylan shook his head. If he had known this place would attract as many curiosity seekers as a Barnum sideshow, he would have stayed in Framingham. There, at least, he had family to hold back the tide of visitors.

He could hear the snuffling and plodding of the horse that pulled the wagon. The arc of lantern light was insufficient for making out the identity of his uninvited guest. Perhaps, he thought, it was no one from Dover Falls, but simply someone passing through who had been attracted to the lighted windows of his cabin. That made a kind of sense to him, though why a traveler was out so late in these conditions was still mystifying.

Dylan hefted his rifle under his arm. The barrel pointed a little wide of the wagon's approach but could be brought quickly to the target if necessary. In his peripheral vision he saw Ulysses pad quietly around the corner of the porch and take the three steps in a single leap. The dog circled Dylan's legs twice, as if trying to make up for his serious dereliction of duty, then sat on his haunches and whined softly for attention, supremely unconcerned by the imminent arrival.

"Where have you been, boy?" Dylan let his fingertips graze Ulysses's head. "Chasing deer? Raccoon? You see we have a visitor, don't you? Perhaps more than one."

Ulysses pushed his nose at the back of Dylan's knee with enough pressure to make the leg buckle.

"Hey!" Dylan scolded the dog softly. "You're going to make me fall." He rested his shoulder against the door and struck what he hoped was a casual pose, not an injured one. "Why aren't you running out there? Something wrong with your howler?"

Ulysses set his cold nose against Dylan's leg again and whimpered.

Dylan looked down at the dog and shook his head. "Pathetic." The wagon would reach the clearing in another minute and Ulysses remained supremely unconcerned. There wasn't enough time to think about whether that boded ill or was, in fact, a sign there was no trouble coming. Dylan relaxed neither his guard nor the position of the Winchester.

Raising his voice so he could be heard over the noise of the horse, the wagon, and the squeaky wheel, he called, "Stop right there." He squinted through the plump flakes of snow and saw the lantern complete its arc, then become still. There was only a lone figure on the buckboard seat and he made a slight silhouette, huddled as he was against the cold. "What purpose do you have here?"

Before there was an answer, Dylan felt Ulysses brush his leg as he got to his feet. The dog ambled to the edge of the porch, stood there a moment as if taking stock of the situation, then jumped to the ground and trotted off in the direction of the wagon. "Traitor," Dylan said under his breath. He almost asked the stranger what he'd done to his dog. Where was the teeth-baring snarl that had sent Reverend Pritchard running? Or the aggressive growl that threatened Miss Henry? What had happened to the crouching and leaping predator that set Mr. Imans back on his heels and then on his backside?

Dylan watched with something akin to horror as Ulysses made the jump to the buckboard's seat and cozied right up to the stranger.

"Your business," Dylan called again. "Come here, Ulysses." The dog whined, but he didn't disobey. He came right back to the porch and put himself at Dylan's feet.

"He's a noble beast," Abby said. "Did you name him after the hero of Homer's epic?"

Dylan thought that after witnessing Ulysses's odd behavior he couldn't be surprised again this evening. Now he realized he had been overly confident. He peered more closely at the figure hunched atop the buckboard. "He's named after the general."

"Oh. Well, you might want to keep that to yourself. People in these parts aren't kindly disposed toward the general."

"I'll keep that in mind."

Abby nodded. "May I bring the wagon up to the porch? I have your supplies." When he didn't say anything, she added, "It's me, Mr. Kincannon. Abby Winslow from the mercantile."

Dylan placed a little weight on his injured foot. It was the equivalent of pinching himself, and when pain shot up his leg from his heel to his hip, he was that much closer to believing this was no dream. "What the hell are you doing here, Miss Winslow?"

"Didn't I say? I've brought your supplies." She lifted the lantern from the hook on the edge of the seat and held it close to her face. "Can you see me, Mr. Kincannon?"

"I can see you." He did not issue an invitation for her to approach the cabin. "I didn't ask you to come out here."

Abby replaced the lantern. "Of course you didn't. How could you?"

Her practical tone made him blink. It was as if she suspected he was the one with bats in his belfry. He could have told her that he'd spent very little time in Dover Falls before learning that *she* was the town's quaintly queer one. Complete strangers had offered that information to him when he merely had inquired about the direction of the mercantile. "Indeed," he said dryly. "How could I?" Dylan lowered the barrel of the Winchester to the ground. "Very well, bring the wagon here."

Abby replaced the lantern and flicked the reins. The mare strained at her halter once, then pulled the buckboard forward. Abby brought her alongside the porch and applied the brake.

Dylan kept his post at the door, but that traitor Ulysses eagerly took himself off again. The shepherd paced off a few feet beside the wagon and made several quick figure eights while he anxiously waited for Abby to alight. Dylan decided there was no harm in finally asking the question. "What the hell did you do to my dog?"

Abby slid to the edge of the bench and jumped lightly to the porch. She bent and scratched Ulysses's head. The dog crooned softly and all but lay prostrate at her feet. Smiling, she glanced up at Dylan Kincannon. "I fed him," she said simply.

One of Dylan's dark brows lifted. "You fed him what?"

Straightening, Abby shrugged. "A biscuit."

"A biscuit."

"Several biscuits, actually."

Dylan jerked his chin toward the back of the buckboard, where his supplies were covered by a large oilcloth tarpaulin. "You gave Ulysses *my* biscuits?"

"Oh, no."

"Then . . . ?"

"I made biscuits for him."

"Of course."

She nodded. "He wouldn't have liked yours." Her broad-brimmed felt hat tipped back a bit and revealed a fringe of gold-and-ginger hair across her forehead. "Do you want me to put your things right here on the porch, or shall I carry them inside for you?"

"Miss Winslow." Dylan addressed her with an exaggerated air of patience. "Do your parents know you're here?"

"No."

"I didn't think so. You—"

"They're dead." She regarded him now with a slight frown creasing her brow. "But then, there's some that say there's no accounting for what those who have passed on know. Do you believe that?"

He was not going to entertain a philosophical discourse here at his front door. "Put the things on the porch." He watched her turn away, seemingly oblivious to his tersely phrased command or the fact that he wasn't going to help her. "Come here, Ulysses. Get out of her way." The last thing he needed was Miss Abby Winslow tripping over his dog and going head over bucket down the steps. Whimpering, Ulysses did as he was told.

Abby loosened the cords that held the oilcloth in place, then peeled it back. It looked as if everything had been kept dry. She dragged a sack of flour close to the edge of the wagon, then grabbed it by the ears and hefted it over the side. "You don't want to let this dampen," she told him. She reached for another sack and repeated the motion, swinging it easily so that it landed softly at her feet.

Watching her, Dylan was struck by the easy rhythm of her movements, the natural grace that was inherent in each twist and turn. He wondered that she did not expect him to lend a hand. He couldn't think of a single woman of his acquaintance, starting with his own sisters and mother, who would have set to work with such straightforwardness. There was no feigned helplessness, no coy look from beneath a fan of lashes. Even in Framingham the females knew something about pretending to be the gentler sex. Apparently it was a lesson that Miss Winslow had no use for.

A sack of dried beans thumped to the floor of the porch, drawing Dylan from his reverie. "Who are the Winslows to you?"

Abby did not stop working. "My aunt and uncle."

"And they know you're here?"

"Yes."

It was hard to believe, yet she didn't strike him as someone who lied so easily. His eyes followed the willow basket she drew from the wagon all the way to its placement on the porch at her feet. "What's in there?"

"Potato bread rounds."

As impossible as it was, he swore he could smell the warm fragrance of the loaves. "No anadama?"

"No."

Apparently she thought no explanation was necessary. Dylan suspected he'd regret putting the question to her. "Why not?"

"It wouldn't suit."

Yes, he regretted it. What she had given him was no answer at all. "Why not?"

"You're surly. It's sweet." Abby climbed into the back of the wagon to remove three small casks and two parcels that were neatly wrapped in brown paper and tied with twine. "There would be an argument in your stomach."

"An argu—" He stopped, shaking his head as if to clear it. "I am *not* surly."

Abby hunkered down in the bed of the wagon. Lantern light washed her features in a pale golden glow. "I suspect it's because you're in pain."

Dylan was quite certain he had not given himself away. "What do you mean?"

With more directness than was her usual way, Abby Winslow merely stared at him. After a moment she jumped softly to the porch. The hem of her dress ballooned a little, revealing the ruffled edge of her petticoat and the oversized boots she was wearing. She quickly smoothed her slicker down and drew her feet closely together.

"Your boots?" he asked.

She shook her head.

"But they're your feet?"

"Yes."

He almost smiled at the gravity of her tone. She didn't seem to know he was teasing her. In light of his surly mood, it surprised him a little as well. "You'll be going now." There was not a question. There was no inflection or even the lift of a single dark brow to punctuate it or make it a friendly inquiry.

"If you like."

"I do."

Abby looked over the supplies she had unloaded. She did not make the mistake of offering to carry them inside a second time. Lowering the brim of her hat, she gave him a short nod. She climbed back on the buckboard and picked up the reins.

"Have a care, Miss Winslow."

"Good night, Mr. Kincannon." She prepared to release the brake.

"Wait a minute." He took a careful step forward and managed not to wince. "How did you know I wasn't coming to town tomorrow to get these supplies?"

"Tomorrow the gap's going to be closed. You'd find it hard traveling to take the roundabout route." Abby hesitated, uncertain if she wanted to say more. She had probably already said too much.

"Hard traveling because . . . ?" His voice trailed off in anticipation of her finishing his sentence.

"Because of your injury."

"My injury?"

"Your foot."

He actually sucked in his breath. "How did you know?"

"You favored it."

"Until a moment ago I hadn't moved."

"That's curious, don't you think? You came outside to confront a trespasser and never stepped away from the door. You didn't help me unload the wagon and didn't move out of the way to let me take your supplies inside." Though Abby made her presentation with a certain matter-of-factness, she was a trifle breathless by the end of it. She added one more observation. "Since you lowered your rifle you've been leaning on it for support."

Dylan's dark brows lifted in unison. "So it wasn't a premonition?"

"A premonition?"

"Second sight."

"Is that what you've heard?"

It was one of the things he'd heard. Having Abby Winslow confront him so directly made him feel a little foolish for entertaining the suspicion, no matter how briefly.

"They say you have a wolf here," Abby said. "Some say you *are* a wolf. People come by peculiar notions in Dover Falls."

That he could believe. "Which is why I like it here in Sperry Gap."

"Alone."

"Yes." He would not apologize for it. He saw her lift the reins. "One more thing, Miss Winslow.

How do you know the gap's going to be closed tomorrow?''

Abby's smile was like quicksilver, transforming her features for the brief moment it was visible. "Oh. *That's* a premonition.''

He winced then, rocking back on his heels. Before he could call her back she had dropped the brake and snapped the reins. Shaking his head, bemused, even a bit enchanted, Dylan Kincannon watched her go.

The first indication he had that something was wrong was Ulysses's incessant pacing. In the beginning he supposed it was because the Alsatian was missing Abby Winslow or her biscuits, or perhaps both. He couldn't remember the dog making up to a stranger so quickly. He called Ulysses over, scratched behind his ears, but the animal apparently didn't find his touch as soothing as Miss Winslow's. Instead of lying down, Ulysses pawed the ground, then let out a high-pitched whine that made Dylan wince.

When Ulysses remained restless, wearing a path from the chair to the window and back again, Dylan was finally moved to look outside himself. The snow was falling more heavily than before and the occasional thin shafts of moonlight merely illuminated an impenetrable curtain. "It's no good, boy. I can't see anything.''

Then he felt it. The ground rolled oddly under his feet so that Dylan actually vibrated with the force of it. There was a groaning and a rattling of the cabin walls as the structure shuddered. Hanging pots swayed on their hooks. The cast-iron skillet clattered on the griddle. In the hearth, the ladle slipped inside the soup kettle. The ladder to the loft shifted sideways. A candle was set askew in its holder. Dylan's journal thumped hard to the floor and the picture above the stone fireplace dropped to the mantel.

It was over in a matter of seconds. Dylan turned away from the window, surveyed the cabin, then eyed Ulysses. Swearing softly, he raked back his dark hair. "You know what that was, don't you?"

Ulysses went straight to the door and began pawing it.

"I suppose you do. Let me get my coat." Even using an economy of motion, Dylan's foot and ankle were throbbing by the time he stepped outside. The sharply cold air made him forget the pain for a moment, but it returned with a vengeance as he saddled Phaedrus. With Ulysses making a nuisance of himself, the gelding was not particularly cooperative about letting Dylan mount. The strain showed on Dylan's features in the small creases at the corners of his eyes and the tightness around his mouth.

Holding a lantern in one hand and the reins in the other, Dylan set off for the gap. Ulysses's pattern of bounding ahead, then circling back, was often repeated on the journey. Dylan didn't try to keep him close. It seemed to him that Ulysses understood both the direction and the urgency of their mission but was unwilling to completely abandon him.

At times the pines and hemlocks sheltered Dylan and Phaedrus from the heaviest of the falling snow. The appearance of the full moon was rare now. Dylan could only make out the suggestion of light from behind the thick clouds. Phaedrus unerringly kept to the trail, though that path was no longer clearly marked. It was for his own benefit, not his mount's, that Dylan kept the lantern raised. Even watching as closely as he was, it was difficult to make out the tracks of Abby Winslow's wagon. He did not want to think ahead to what he would have to do if they disappeared entirely.

It did not come to that. Ulysses found her first. A great deal of excited barking accompanied his discovery, and to be certain Dylan did not mistake his meaning, the shepherd circled back and ran tight rings around Phaedrus before he bounded off again.

Dylan caught sight of the buckboard before he saw her. The wagon was standing a short fifty feet from where the wall of snow and stone had finally come to rest. Because of a broken axle and two shattered wheels, the wagon was canted at a forty-five degree angle. A large boulder lay beside the buckboard and splintered wood from the wagon's bed and wheels were scattered around it.

He thought she was dead, struck down by flying debris or perhaps from a glancing blow of the same rock that destroyed the buckboard; then he realized that her position was all wrong. She was not sprawled facedown in the snow yards away from the wagon or forever frozen in a rictus of pain that told of her last breath.

What she was, was sleeping.

Abby Winslow had survived the avalanche that had shaken the foundation of his cabin five miles distant and was now faced with the danger of freezing to death. She had made a decent shelter for herself in the lee of the canted buckboard, but she had overestimated the oilcloth's ability to protect her against the cold. The tarp that had been spread over his supplies was now Abby's ground cover and blanket. She lay huddled with her chin tucked and her knees drawn close to her chest. She looked

small and infinitely vulnerable in the shadow cast
by the wagon against the lantern light.

Ulysses threw himself on the ground beside her,
lending his furry heat to her body. Dylan urged
Phaedrus closer before he dismounted. Dropping
to his haunches, he placed one hand on Abby's
shoulder and nudged her. "Miss Winslow?" She
stirred but did not open her eyes. He tapped her
cold cheek lightly with his index and middle fingers. "Miss Winslow?" Like a kitten in want of
stroking, she moved against his touch this time,
lifting her face so her cheek lay cupped in the palm
of his hand.

Dylan let his hand fall back to her shoulder. He
gave her a second shake, more insistent than the
one before. This time her lashes fluttered open.
She raised her chin above the edge of the oilcloth
and gave him a sleepy, unfocused smile. "So you've
come for me."

"Another premonition?"

Abby shook her head slightly. "No," she said.
"Hope."

He had to brace himself against that softly spoken
word. Hope was something he hadn't allowed himself to feel for so long it hadn't occurred to him
that he might extend it to others. He set the lantern
on the ground so the circle of light spilled over
the snow. "You should have hoped for something
better than me," he said roughly. "Can you get
up?"

More alert now than she had been moments
ago, Abby nodded. "Yes. Of course." She pushed
herself upright without any assistance from Dylan
and unwound the oilcloth. Abby bit down hard in
an effort to keep her teeth from chattering, or
at least to keep him from hearing it. It worked,
although the rest of her slender frame shook in

response. Beside her, she heard Dylan Kincannon grunt, as if he suspected the attempt she was making and did not approve.

Abby shed the rest of the oilcloth and rose to her knees. The unfamiliar chill made her bones ache deeply and she was put in mind of Mrs. Imans, the banker's wife, whose rise from a sitting position was slow and stiffly awkward.

Dylan held the edge of the buckboard as he pulled himself to his feet. He allowed most of his weight to rest on his left foot as he extended his free hand to Abby. "Take it," he said when she hesitated. "This much I can do."

Afraid of offending him, Abby slipped her gloved hand into his. She was pulled up so quickly and easily that for a moment she thought she would simply fall forward into his arms. She stopped just short of that, coming to stand almost toe to toe with him. When he released his grip she hugged herself in spite of the peculiar heat that was beginning to warm her.

"Can you ride?"

Abby nodded. She had unhitched the mare from the buckboard earlier, but the animal hadn't gone far. "Sally was skittish after the slide. She wouldn't let me on her back."

Dylan accepted this explanation without comment. He had wondered why she hadn't tried retracing her route to his cabin. He picked up the lantern and swung it upward to get a better view of the rock and snow that filled the gap. It was clear to him why she hadn't attempted to go over it. The face of it was daunting, a craggy mass of icy boulders and snow-packed crevices. Even as he studied it there was shift somewhere in the wall. A fissure appeared, and the loosened rocks rolled down the face in a shower of white powder, bouncing, grinding, groaning, until they landed at the foot not far from where he and Abby stood.

Casting a suspicious sideways glance in Abby's direction, he asked, "You didn't bring it down, did you?"

Abby's mouth flattened at the absurdity of the question. "Those last few rocks?" she asked. "Or do you mean the entire hillside?"

Her quiet sarcasm was not lost on Dylan. Lowering the lantern, he gave her a considering look. "You did tell me you expected it to come down."

"So I did. Tomorrow."

"It is tomorrow."

"Oh."

"And here you are."

"Yes," she said. "I am. But I expected to be on the other side." Abby felt Ulysses rub against her leg. She bent slightly and scratched his head. "Your dog's not afraid of me."

The observation made Dylan blink because there was something in her tone that implied that the same could not be said of him. It was on the tip of his tongue to tell her that he certainly wasn't afraid of her, but she glanced up then and her eyes, for all their guileless appeal, seemed to know far more than he did. What he might have said came to nothing. Instead, he turned away and mounted Phaedrus, glad that she could not glimpse his pained expression as he did so.

Abby picked up the oilcloth and neatly folded it to serve as a blanket over her dappled mare's back. She did not expect or ask for help mounting the animal, but eased Sally's restlessness by stroking her neck and standing on tiptoe to whisper in her ear. Taking hold of the harness, she led the calmed mare over to the wagon and used one of the broken wheels to give herself a leg up. Once mounted, she nudged Sally forward.

Dylan watched this without saying a word. It had been his intention to draw her onto Phaedrus once he was settled. Now her self-possession gave him pause. What sort of woman was it that allowed herself to hope he would come yet expected nothing of him?

As soon as Abby had drawn close Dylan flicked the reins and Phaedrus moved ahead, picking his way around the splintered wood and scattered rocks. They rode without speaking, even after a second resounding crash made the earth rumble under them. Dylan imagined Abby's buckboard shelter crushed beneath the weight of the rocks and snow. Judging by the paleness of her complexion when he glanced back at her, she was imagining the same.

When they arrived at the cabin Abby drew abreast of Phaedrus and relieved Dylan of the lantern. She watched his painful dismounting in silence. "I'll see to the horses," she said. Before he could decide differently, Abby slid off Sally's back, placed the lantern on the steps and led both horses off in the direction of their shelter.

Dylan did not go inside until she returned. He opened the door and waited for her to enter the cabin before he did the same. "Let me have your coat," he said. "Then warm yourself at the fire."

Abby slipped off her slicker and gloves and handed them over. She had already taken a step toward the hearth when she felt him pluck the broad-brimmed hat from her head. Her thick braid uncoiled and dropped in a straight line down her back. Self-consciously, Abby's hand lifted to her scalp. She smoothed the crown of her gold-and-ginger hair before she brushed at the loose strands that had fallen over her cheeks.

Aware of Dylan's regard, Abby quickly closed the distance to the fireplace and thrust out her hands. The tips of her fingers tingled as heat flushed her skin. Ulysses joined her, dropping to the braided rug with a snort of contentment.

"His work's done," Dylan said dryly. "And he is pleased." He finished shrugging out of his own coat and hung it up. His cane was lying on the floor. He bent and picked it up, using it for support while he stood there and contemplated his chances of crossing to the rocker without an ignominious fall.

"May I help?"

Her soft query did not register with him at first. It was the echo of her words that he heard coming out of his reverie. He nodded once and held up his arm, slightly bent, so that it would fit around her slim shoulders. She did not look as though she could bear his weight, but he knew differently. Miss Abigail Winslow, graceful reed that she was, took him on with steel in her spine.

After hobbling to the rocker, Dylan was grateful to sink down onto its worn seat and against its smoothly spindled back. Abby dropped to her knees in front of him and pushed the three-legged upholstered stool under the foot he had favored. When she looked up at him she saw his jaw was tightly clamped. The pain that he would not let her hear was around his eyes for her to see.

"I should cut away your boot," she told him.

"Like hell."

His reply was not unexpected. They were a fine pair of leather boots he was wearing, comfortably creased but not worn to cracking. Droplets of melted ice beaded on the toe and instep. "Very well," she said. "Do you want to take it off yourself or let me?"

He didn't want to take it off at all. That apparently was not a choice she was willing to give him. "I'll do it."

Abby sat back and watched as he slowly worked off the boot. At one point she offered him the bootjack, but he declined. She realized he did not want to place more pressure against his heel and ankle than he had to, and when she saw the size of the swelling, she understood why. Cupping his heel in her hand, she lowered it gently back to the stool, then carefully rolled up the leg of his trousers and removed his sock.

She had expected bruising, but what she saw was more than the livid discoloration of a sprain. There were deep cuts in the flesh above his ankle and along the side of his foot. The removal of the sock had reopened some of the wounds and now they were bleeding. The spacing of the cuts, their shape and size, told Abby what had happened to Dylan Kincannon as clearly as if he'd explained it in words.

Abby glanced sideways at the boot he'd dropped beside the chair. There wasn't a single tear in the polished leather. "You weren't wearing that when you stepped into the trap," she said.

"More's the pity." His voice was taut. "It would have hurt a hell of a lot less. I was wearing buckskins."

Abby's feathered brows lifted in tandem. "Then the wonder of it is that you have a foot at all."

He looked down at the offending appendage. Though it rested on the stool, Abby still cradled it lightly between her hands. It throbbed as heavily as if his heart had settled there. "A wonder," he said, a certain irony in his tone. His eyes lifted to Abby's face and he held her questioning gaze directly. "Tell me, Miss Winslow, have you ever assisted at an amputation?"

Chapter Two

Abby stared at him for a long moment, then at his foot. His question was not made in the vein of dark humor. He was truly contemplating the loss of part of his limb. Abby's mouth flattened briefly as she considered the consequences of such a loss.

Since the war she had seen a fair number of men who were missing an arm or a leg. Mr. Malley had nothing below his right knee and Brenton Harris, who owned the feed store, had lost an arm at the shoulder. Men passed through Dover Falls looking for work, struggling with a crutch or a sling and bent on proving they could still manage with one limb what they had always managed with two. For a while her uncle had employed a young man whose hand had been shattered by a lead ball at Cross Keys in '62, but he had moved on when Abby turned down his proposal of marriage for the third time.

Some of the men were still whole after their loss. They made their peace with it and carried on because life, in their opinion, meant living, and no other choice came to mind. Other men became something less than they had been. It happened first in their own thinking and then in the way they were thought of. They struggled on, objects of pity because they made no objection to being pitiable. Finally there were those caught somewhere between bitter, angry, sometimes hateful, and they stayed among the living out of sheer cussed meanness.

Abby wondered about Dylan Kincannon and the kind of man he was now. It would have everything to do with the kind of man he became. It surprised her that he suggested amputation. She would have supposed he was so purely stubborn that putting himself under a surgeon's saw would never present itself as a possibility.

"I've never assisted in a surgery," she told him.

"Never? I thought the Rebs conscripted most of Dover Falls to help with the wounded. There was fighting around here, wasn't there? At Cross Keys?"

She nodded. "And Port Republic. Our men and boys fought and our women and girls helped, but tending to the wounded isn't the same as being in the surgery. I wasn't allowed in that tent." Abby hesitated, uncertain if she wanted to take issue with him. Still, some things should be said. Some things were a matter of pride. "We weren't conscripted. We volunteered."

Dylan regarded her, one eyebrow faintly cocked. He gave her full marks for not turning away. "I apologize," he said finally. "You're right. There never seemed to be a lack of volunteers." Even at the end, he thought, they came from all over the South, some as young as eleven and twelve. They came in spite of the fathers and brothers that had gone before them; sometimes they came because the fathers and brothers had not returned.

Abby saw a passing sadness in his eyes and heard the same in his voice. He seemed to know she caught the hint of it because his expression became shuttered and whatever more he meant to say remained unspoken.

"You saw fighting?" she asked.

He did not say anything for a moment. "No, not the way you mean."

Abby simply regarded him patiently, waiting for a better explanation than the one he had offered.

"I saw the aftermath," he said finally. "At Bull Run. At Antietam. At Chancellorsville." He watched a small furrow appear between Abby's brows as she puzzled out his meaning. Her unusually colored violet eyes darkened briefly. It was when he saw them clear that he knew she understood.

"You're a doctor," she said.

"Wrong tense. I *was* a doctor."

Abby glanced down at his injured foot, then back at him. "A surgeon?"

"When I had to be." He began to withdraw his foot from the soft cradle of her palms, stopping when he felt her fingers tighten on his heel and ankle. "Miss Winslow, the foot still belongs to me. I would like it back now."

Nothing about Abby's grip changed. "You mean to cut it off."

One corner of his mouth curled, making his half smile darkly sardonic. "Not just at this moment."

Abby did not share his black humor. "You cannot."

"Probably not. At least not easily. That is why you will have to do it." He did not say the words to make her let him go, but that was their effect. Freed of her hands, Dylan gingerly set his foot on the floor and started to rise. The pain made him audibly suck in his breath.

"Sit down," Abby said.

He did.

She took his heel again and lifted it onto the stool. "Do you have a pressing engagement, Mr. Kincannon?"

The soft edge of Abby's sarcasm was almost lost on Dylan as he struggled with the needles of fire that were pressing into his foot and then pricking him along the length of his leg. "The pleasure of a dance with you?" He saw the curves of her lush mouth flatten in annoyance. "I meant to add wood to the fire, Miss Winslow. It may have escaped your notice, but you are shivering."

Was she? Abby looked down at herself and saw the light tremor in her hands. Her jaw ached from straining to keep her teeth from chattering and her shoulders were taut with the same effort. That he should be aware of her discomfort only added to it. "I'll get the wood," she said. Rising somewhat stiffly, more in an effort to affect some dignity than out of any complication, Abby went to the hearth and placed two logs on the glowing embers. She allowed the burst of heat to penetrate the damp hem of her gown until she could feel it against the skin of her ankles and knees. When the warmth finally went as deep as her marrow, Abby turned away. She didn't expect to find Dylan Kincannon watching her. She hadn't once felt his eyes on her or given a thought to his observation. It would have been reasonable to pretend that the flush coloring her face had something to do with the fire, but Abby suspected this man knew differently.

"You are staring at me, Mr. Kincannon."

Her straightforwardness made one corner of his mouth lift in a slight smile. "Yes," he said, "I am."

When he did not have the grace to look abashed or offer a modest apology, Abby felt the flames in her cheeks grow hotter. She was used to having people watch her, but it was generally done without Dylan Kincannon's frankness. The glances that followed her in Dover Falls were most often sideways ones. People were not so impolite as to stare openly. Their watchfulness was in anticipation of her treating them to some peculiarity of thought or action, and they managed it out of the corners of their eyes. In the main, she pretended not to notice the surreptitious stares. That was not as easily accomplished here.

"Perhaps you have not been told it is impolite," she said.

"I've been told."

Abby was uncertain how to respond to that. She stared back.

The faint smile playing about Dylan's mouth deepened, and for a moment the shadow of pain vanished from his features. "Good for you, Miss Winslow."

Embarrassed, but oddly flattered at the same time, Abby was glad for the distraction Ulysses provided by rolling onto his back and presenting his belly. She bent and gave the Alsatian a brisk rub. With her attention on the dog, she asked, "Will you allow me to tend your wounds, Mr. Kincannon?"

He was tempted to dismiss her request out of hand. Dylan heard himself ask instead, "What do you know about it?"

"I have no formal learning."

"That isn't what I asked."

"I know something about healing."

Dylan's dark eyes narrowed slightly. It seemed to him that she was saying rather more than he was hearing. He wished she would stop playing with

Ulysses and look at him again. It was her eyes that would give him some hint of what she was thinking. "Do you mean to save my leg, Miss Winslow?"

She did look at him then. "If that's where I have to start."

The fragrance of bread dough rising lifted Dylan from his dream to full wakefulness. His nose twitched as the blankets were slowly pulled over his face. He turned away from the damp, rough pad of a tongue lapping at his cheek. "Ulysses." Dylan batted the dog on the tip of his cold nose. "Move."

The shepherd immediately dropped to his haunches and placed his forelegs over Dylan's chest, pinning his master down to the floor pallet.

Dylan heard the unmistakable melody of laughter from the kitchen. At first the sound was as disorienting to him as the warm yeast fragrance; then he remembered that the one had something to do with the other. He glanced toward the window and saw that it was not yet fully light, but that the edge of dawn was breaking over the treetops. "You are an early riser, Miss Winslow."

Abby dusted off her floured hands on her apron and skirted the corner of the table. "You may call me Abby," she said. "There really is no point in formality any longer."

"Very well . . . Abby." Dylan pushed Ulysses off his chest and turned on his side. He propped himself on one elbow and regarded his guest with heavy-lidded eyes. Now that he was awake he could feel the slow throbbing of his injury. It was only moderately less painful than it had been before he had fallen asleep. He had no expectation that he would see the day out in less pain than that in which he had started it. "You found the bed comfortable?" he asked.

She glanced toward the loft. "Yes. Thank you. It was good of you to give it up for me."

Dylan's smile was little more than a grimace. His offer had hardly been a chivalrous gesture. The climb to the loft was more than he could easily manage in his condition and Abby must have known it. Her thanks seemed a bit disingenuous. "If you prefer to believe I was being gallant," he said, "then I have no objection."

Abby surrendered a little sigh. She supposed he meant to be disagreeable this morning. It was probably pointless to argue with him. Crossing the room, Abby dropped to her knees at Dylan's feet. "May I?"

He shrugged.

Taking that for agreement, Abby folded back the woolen blankets. The bandage she had placed around his foot the night before still looked fresh. There was no evidence that the wounds had wept during his sleep and no odor of putrefaction. She unwound the strip of cloth carefully, then examined his injury. Some of the smaller cuts were merely pink at the edges where the skin had begun to knit. Without announcing her intention, Abby rose and retrieved a basin of fresh water. "You may as well lie back," she told him. "It only makes me clumsy when you watch."

He couldn't recall that she had made a single graceless move the previous night. Her ministrations were executed with a minimum of fussing. She was cool and practical, as gentle or as firm as she needed to be. Women with her talents had been in short supply in the army hospitals. In the field they were almost nonexistent.

Dylan let himself fall back because it was a more

comfortable position. He glimpsed her small smile before his head came to rest on the pillow. She probably thought he was doing it because she had asked him to. He wasn't certain why he didn't tell her that that had nothing to do with it. Maybe it was only that he liked catching sight of that shy smile of hers.

Abby saw that Dylan had closed his eyes. She lifted his foot onto her lap and began cleaning the wounds. There were several that should have been stitched and she wondered why he hadn't. He must have had the skill to do so. "Will you permit me to close two of these deepest cuts?"

He shook his head. "I don't care about the scarring."

It seemed to her that he didn't care about losing a good portion of his leg either. She began to dry his foot. "Did you perform a great many amputations in the field?"

Dylan's mouth tightened. He did not look at her, but kept his eyes closed instead. "My share. Same as any other sawbones."

"Then you saved lives."

"That's one perspective."

Abby sensed the subject was closed. She finished drying his foot and applied the willow bark salve she'd brought with her. He flinched a little when the cool ointment touched his skin, but then she felt him relax and allow her to have her way. She appreciated that he was more cooperative this morning than he had been last night. He must have satisfied himself that she meant to do him no harm.

"It doesn't seem to help," he told her.

"You can't have it both ways," Abby said.

"What do you mean?"

She sat back and unrolled a fresh bandage. "I

mean that you'll have to decide if you're more fearful of dying at my hands or living by them. Last night you didn't want me to put the salve on you and this morning you're complaining it hasn't helped."

Dylan's smile was wry. "I suppose you think that's unreasonable."

Abby was hard pressed not to laugh. She applied the new bandage, gently tied it off, then rose to her feet. "May I help you up?"

Opening his eyes, Dylan saw she was standing over him with her right hand extended. "I can manage."

She nodded and let her hand fall away. Turning her back to let him struggle on his own, Abby picked up the basin and ointment and went to the kitchen. She washed her hands and applied herself to her bread. She removed the blue-and-white-checked towel over the bowl, took out the dough, and punched it down on a lightly floured board. When Dylan limped past her on his way to the privy Abby didn't look up from her work, though she smiled as Ulysses trotted after him. By the time they returned she had kneaded the air bubbles out of the dough and was placing it near the hearth for a second rising.

"Coffee?" she asked.

"Yes. It's in—"

"I know. I saw it when I was collecting what I needed for my bread." When Dylan continued to hover near the table, she added, "You may as well sit down. Your leg should be up."

"I only came back in for my boots. I have to get some wood."

"I'll do it."

"Like hell."

"I'll *do* it." Before there was further discussion,

Abby took her coat from the peg by the door and hurried outside as she was shrugging into it. She heard Dylan calling her back, but she ignored him. There was a cord of wood on the side of the cabin and Abby managed to load an armful. Dylan was waiting for her just inside the door, his expression thunderous.

"If you mean to abuse my hospitality, then you can find your way over or around or through that damned avalanche, because you'll not be welcomed here." He delivered his pithy speech in brittle tones, then took the stack of wood from her arms. His progress to the fireplace was uneven and halting, but he managed it without mishap.

Abby slipped inside, removed her coat, and retreated quickly to the kitchen. She wished she had another bowl of dough to punch. It would have been an immensely satisfying activity. She had to occupy herself instead with preparing the coffee and cutting slices from the potato rounds she had baked the day before. There was sweet butter that melted on the warmed bread, and she added a smear of her aunt's raspberry jam to each piece.

When the coffee was done she poured two cups and set them on the table along with the bread. She did not invite Dylan to join her, but sat down herself and supposed he would eventually arrive at the idea of coming to the table on his own.

Ulysses came first, settling himself under the table at her feet. Abby pushed the tips of her shoes under his furry belly to warm her toes and knew herself to be passingly content before Dylan Kincannon came to take his seat. Once he was slouched in the chair at a right angle to hers, her settled feeling fled.

Dylan held his mug in both hands. "This coffee's good."

Abby thought his observation was offered rather grudgingly. She accepted it politely, though not graciously.

He regarded her openly, permitting himself a small wry smile when she did not once glance in his direction. In her own way she was licking her wounds, and he wondered that she was so tender-hearted. "When I push," he said casually, "sometimes you have to push back." He saw her brow crease as she considered his advice, but her expressive, otherworldly violet eyes remained downcast and he could not divine what she was thinking. Dylan put down his coffee and picked up a slice of warm bread. He bit into it and his mouth immediately wrapped around the distinctive flavors of sweet butter and jam. More deeply, there was the fine-grained texture of the bread, the hint of potatoes and molasses and caraway seeds and . . . and something else he could not name.

"A taste of heaven." Dylan noticed that Abby seemed to accept this fulsome praise in stride. Perhaps she was used to compliments of this nature. "Did I ever tell you how much I enjoyed the anadama bread?"

"No," Abby said. "You never did."

"Then I was remiss."

She shrugged lightly. "You came back to my uncle's store."

He had. "I needed supplies." Dylan noticed the corners of Abby's mouth edging upward. The curve was so faint that it was more a suggestion of humor than an actual smile. She had secrets, this Abby Winslow. "You expected me to return, didn't you?"

"You ate the bread."

The connection between one thing and the other was not as clear in Dylan's mind as it appeared to be in Abby's. Still, he let it pass without comment.

He dropped the last bite of bread into his mouth and picked up a second slice. "We should discuss what we're going to do about getting you back to Dover Falls. The town is probably organizing a search party for you."

"No, they're not."

"Another premonition?"

"Common sense. I told my uncle I would come back safely."

"You expect him to accept that when you didn't return last night?"

"Of course. He will have to convince Aunt Georgia and perhaps a few others who might want to mount a search, but he'll have his way in the end. There's really little for them to do. The snowfall will make travel difficult and the rock slide makes the gap impassable. He won't let anyone risk their lives when he knows that I'm quite safe on this side of things."

Dylan realized Abby Winslow possessed the uncanny ability to take the wind right out of his sails. "Extraordinary."

"Hmmm?"

Until her murmured inquiry, he had not known he had spoken aloud. "I was thinking that you are quite extraordinary."

Abby was silent for a moment, thoughtful. "Is that better or worse than being peculiar?"

He managed not to choke on the bread he was swallowing, but it was a narrow thing. To be on the safe side, Dylan washed it down with black coffee. "I guess it must be better," he said finally, "though I suppose it's all in the way one thinks about it. There are worse things than being peculiar."

"Oh, I know that. I don't mind, not really. I suspect there are even some advantages. People don't expect much except that I should do the odd thing from time to time. Apparently I excel at it. Aunt Georgia says I will be the town character if I don't change my ways." Abby turned to Dylan and gave him the full benefit of her frank regard. "Though she hasn't mentioned it since you came to Dover Falls."

Dylan's mouth twisted wryly. "What qualifies me for the position of town character?"

"I'm not certain," Abby said. She pressed her lips together as she gave the matter serious consideration. "Perhaps it is only that you're a Yankee."

"That is merely a matter of geography."

"You keep to yourself."

"Yes." He paused a beat. "Though that seems to be changing."

Abby's cheeks pinkened and her eyes darted back to her plate. "People say it's because you killed your wife."

Dylan suspected his foot had been throbbing all along, yet he hadn't been aware of it since he'd taken that first bite of Abby's manna. His plate was empty and he was sorry for that, because the pain in the lower part of his leg was fast becoming pure agony. "Do they say how I killed her?"

"Strangulation."

Grunting softly, Dylan used his good foot to push his chair away from the table. He stood, bracing himself briefly, then hobbled to the rocker near the fire and sat down. He immediately raised his injured foot and placed it on the small stool.

Abby rose, freshened Dylan's coffee, then carried it over to him. "Some say you pushed her from the top of the stairs of your Beacon Hill home."

"I see. And I did this because . . . ?"

"You wanted her money."

"Then she was rich."

"That's what they say."

"I thought it might be because she was making me a cuckold."

"No," Abby said blithely. "It was because she had money." She returned to the table and began clearing it. "But that story's gone out of favor."

Dylan's tone was dry. "Really?"

"Now the talk is all about your wolf."

Cocking his head slightly, Dylan could see Ulysses stretched out under the table. His head rested on his front paws and his eyes were closed. He pointed to the dog. "That wolf?"

Abby followed the line of Dylan's sight. "I suppose so. Reverend Pritchard, Miss Henry, and Mr. Imans all say they were attacked by a wolf. People can't decide if he's your familiar or if you're the wolf."

Dylan's mouth flattened and he shook his head. "And these same folks call you peculiar."

"Yes."

"It's hard to know what to make of that."

She smiled. "Isn't it just?"

Dylan kept the shapely tilt of Abby's lips in his mind long after she turned away. She had a beautiful mouth, he thought. It was hard to believe it was not the first thing he'd noticed about her. When he'd seen her standing at the back of her uncle's store, looking as if she was working up the courage to approach him, it was her eyes that had caught his attention. Shy and direct by turns, she had tried to study him without calling notice to herself. It wasn't possible. If she hadn't finally shown her mettle, he would have made a point of speaking to her, if for no other reason than to assure himself that she was quite real. His reluctance had everything to do with discovering that quite the opposite might be true.

Abby Winslow had a bit of the fairy-fey about her. That's what his mother would have said, and he was inclined to believe her about otherworldly matters. She knew all about the wee folk and what mischief they might get up to. Dylan had grown up listening to the tales, expanding on them sometimes for the benefit of his sisters when his mother grew weary of the telling. He had been twelve years old before he questioned his mother's absolute belief in the fairies, but when he'd gone to his father there was confirmation for everything his mother said.

"You're smiling," Abby said.

Dylan blinked. "Was I?"

"Hmmm."

He watched her turn back to her work. While he had been in his reverie, fixed first on the shape of her mouth and then on all that was the rest of her, she had fetched water to clean the dishes and was now replacing mugs and plates on a shelf above the stove. "Did I fall asleep?"

She nodded. "Only for a little while."

He didn't remember slipping away or even that he had been tired. "I'm sorry."

"There's no reason you should apologize. Sleep is healing."

Dylan wondered how many times he had said that very thing to his patients. So convinced was he of the truth of it that he prescribed laudanum to ease them to sleep when they could not accomplish it on their own. "What did you put in my coffee?"

Abby slowly set the bowl of risen dough on the table. "Why do you think—" She stopped because he was looking at her with one arched brow, his features set with such patent skepticism that Abby knew he intended to shame the truth from her.

She would give him that, she decided, but had little expectation that he would believe her. "Nothing. I didn't put anything in your coffee."

His eyebrow remained exactly as it was.

Disappointed that she had been right, Abby lied, "A bit of crushed poppy."

Dylan's features relaxed. "Why?"

Abby took the dough from the bowl and began shaping it for baking. "You did not sleep well last night. I could hear you tossing. Your injury won't heal if you don't rest."

Everything she said was true, but that hardly made it more palatable. "You should have told me."

Abby merely nodded. She placed the dough in a greased loaf pan and carried it to the oven. Using her apron like an oven mitt, Abby opened the hot door and set the pan inside.

Studying her, Dylan decided she was more than simply competent in his kitchen. She was comfortable. That could not possibly bode well for his peace of mind. "How long before you'll be able to get back to Dover Falls?"

Abby ignored the rough way the question was put to her and concentrated only on what was asked. "I suppose that hangs on whether you mean for me to leave this afternoon or when there's a thaw."

He glanced out the window. It was beginning to snow again. "Of course I don't expect you to leave today."

"Then it depends."

"On what?"

"On when there's a thaw."

He actually ground his teeth then. Somehow he felt the pain all the way to his toes.

"You look as if you want to swear, Mr. Kincannon."

"I sure as hell do."

Smiling to herself, Abby turned and searched out her next chore.

Dylan faced the fire in the hearth and watched the flames lick and flicker around the freshly stacked logs. Adding the wood was the last thing Abby had done before she climbed the loft ladder. Now she was up there preparing for bed. His bed. He had found himself thinking more about that these last few nights. She was sleeping in his bed. He was almost certain he'd be able to climb the ladder if she invited him.

She hadn't, though.

She didn't seem to be aware of herself as a woman, or at least as a woman he might desire. He couldn't recall that she had ever flirted with him. The occasional wary smile or surreptitious glance in his direction hardly counted, though he found himself trying to provoke those responses from her. That smile, when it came, could be perfectly arresting.

Abby Winslow was a curiosity. In the ten days since her unexpected arrival, Dylan had not changed his opinion about that. What precious little he had learned about her only made him want to know a little bit more. He had the sense she was mostly left to herself in a town brimming with busybodies. She was not oblivious to the fact that she was set apart or in danger of becoming the town character, but neither did she pay it much mind. He thought she might have even been amused by it. The town had always been a little inclined to keep her at arm's length, she'd told him, because of who she was. It begged the question of whom exactly the gossips thought they had in their midst, but Dylan didn't ask. He cared more for his own opinion than the one held collectively by Dover Falls.

Abby was unassuming, unfailingly polite, and patient to a fault. It seemed to him that even when he was at his very worst, she took it in stride. She had learned when to stand her ground and when to return fire. Even more importantly, she knew when retreat was the better strategy. Her ability to gauge his moods as well as the bent of his mind was nothing short of uncanny.

It occurred to him that there was something of the witch about her, and when he announced this conclusion she had laughed. That, of course, was all he had wanted.

Dylan rolled onto his back and cradled his head in his hands. He stared at the rough-hewn cabin ceiling, but in his mind's eye he was in the loft with Abby, sitting at the foot of the bed while she completed her nighttime rituals.

He knew her routine, had memorized it over the course of these successive evenings. She would have removed her gingham dress and stockings by now. He imagined she folded them neatly over the ladder-back chair, examining them for stains or tears before she did so. She would be standing in her chemise, hugging herself against the cold, before she turned down the comforter or fluffed her pillow; then she would quickly run a brush through her thick hair and plait it loosely. Only then would she slip into bed.

He wondered if she slept on her side. He liked to think that she did. It was easier to imagine her curled along the length of him in that position, her small breasts pressed to his back, her thighs cradling his. She might even put her arm around his waist or insinuate her knee between his. Her breath would be warm on his skin, and her lips . . . her lips would be sweet.

Dylan tilted his head backward so he could see the loft. He was just in time to glimpse the candlelight being extinguished. He really did know her routine. It should have made him smile. It didn't.

He made up his mind right then that she would have to go.

She had been doing something to him since she came, not just with his injury but with *him*. He wished he understood it better because he would have stopped her. He had come to Tucker Maddox's cabin at Sperry Gap to be alone and she was making him think that maybe that wasn't what he wanted at all. Abby Winslow had a way of getting under his skin that was only marginally more pleasant than a tick. He'd told her that, too. Instead of being offended, she'd given him one of those little smiles of hers and a sideways glance. It made him think she was expecting that comment long before he got around to making it.

When he was being fanciful, it occurred to him that the changes she had wrought had something to do with her baking. She made bread every day, small loaves usually, just enough for him to have with his meals. Sometimes it was anadama that she slid into the oven, and the fragrances familiar to him from his youth would fill the cabin. She baked wheat and rye and cinnamon bread. She made bread with nuts and anise and sunflower seeds. He watched everything she did, looking for that one special, mysterious ingredient that made her bread different from anything he had ever tasted, but he'd never seen her add a thing that shouldn't have been there.

He recalled that first morning when he had nodded off after breakfast. He'd thought then that it had been something she'd put in the coffee, but now he was not so sure. When he hadn't been able to find any crushed poppy among her spices, it occurred to him that she had only been humoring him, telling him what he expected to hear because the truth wasn't as easily swallowed.

He had to admit to the possibility that Abby hadn't put anything in his coffee to encourage him to sleep. Whatever had been done, had been done to the bread, and that made no kind of sense to him. The bread he had eaten that morning—the moist potato rounds—were what she had brought with her to Sperry Gap. She had baked them before she could have known he was injured.

If there was an alternative explanation, it had to be in the fact that Abby Winslow was something of a witch after all.

Dylan turned on his side again, this time with his back to the fire. Closing his eyes, he told himself he was making the right decision. She would have to go.

"It's healing," Dylan said. He rolled the woolen sock back over his foot and removed it quickly from the stool where Abby had been examining it. "I can put weight on it."

Abby didn't say anything. She had been able to see the color was healthy and that even the deepest cuts had fleshy scars pulling the skin together. But Dylan had also flinched when she touched him, and that did not strike her as a good sign. She wondered if he could really place his weight on the foot or if it was only wishful thinking.

Dylan pushed himself out of the rocker and

stood. He shifted his weight from one leg to the other to prove that he could. Abby, he noted, didn't watch his foot, but kept her attention on his face, looking for the grimace or the slight narrowing around his eyes that would have told its own story.

"See?"

"Hmmm."

"I hoped you would be more impressed."

"Hmm."

"Actually, I thought you might say something."

"Hmm." Abby stood and returned to the table, where she had been cutting potatoes and onions for venison stew.

Dylan watched her pick up the knife and resume working. There was nothing fussy about her movements, not a single wasted motion. It was a pure pleasure to watch her hands move with that fluid lightning grace.

Neither pausing nor looking up, Abby said, "You could make yourself useful, you know, and bring in the venison from the curing shed."

It was the first time she had suggested he do anything outside the cabin. Until now their daily argument had been about him staying off his foot. "All right." He expected it was some sort of test, but when he turned at the door to see if she was looking after him, he only saw that her head was bent over her task.

As soon as he was gone, Abby went to the window and watched from one corner of it, marking Dylan's progress from the porch until he turned out of her sight at the edge of the cabin. Ulysses did his best to trip his master, winding in and out of his legs and generally making a nuisance of himself. It was quite remarkable that Dylan never made a misstep, even when Ulysses threw himself prostrate at Dylan's feet and whined for a romp in the snow. Dylan obliged, hurling a snowball so deep into the pines that Ulysses didn't impede his progress for at least another ten yards.

Abby was back at the table by the time Dylan returned. She pointed to where she wanted him to put the venison. Her silence chafed at him because to his way of thinking there was no good reason for it. "Are you angry?"

That made her look up. The surprise in her voice was genuine. "No. Why do you think so?"

"You seem suspicious."

"Oh. Yes, well, I am."

"Then . . . ?"

She frowned. "They're not the same thing at all."

"You're saying very little about my recovery."

"I thought I just explained that. I'm suspicious."

"Of my foot?"

"Hardly."

"Of me, then."

She lifted both hands, palms out. "If the shoe fits."

Dylan chuckled. "Plainly, the shoe does fit. You should take some comfort in that. I can escort you out of Sperry Gap."

Abby said nothing while she struggled to keep her expression neutral. He would be careless of her heart if she handed it to him. It had not yet occurred to him that he might want that from her. He was only honest enough with himself to know that he desired her in his bed, and still gentleman enough to want her to leave because of it. He must have been wrestling mightily with his conscience last night. "You don't have to escort me. I can find my own way. I always could."

That did not mean it wouldn't be dangerous for her. "I won't let you go alone."

"Are you going to be difficult about this?"

"I expect I am. Are you?"

"Yes. I believe so."

The look he gave her was a sour one. They were at something of an impasse, and she realized it as well as he did. If he insisted on escorting her, she would find a way to leave on her own, knowing he couldn't keep up with her. She was practically daring him to admit his leg wasn't as without pain as he would have her believe. If he didn't want her to go on her own, he couldn't let her leave at all, at least until the route was much safer. "All right," he said grudgingly. "You can stay."

Abby went back to chopping.

Grunting softly, Dylan abandoned the pretense of being fiddle-fit and hobbled to the front door to let Ulysses in. Had he looked back over his shoulder he would have caught Abby's fleeting, satisfied smile. He imagined it anyway.

"It's your turn." There was a hint of impatience in Dylan's voice. It seemed to him that she was taking an extraordinarily long time to make her play.

"Yes, I know."

"Well?"

"I'm thinking." Abby rearranged the cards in her hand, mentally recounted the trump that had already been played, and chose the four of hearts to place on top of his lead card. "That makes it my trick, I believe."

He scowled. "Yes."

Abby was oblivious to neither his tone nor his expression, but she had been studiously ignoring both. It was with the onset of dusk that she noticed a shift in his mood. If he could have paced the length of the cabin comfortably, it was what she imagined he would be doing. His suggestion that they play cards was a poor second choice. It did nothing to allow him to contain or express the breadth of his edgy energy.

Occasionally she would glimpse him watching her. His gaze was intense, almost predatory, and more than once she found herself held perfectly still by it, wary and just a little frightened that any movement on her part would make him pounce. In those moments she could believe what everyone in Dover Falls said about him was true.

"It's your turn." He fairly growled the words and was not at all displeased when Abby actually jumped. She was too composed by half, he thought, senseless of the danger he posed to her. A more knowing young woman would have hightailed it up the ladder by now or plainly offered herself to put him out of his misery. Abby Winslow did neither. She just sat there across the table, delicately fingering her cards, worrying her lush lower lip while she decided on her next play. He'd been to bawdy houses where the whores weren't half so skilled at seduction as Miss Winslow.

Abby chose a card and laid it down. The small crease between her brows deepened as she watched both of Dylan's brows go up. "Have I made a bad choice?" She was only learning this game from him. Apparently euchre had been a favorite of the soldiers at his camp, though why anyone would have invited him to play was baffling. "Perhaps we should—"

"Quit?" he asked. "No, that would not be sporting. I should have an opportunity to win my money back." Dylan tossed down his last card, then pushed the trick to Abby's side of the table. "You win that hand."

Abby watched him note the score on the pad of paper he kept by his elbow. She felt compelled to point out, "It's all your money."

He shrugged. "I gave you a stake. The winnings are yours."

"Yes, but—"

"Yours," he repeated. Dylan looked up and regarded her directly. "Unless you'd like to play for something else?"

There was no mistaking that predatory gleam in his gray-green eyes. "Yes," she said. "I think I would."

Her answer surprised him. "You have something in mind?"

"Yes." She carefully counted out the stake he had given her and returned it to him. The winnings she kept for herself. "If I take the next hand you'll answer a question for me."

It was hardly what he had in mind, but he suspected she knew that. She wasn't entirely naive, he decided, but she did attribute him with more in the way of gentlemanly honor than he deserved or wanted. "And if I win?"

"I'll answer any question you put to me."

Dylan supposed that could be interesting, perhaps even entertaining. He could think of several things he'd like to know about Miss Abby Winslow.

She watched him think it over. "Truthfully," she said. "We have to answer the questions truthfully."

It was uncanny the way she seemed to know he was considering doing the very opposite. Dylan grudgingly gave his agreement. "You are putting too much stock in the truth."

"I don't think so."

Shrugging, Dylan picked up the cards and began to shuffle. He dealt them out one at a time, five cards each and a hand for the dummy. They both took a moment to examine their cards before Abby made the first play. The dummy won the trick. "I don't suppose you've thought of what we'll do if the dummy takes the hand."

Abby smiled. "We could put a question to Ulysses."

Dylan glanced over at the shepherd. Ulysses was basking in the heat of the hearth, his eyes closed. He looked sublimely content. "I don't think you can depend upon him answering anything."

"Probably not." She laid a card down for the dummy and waited for Dylan to follow suit. She ended up taking the trick, but Dylan took the next three and won the hand. Abby felt her heart race a little as she wondered what question he would put to her. She expected him to require some time to think it through. He surprised her by having it at the ready.

"How is it that you've been able to save my leg?" Dylan was gratified to see Abby blink. Clearly she hadn't been anticipating this query. It was comforting to realize that she was not privy to every one of his thoughts after all.

"I don't know."

Dylan gathered the cards and fanned one corner of the deck with his thumb. "That's a disappointing response to a reasonable question."

"It's the truth."

"I was a physician, Abby. I've seen enough wounds to know what I could have expected if you hadn't come here. I was prepared to make the cut myself without benefit of help from anyone. You saw for yourself today that I was able to walk." He held up one hand, palm out, when she looked as if she meant to interrupt. "I admit that I was overreaching, but it's plain I'm getting better. In a few more days I won't have to pretend I have no limp. It would go a long way to putting you back in my good graces if you'd tell me how it was accomplished.''

Abby had not realized she had ever been in his good graces. "I think you give me too much credit for your recovery," she said. "Providence had more than a little to do with it."

"Providence sent *you* here. I think what you made of it is your own doing."

She sighed. "I really don't know the answer to your question."

"It's the bread, isn't it?"

"Why do you think that?"

"Because it's . . ." He shook his head. Abby was watching him expectantly, waiting for him to finish. "People must have commented on it before."

"Yes," she said. "Frequently."

"And?"

"And it's simple, really. They encourage me to open my own shop." Abby indicated he should deal a second hand. "There's no sense in that."

Dylan shuffled the cards. "Why not?"

"How would people know which loaves were meant for them?"

He stopped shuffling and regarded her for a long moment. "How would people know . . ."

Abby took the cards from his hands and dealt them. "You can roll your eyes if you like. People often do."

He did not roll his eyes. "It doesn't matter if I don't understand," he said quietly. "You deserve better." Reaching across the table, he laid his hand over both of hers. "Forget the game, Abby. Ask me anything you like."

Her fingers uncurled around the deck and she let the cards slip from her grasp. "I was wondering about your leather satchel."

Dylan looked past Abby to where his satchel hung next to his coat. He'd had no idea that she was at all curious about it. "Do you have a specific question, or would you just like to look inside?"

"May I?"

He nodded.

Abby eased her hands out from under his and went to the door to retrieve it. It was heavier than she expected, and she slung it over her shoulder in the same manner she had seen him do. "You always carried it with you when you came to town."

"Yes."

She set it on the table and started to lift the flap.

Dylan sat back in his chair, his arms crossed in front of him. "Have you considered it might hold my murdered wife's remains?" He chuckled when she rolled her eyes. "Go on. It's nothing so interesting as that."

Abby let the flap fall back and reached inside. She could identify the contents by touch alone. "Books."

"Disappointed?"

"Not at all." She pulled one out. "I think it is very telling to know what a person reads."

"Hmmm."

Abby regarded the slim leather-bound volume she had in her hand. There was nothing on the outside to indicate the title or the author. She had just begun to open it when Dylan plucked it from her hands. "Why did you do that?"

"I said you could see what was in the satchel. We made no agreement about the contents of this book." He watched her reach for another. "Or that one." He held out his hand and she reluctantly placed it there. He allowed her to continue in just that manner, taking the books as soon as she pulled them out until the satchel was empty and there was a stack of eight in front of him.

Abby sat down again and stared at him. She rested her elbows on the edge of the table and propped her chin on her fists. "I suppose you think you're very smart."

"I studied medicine at Harvard."

One of Abby's brows lifted as she dryly pointed out, "You were going to amputate your own foot."

Dylan was amazed to realize one corner of his mouth was actually edging upward. He would not have suspected it was something he could have smiled about. "Is it your plan to remind me often?"

"I believe so, yes." She glanced at the books. "Perhaps if you'd let me—"

"No."

Abby expected him to refuse. "They're journals, aren't they?"

"Yes."

"How long have you been writing in them?"

"Four and a half years."

Mentally counting backward on her fingers, Abby came to the beginning. It made a sad sort of sense to her. "Of course," she said softly. "Gettysburg."

Chapter Three

Dylan looked at Abby for a long moment. He was no longer surprised that she had grasped some fundamental fact about his life. She always seemed to know what thoughts hovered at the edge of his mind. What struck him as vaguely odd was that for the first time in four and a half years he wanted to share those thoughts with someone.

He glanced down at the neatly stacked journals in front of him. He chose the one whose burnished leather spine showed the most wear. "This is the beginning," he said quietly. Dylan pushed it across the table toward her.

Abby did not pick it up. "Tell me," she said.

It was not a demand, not the way she put it to him, yet Dylan hesitated. To say the words aloud, to reveal things he had only placed on paper—he wasn't certain he could get his mind or his mouth around that idea. But Abby was watching him in that quiet way of hers, and he was not immune to the serene scrutiny of those violet eyes.

So he told her. He told her about the cannons and the smoke and the relentless heat. He described three days of battles that started with bravado, then quieted to trepidation, and finally became for each man a peculiar and vital turmoil of emotion that some called courage and some had no name for. It ceased to matter to Dylan how the men set off in the morning, the day inevitably ended in his surgery for too many of them. Big and Little Roundtop. Devil's Den. Pickett's charge. Men who could not be helped were left in the fields and woods where they fell. Men with a chance of survival were brought to the tents where the surgeons waited with saws and ether, and sometimes only with saws, to tell these luckless souls that they had not yet given enough, that further sacrifice was required in the form of a hand or an arm, a leg or a foot. And if not one of these, then their life.

The orderlies could not remove the bloody stumps as fast as they collected. The cannon fire was a diversion for which they were grateful because for the few seconds those reports thundered in their ears, they were all deaf to the screaming. Men wept and whimpered and prayed. They cursed and flailed. Some threw themselves from the stretchers when they saw what was waiting for them.

There was no relief. No silence. No escape. Someone was always moving, tossing, moaning. Sleep came infrequently and always on the heels of exhaustion, yet it was still not powerful enough to quiet the screams that stirred inside the surgeons who cut, the orderlies who carried, and the commanders who would order the next day's fighting.

Dylan met Tucker Maddox the afternoon of the very first day. Tucker was with the Army of Northern Virginia, one of the near casualties at Cemetery

Hill. He was brought to the Yankee field hospital by an orderly with more compassion than good sense and it was left for Dylan Kincannon to care for him. Maddox didn't require a surgeon's saw. He was gut shot, and no amount of cutting could have saved his life. He was going to die slowly and in more pain than any man should have to bear. During every pause in the work that day, Dylan went to Tucker Maddox's cot and stayed at his side, drawn there as if by some force outside himself and compelled to remain for reasons he didn't understand.

In faltering, sometimes whispered speech, Tucker Maddox described Dover Falls and his cabin at Sperry Gap. He told Dylan how spring came to the mountains, how the trees budded before the last frost as if they could not bear to wait for winter to be gone. He spoke of the solitude a man could have if he had a mind to be alone, and the companionship that was available at Mrs. Abernathy's Parlor House when he didn't.

Abby's cheeks flushed a little at the mention of Mrs. Abernathy. "I think he was sweet on the widow," she said.

Dylan smiled a little crookedly. He suspected it was more of a business arrangement than romantic attachment, but he wasn't going to disabuse Abby of the latter. He hadn't visited the euphemistically named Parlor House since his arrival, but he decided Abby knew that. It was just the sort of thing the locals would have gossiped about, especially in light of their rumors that he had murdered his wife and was more wolf than human. "Did you know Tucker Maddox?" Dylan asked.

"Everyone knew him," Abby said. "He used to be the town character. Tucker lived here all his life, though he didn't come to town as often as you. He was more . . ." Her voice trailed off and she ducked her head, embarrassed that what she meant to say would have insulted him.

"Self-sufficient?"

Abby looked up, saw he was grinning, and nodded. "You're a city boy."

"Hardly."

"You're not a farmer or a trapper."

Under the table Dylan wiggled the toes of his injured foot. "Definitely not a trapper." His smile faded. "And definitely not a boy."

It was odd, Abby thought, the things that made her grow warm and the things that did not. She had flushed at the thought of Dylan Kincannon lying with Mrs. Abernathy, but when he looked at her as if she was as tasty a morsel as her anadama bread she was not at all disturbed. In fact, she was emboldened. She simply stared back, not in a shy flirty fashion, but as one who was just a little curious about a man's full appreciation.

Dylan decided he was the one who would have to close the shutters on all that frank interest. He blinked once and shifted slightly in his chair. "Is there any more of that honey bread you made for supper?"

Abby felt her heart give a little start before its beating slowed. Recovering quickly, she nodded and began to rise.

"I'll get it," Dylan said.

She let him because it occurred to her that while there was no hint of color in her face, her knees felt a little weak. She might not have known it at all if she hadn't tried to stand. "Tucker Maddox never came back," she said as Dylan cut one heel from the remaining loaf. "No one knew what became of him, except we supposed he was killed in the war." Abby touched her throat with her fingertips to press back the small ache that had risen there. It wasn't true that no one had known Tucker's fate. She had, but nothing good could come of explaining that to Dylan now. "Is he buried in Pennsylvania?"

Dylan paused, the knife deep in the hearty grain of the bread. "That's right." He finished his cut and put the knife down. His hand was trembling slightly. "I saw to it myself."

"That was good of you," Abby said. Her throat seemed to want to close over the words. She followed the movement of Dylan's hand before he let it drop to his side. "Then he wasn't by himself at the end."

"No. I sat with him. Heard him out. The chaplain couldn't be everywhere and it wasn't right that he should die alone." It had been late on the third day before Tucker's grievous wounds took him. He was more than ready to go by then. He had asked, then begged, for Dylan to show him the same consideration he would have shown a suffering animal. It would have been a mercy to have complied. Perhaps it would have even been easier to live with, but it was not something Dylan Kincannon the healer could do. Tucker Maddox had understood, had in fact pitied him for it, and when Dylan put his hand in Tucker's, it was the dying man who offered comfort to the doctor.

"He gave me this cabin," Dylan said. "And his land. He said no one would be much interested in it and I would have it free and clear. He dictated his will to an orderly and made his X in front of witnesses. I didn't want the place, had no intention of ever laying claim to it, but I accepted it because he was a good man and it was important to do this one thing for him when I could not do the other."

"Folks wondered how you came to take up here."

In light of all the things they'd said of him, he imagined he knew one of the less kind epithets. "I'm not a carpetbagger."

"I never thought so."

"But people did."

"Some. Does it bother you?"

"A little more than them thinking I'm a lycanthrope, but not so much as them thinking I'm a murderer." Dylan turned away to spread jam on his bread. "Do you want some?"

"No. It's for you."

That gave him pause, but not so much that he considered not eating what he'd prepared.

Schooling her features so he could not see that his hesitation had amused her, Abby said, "I think Tucker would be glad you found your way here. He must have wanted you to or he wouldn't have passed it on. It's a good place for a soul to rest."

Dylan limped lightly back to the table and sat. "Is that why you think I came? Because my soul requires it?"

"I don't know. Does it?"

He did not answer immediately. It was true in the beginning. "Yes," he said finally, quietly. "Exactly that." Did it still? he wondered. He was no longer certain. "Things are different now." He did not say that he was different, but that was what he meant. He might have told her, but she seemed to already know because she was watching him with that small, secretive smile hovering at the corners of her mouth. "I went back to Framingham after the war," he said. "My family was there. My mother and sisters. My fiancée. I reopened my office and closed it again after a few months. I couldn't practice medicine any more. My mother professed to understand. My sisters were worried on my behalf. My fiancée married a lawyer." He noticed Abby was no longer smiling and he realized he already missed that faint curve of her mouth. "And no, I wasn't moved to murder either one of them."

She matched his wry tones perfectly. "Good for you."

Dylan grinned because she made it so easy for him. He took a bite of bread and tasted honey on the tip of his tongue. It would be the same if he kissed Abby, he thought. She would be warm and sweet and liquid. He tried not to think of her mouth against his or their tongues touching or their breath mingling. "For a while I tried my hand at business. Then farming. Shipping. The railroads. None of it fit."

"Of course not. It's like having your shoes on the wrong feet."

Dylan couldn't have described it better. He simply nodded in agreement, no longer surprised that she was quick to understand what had taken him so long. "I came here to try another pair of shoes."

Abby supposed it would take him a while yet to discover he had only one pair of feet. Her glance fell to the journals. "You think you're a writer?"

"Maybe."

"A good one?"

"I don't know."

She rested her chin on her hands. "You should be sure about a pair of shoes. I've noticed you can't really break them in the way folks say. An uncomfortable pair is always uncomfortable. They break you, not the other way around."

Dylan's dark brows creased his forehead. "What are you saying?"

"Hmmm. Maybe you're not so smart."

"Maybe I'm not."

"Dover Falls needs a doctor."

"No."

"You're a doctor."

"Not anymore."

"So you say." She pointed to the journals. "I bet these say different."

Dylan didn't take the bait. "You're not reading them now."

Abby shrugged. "Dover Falls hasn't had a physician since Doc Meriwether got kicked in the head by the reverend's mule."

Dylan guessed that a doctor in these parts treated as many four-legged creatures as he did the two-legged variety.

"In the spring it will be six years since Doc Meriwether was around to deliver the babies."

When he heard the hint of wistfulness in her voice, Dylan's eyes narrowed.

"Have you delivered babies?" she asked.

"My share."

Abby ignored his terseness and went on blithely. "And what about typhus and the measles? Have you doctored for them?"

"Yes."

"Liver and heart ailments?"

"Yes."

"Can you treat gout? Mr. Kinsey has the gout."

"Yes to all of it, Abby. Gout. Pox. Stones. Boils. Bunions. Bones."

"And babies. Don't forget babies."

"Headaches. Sleeping illnesses. Tuberculosis. Pneumonia. Mumps. Fevers."

"Then you could be our doctor."

The outer ring of Dylan's gray-green eyes turned flinty. "No, I couldn't. Is that why you came? Did the whole town put you up to it?"

"No one put me up to anything."

"But it's why you came."

Understanding that he meant to pick a fight

with her, Abby responded with patient practicality. "How could I have known you were a doctor?"

Her question stopped him cold. Taking it at face value, there was no reasonable answer. Abby Winslow *couldn't* have known. Still, having learned a fair bit about his guest since she'd been under his roof, Dylan hesitated to believe it was strictly a rhetorical matter. "How do you know any of the things you do?"

Abby reached for the playing cards and began to shuffle. "Will you play another hand?"

"Same stakes?" he asked. "If I win, you'll answer my question?"

She had managed the initial shuffling with deftness. Now she was all thumbs. A third of the deck simply flew out of her hands and scattered on the tabletop. She gathered them up quickly, very much aware that Dylan was watching her with even more interest than he had been earlier. "I think I'll play solitaire."

"Coward."

Abby was not at all offended. "Yes," she said. "Sometimes I am."

There seemed to be nothing to say to that. He'd never met anyone who was so difficult to provoke. Shrugging, Dylan returned the journals to his satchel. He rose and carried it to the door where he exchanged it for his coat. "Ulysses needs to go out."

Turning slightly in her chair, Abby nodded. The shepherd had left his place at the hearth as soon as Dylan started for the door. Now Ulysses was nosing Dylan behind the knees, urging him to move faster. Abby waited until they were gone before she stopped her idle shuffling and came to her feet. She swept the crumbs from Dylan's bread into her palm and carried them to the fireplace.

Brushing off her hands, the crumbs sparkled blue and green and gold as they were caught by the flames in mid-air.

Fairy dust was what her uncle called it.

It was the shout that woke her. Abby bolted upright and quickly rolled out of bed to her feet. She was at the edge of the loft, both hands on the ladder posts, before she was fully aware of what she was doing. Below her, she could make out Dylan's huddled shape in front of the hearth. He was turned away from the fire so his face was in shadow. It didn't matter that she couldn't see him clearly. His low moan spoke to his pain.

Abby hurried down the ladder, missing a rung at the bottom so that she stumbled and almost fell facedown beside him. She managed a graceless drop to her knees instead, bruising the right one on a buckled floor plank. In other circumstances she might have cursed, but in these conditions, when she was focused on someone else's distress, she was hardly conscious of her own injury.

Sidling closer on her knees, Abby laid one hand on Dylan's shoulder. She said his name softly and waited for her voice to have an impact on his restlessness. It had none. He shrugged off her hand and burrowed more deeply under the blankets. Abby touched his forehead with the back of her fingers and found his skin was cool and dry. His lips moved around some words she could not make out by the shape of them.

She said his name again, more firmly this time. It was a tone she had heard Miss Henry use in the classroom with the undisciplined boys. Dylan Kincannon would have gotten a ruler rapped across his knuckles for all the heed he gave it.

Abby lifted the blanket at Dylan's feet and examined his injured foot. She realized immediately that this was not the source of his pain. It would only be a matter of days before he was able to put his full weight on it without pretending it no longer troubled him. The color was good, and even the wounds that he had not allowed her to stitch were knitting. She covered his feet again and moved back to his side. This time she did not try to wake him, but lay down instead, fitting herself snugly against his taut frame and taking one corner of the blanket to draw around her hips. She found his arm and pulled it across her waist and held it there, keeping him close to lend him her body heat. She could feel the heavy thudding of his heartbeat against her back and the unfamiliar warmth of his breath on the nape of her neck.

The entire line of his body was tense with cold, and though there were times he vibrated against her like a plucked string, Abby never once felt the accompaniment of a single sweet note. She pulled him closer so that her head was tucked under his chin. Finding his fingers, she laced hers between them and whispered as much to herself as him, "You're sorely out of tune, Dylan Kincannon. Sorely out of tune."

Against the curve of her bottom she felt the hard outline of his erection. Apparently there was nothing wrong with his bow.

She was every bit as pliant as he thought she must be. She turned easily in his arms and encircled his neck with her own. Her mouth lifted and her lips parted. He knew she would taste like warm honey and her tongue would wind around his with the same slow, sweet heaviness.

Her small breasts rubbed against his chest. He could feel the pebble hardness of her nipples through her thin chemise and the slightly uneven ridge of her teeth against his bottom lip.

He was between her damp thighs, his hips caught in the cradle she made for him. There was need here. His need. Hers. There would be no denying that she wanted him, or that he wanted the same. This urge was primal and essential.

Neither one of them had opened their eyes.

He heard his name. It came to him as if from a distance, the final consonant resonating faintly. The sound of it made him start and tilt his head, as if he might find the source and hear the whole of it clearly.

The perfect stillness of his body made her heavy eyelids lift. The dark centers of her violet eyes were wide and her slumberous stare was largely unfocused. She was aware of him in so many ways that had nothing to do with sight that it took more than a few moments to orient this new sense.

"Dylan." She said his name and upon saying it realized it was not the first time she had done so. She had the memory of it on the tip of her tongue, along with the taste of him. Her arms were around his neck and she made no move to let them fall to her side. She felt the press of the warm taut flesh of his back against her fingertips and her nails made tiny crescents in his skin.

Her chemise was rucked up to her hips and he lay naked between her legs, his muscular flanks pressing against the softness of her inner thighs. It was all she could do not to move against his heavy erection.

"What are you doing here?"

It was the same question he had asked when she arrived on his doorstep. She almost answered it the same way, but some remnant of good sense told her he would not be amused. He wasn't angry with her, at least not yet. Abby thought she had better not provoke the beast. "You had a nightmare," she said. "You called out in your sleep and it woke me. I came to see if you were all right and I stayed because you weren't."

"You should have woken me."

"I tried," she said. "I couldn't. You were cold, so I crawled in beside you."

He grunted softly, as much in frustration as disbelief. "There are extra blankets in the trunk over there. And there's plenty of wood for the fire."

All of that was perfectly true. "I was cold, too."

Dylan closed his eyes briefly. She was yielding under him. He could feel the slight spread of her thighs and the gentle lift of her hips. "Abby."

"Hmmm?" It was difficult to think when all she wanted to do was feel. How could it be any different for him?

"Abby." His tone was rough, impatient.

"Yankee." She made it an endearment.

"Abby, if you don't tell me to stop, I'm going to—" He didn't finish because she was drawing him closer. He didn't realize until then that such a thing was possible. The touch of her mouth was shy at first, just like her smile, but that hesitation vanished quickly and she kissed him as if she'd been hungry for him all her life. She nibbled on his bottom lip and ran her tongue along the soft underside until she felt him not just give himself up to it but take the lead. The sheer joy of it made her want to laugh. Her breath hitched instead, and the bubble of pleasure burst in the back of her throat and tripped lightly down the length of her spine. She shivered in his arms, not because she was cold but because she wasn't. He was kissing her hotly and deeply and with no sense that it should ever end.

She took him into her without fear, only wanting. There was pain, then there was none. He moved slowly, held her head in the cradle of his palms, his fingers threading between thick silky strands of her rich gold-and-ginger hair, and waited for her to accommodate his entry. He liked it that she seemed to be holding her breath, that it was caught again at the back of her throat. She was watching him, her eyes searching his face, anticipating his movement, wanting it, perhaps even a little greedy for it.

"Is this why you came here?"

Abby's breathing came back to her full measure and she laughed easily. "You flatter yourself."

He could have expected a more sensible woman to be angered by his question. Abby was not so readily riled, or maybe, Dylan thought, she simply was amused that he could take himself so seriously. Why had he ever thought that she was naive when in so many ways she was wise even beyond his years?

He kissed her again. Easy this time and more slowly than before. He showed her with his mouth what he intended with his body. She never once shied away.

A draft eddied under the front door of the cabin and pinwheel flakes of snow danced into the room on their crystalline points. The lovers didn't notice the cold intrusion or that Ulysses moved from his position under the table to prostrate himself against the crack. Burying his nose against his fore-paws, he closed his eyes.

Abby arched her throat as Dylan's mouth made a foray along the line of her neck. The vibration of her humming pleasure tickled his lips. He nuzzled the curve of her shoulder and sank his teeth gently against her skin. She sucked in her breath as the intensity of pleasure teetered on pain.

He drew back and searched her face. "Did I hurt you?"

"No." It was more an expulsion of air than an answer. She said it again so he would know that she meant it. "No. It was unexpected."

A half-smile edged Dylan's mouth and he ducked his head, nudging her with his nose, then dropping a kiss on her parted lips. "I was beginning to think nothing could surprise you."

"It's quite the opposite," she whispered, pulling him back to her mouth again. "Almost everything does."

Dylan didn't care that he didn't understand. What he knew for a certainty was that he wanted to be with her, and it was that which had the capacity to surprise him. It was not merely that he wanted her, but the very rightness of wanting her.

Their bodies moved together. Claiming. Surrendering. What she gave he took selfishly and eagerly, for there was no shame in grasping at this pleasure. He taught her the same, so that she was greedy for not only what he could do for her but all the ways he could do it.

The blankets fell to the side and firelight caressed his naked back. Abby's chemise slipped over her shoulder and he made the curve damp with the edge of his tongue. He lowered his mouth to her aureole, making the pink tip wet through the thin cotton fabric. She wriggled out of the chemise until her breasts blossomed in his work-roughened palms. He took one in his mouth again, this time with nothing between them.

Closing her eyes, Abby breathed in the fragrances that clung to his skin, the smoke from the fire and the musk of his sex. Each ingredient was vital to the texture of this man, and when she tasted him, she caught the hint of each. He moved in her slowly, rocking her with each thrust. She lifted for him and carried him when he came so deeply inside her. Her fingertips slipped along his spine and clutched him at the small of his back. He growled softly against her ear and she thought of the wolf. It made her smile that he was so gloriously human an animal.

The spiral of pleasure wound itself more slowly around Abby. It teased her at first, darting under her skin from her shoulder to her wrist when he kissed the soft and sensitive underside of her elbow. She felt it skip lightly across the flat of her abdomen as Dylan's mouth moved from her breast to her navel. It was there in the hitch of her breath, in the swelling of her breasts, and in the flush that pinkened her cheeks. She gave this pleasure sound at the back of her throat with inarticulate murmurings and whimpers. What she thought she knew about the joining of a man and a woman was inadequate preparation for the reality of what was done to her.

For all of Abby Winslow's imaginings of how things might come to pass, she had not been able to grasp this truth.

She buried her face in the curve of his neck as her body shuddered beneath his. Whatever she cried out was smothered by the press of her mouth against his warm flesh. He cradled her close, buffeting the storm of sensation her body had become, and when she shied away from it, more afraid of the release than of all the tension that pulled her taut, she was glad for the shelter of his arms.

Drifting away from pleasure as if floating in a warm current, Abby became aware of things outside herself first, like the heavy beat of Dylan's heart, the way he watched her with eyes that were dark mirrors, and the mouth that curved slightly at the corners but could not be named a smile. She moved past him to awareness of things beyond: the crackle of the fire, Ulysses's soft snuffling by the door, the wind slipping through a crack and fluttering the edges of the curtain at the window.

"What are you thinking?"

Abby looped her arms loosely around his neck. "Nothing," she said quietly, a softly wry smile changing the shape of her lips. "I'm not thinking about anything." It was true. This pervasive sense of peace was something largely unknown to her. She was not often a mind at rest. The novelty of being so replete was something to be savored for the moment.

Her mouth was damp and slightly swollen from his kisses. Dylan bent his head and touched his lips to hers. It was all he had been thinking about, this need to kiss her again, to touch her dewy mouth and know that she was quite real and that nothing that had come before was the extension of an elaborate and very satisfying dream.

Dylan rested his weight on his forearms. His fingertips sifted through Abby's unbound hair, smoothing silky strands around her ears and the nape of her neck. His gentling touch made her shiver lightly. Her abdomen retracted as she caught her breath. She stirred under him.

"Don't move," he whispered. "I don't think I can—"

Everything about Abby stilled except her mouth. "Is it your leg? Your foot? Have I—"

This time his kiss had a different purpose. She was quiet and just a little dazed when he finished. "There's nothing wrong with my leg," he told her. "Nothing."

She was suspicious, and one brow arched to underscore what she was thinking.

"You shouldn't doubt it," he said, touching his forehead to hers. "You're responsible."

"No." Her nose bumped his as she shook her head. "I'm not."

Dylan eased himself from Abby and rolled onto his back. He did not have to encourage her to shift her position and curl into him; she did it without prompting, finding the natural curve of her body that fit the planes of his. Her head rested on his shoulder and one arm slid around his waist. Her knee rose to lie against his thigh. Dylan pulled the blankets as far as her bare shoulders. Her breath felt warmer on his skin than the fire in the hearth.

"Who *are* you?" he asked quietly.

She smiled. "You know that. I'm Abigail Winslow."

It occurred to Dylan that he was asking the wrong question. *"What* are you?"

Her head tilted back a fraction so she could glimpse his profile. "What do you think I am?"

"A sprite. A pixie."

She laughed softly. "Not a witch, then. It's what you thought before."

"A fairy witch."

"Is it so difficult to believe I'm simply a woman?"

"But not a simple woman."

"No woman is that," Abby chided him. "We all have our ways, obvious or not. Some of us are not so shy about using them."

"You were. I didn't think you'd ever speak to me."

"Talking's different. I baked anadama bread for you, remember?"

He remembered. The fragrance of that bread had flooded him with memories. One taste had drawn him in. "Tucker Maddox told me about your bread."

"Did he?"

Something in Abby's tone made him suspect she had known all along. "You expected it."

"You said many of his last thoughts were about Dover Falls. He liked my bread just fine."

"What he said was that he couldn't forget it."

"I baked a lot of bread with scallions and garlic for him. He was partial to it."

Dylan smiled. "That would explain it." His palm lay on the curve of her hip and his thumb idly passed back and forth across her skin. "What explains what you did to me?"

"I'm not certain what you mean."

He didn't believe her. "I asked once if you meant to save my leg. You said, 'If that's where I have to start.'"

Abby lifted her head and looked at him. "And?"

"And I think you knew from the beginning it was more than my leg that was troubling me."

"So I did," she said. "It's a thing not so easily hidden."

"From you, perhaps. Not everyone sees what you do."

"My uncle did." Abby's head dropped back to Dylan's shoulder. "He thought I should come here."

Edward Winslow seemed a nice enough sort to Dylan's way of thinking, but to learn that he shared some of Abby's fey ways was not at all expected. "So he *did* send you."

"No. Of course not. It was my choice. I wanted to come and . . ."

After a few moments' silence, he prompted her. "And?"

"And you needed me."

If she had told him that so baldly the first day, he wouldn't have let her in, but now he knew it was true. "Is there more?"

She nodded faintly and spoke on a mere whisper of sound. "Of course there is. You should never doubt that I needed you."

His mind could not get around the idea, but his heart embraced it immediately. She had become part of him in a manner that had no easy explanation, but then how was attraction ever explained by the poets and mystics if not by magic?

"It might be a week or more before you can return to Dover Falls," Dylan said.

"Probably."

People will expect a marriage."

"Some will."

"Shotguns?"

She smiled. "Not many."

"I think I'd like to marry you, Abby Winslow."

Abby ran her fingertips along the back of his hand. Her eyelids drooped sleepily. "You let me know when you're certain."

She made four-grain orange bread for him the next day. He sat at the table watching her fold the rye, barley, and wheat flours into the warm molasses, yeast, and oatmeal mixture. She sprinkled the tabletop with a light layer of flour, then did the same to her palms. Finally she turned out the dough, shaping it in a round ball before she set it down. Glancing in his direction, she pressed the heels of her hands into the dough and made a rolling motion away from her. "You're watching me," she said.

"Yes."

"Do you still think it's something about the bread?"

"Yes, but I've changed my mind about what it is."

One of Abby's brows lifted. "Oh?"

Dylan nodded, but he didn't elaborate.

After a moment Abby went back to her work, and in time she forgot he was there. She folded the dough toward her, gave it a quarter turn, and pushed it away again with her heels. There was a rhythm to the pushing and folding and turning that she found soothing and she gave herself up to it, unaware of the glow that touched her features, the half-smile that played about her mouth, or the way her violet eyes darkened with dreamy appeal. Dylan noticed all these things, and that was how he came at last to understand the nature of Abby's bread.

The intrinsic ingredient was Abby.

He was waiting for her when she put the covered dough aside to rise. He set her against the flour-dusted tabletop and lifted her skirts and quieted her laughter with the hard slant of his mouth across hers. She left a trail of white fingerprints on his chambray shirt and later on the button fly of his trousers. The ghost of them showed up again on the narrow curve of his naked hips.

The table rocked uneasily yet still managed to hold their weight. The legs scraped against the uneven floor, but the sound of it was lost to the ones they made. Ulysses circled Dylan's legs, brushing up against them until Dylan was almost put off his feet. Abby's laughter returned, and the musical sound of it made Dylan oblivious to everything else. This time he did not try to quiet it but absorbed it instead, embracing it in the same manner he did the fey, lovely woman in his arms.

"It's you," he said afterward. He had drawn her down to the floor because in the end his own legs proved less reliable than the table's. He leaned against the wall and she sat between his splayed thighs, her back resting against his chest. His arms were folded across her apron just below her breasts. The fragrance of the rising dough filled the cabin, but it wasn't what caught Dylan's attention; rather it was the fragrance of Abby's hair with its sweet light scent of lavender.

"Me?" she asked.

"Yes. I watched. You make the bread."

"Of course I do."

"No," he said. "You *make* the bread."

"Aaaah." Her voice was soft, her smile gentle.

"You make it . . . different. Something more than it is." He paused, hearing the words aloud for the first time. "That's what you've done to me, isn't it?"

"If you'd like to think so."

Her enigmatic answer made him tilt her face back so he could see the expression that went with it. Sure enough, it was the cat-in-the-cream look of sublime satisfaction. Dylan laughed and kissed the crown of her hair. "I don't know why Dover Falls needs a doctor when they have you for whatever malady ails them."

Abby sat up straight and moved to one side, coming up on her knees as she faced him. She didn't let Dylan catch her elbow when he would have pulled her back into his arms. "I can't do what you do," she said. Her features were set earnestly now. It had never been so important that he believe what she meant to say. "What I know about doctoring wouldn't halfway fill a thimble. But I was honest with you at the outset. I told you I know something about healing, and I do. I know when a body is in want of a spirit. You left your spirit with Tucker Maddox at Gettysburg, or maybe he just stole it from you, but you were walking wounded long before your foot found that trap.''

It was true, all of it. He had been walking wounded. Abby was regarding him almost challengingly, daring him to say different. Dylan simply stared at her and said nothing at all.

''My mother had the gift of knowing things,'' she told him quietly. ''She ran away from Dover Falls with my father thinking she could leave it behind. I was born in Richmond, which is about as far as she thought she had to go. Uncle Edward came and got me when my parents died, and he had to go toe to toe with the town to do it. There are times I think about leaving just like my mother did, though I haven't precisely her same gift. I'm told I haven't the same gift as any of her kin.'' She shrugged lightly, as if it could not matter that even in her own family she was set apart. ''I learned early on that wherever I go, it will be there, too. I'll be as much an oddity in Richmond or Boston or Atlanta as I am in Dover Falls. Uncle Edward understands a little better than most that it's just my way and he doesn't mind much.'' One corner of Abby's mouth lifted slightly. ''He was sweet on my mother, I've heard, or at least that's what Aunt Georgia believes. She never fails to remark on it when she thinks he's indulging me.''

''Do you hear it a lot?''

Her smile continued to hover. ''You're asking if my uncle indulges me often and the answer is yes. He didn't stop me from coming here, for instance.''

Dylan's dark brows pulled together and the crease deepened between them. He thought he remembered Abby telling him that her uncle had wanted her to come to Sperry Gap. She'd said he hadn't sent her, that it was her choice, just that he had wanted her to come. There was something he didn't understand, that much he was sure of, but a lifetime in Abby's company wouldn't make some things any clearer. That much he was sure of, too.

"What is it?"

Aware of her worried glance, Dylan's bemused expression disappeared. "Nothing," he said. "It's nothing."

She gave him an arch, expectant look.

Laughing, he caved. "I was thinking I'd like to spend a lifetime puzzling you out, Abby Winslow."

Her smile perfectly serene, Abby rose to her feet to fetch her bread. "Let me know when you're certain."

The winter thaw arrived without warning and much too early to suit Dylan Kincannon. He glanced at the sky worriedly, watching a bank of clouds move off to the northeast and leave nothing but blue and sunshine behind. A day was all he had left, two at the outside. If he wanted her to stay he would have to say so. He couldn't pretend any longer that it was too dangerous for her to travel out alone. His foot wouldn't prevent him from accompanying her unless he found another trap to step into.

He must be a little crazy in love if he was thinking that was a reasonable solution.

Dylan grabbed his coat and muttered something about cutting wood and Ulysses needing to run before he slammed out of the cabin. He didn't look back at Abby, but he imagined she was amused, knowing just what was wrong with him and waiting for him to say it.

He picked up the ax leaning against the woodpile and chose a log for splitting. The accompanying thwack and splintering was not nearly as satisfying as he wanted it to be. He chose another and hefted the ax again while Ulysses darted off and marked his familiar territory.

The work felt good. It stretched his muscles and eased his mind. The journals had not been as helpful of late. He'd been reading through them at night after Abby had fallen asleep. He hadn't thought about writing again; just reading was enough to help him take the long view. He was a good writer, he knew that now, but he was a better doctor. It was in the rereading of his own thoughts that his shortsightedness was corrected, not in anything Abby had done.

He swung the ax, his smile a bit more rueful than crooked. It was truer, he thought, that it was not *all* Abby this time. In her own quiet way she had dared him to decide how the shoe fit. Writing, he discovered, was like a pair of old slippers, comfortable and warm. He could be easy in them. But there was no mistaking that what he wrote came from his healer's soul. He had forgotten until now that being a doctor was who he was, not only what he did. He could waste a lifetime trying to find the right shoes and never be comfortable in his own skin.

Or he could go barefoot.

Dylan let the ax stay wedged in the partially split log and glanced back at the cabin. Abby was standing on the porch, watching him. She did not look so different than she had the first time she'd struck up the courage to talk to him. The smile was there, though not as wary as before, and the violet eyes were watchful, but no longer timid. She had a basket tucked under her right arm with the blue-and-white towel lifted at one corner, and he could smell the molasses and cornmeal from where he stood.

Anadama bread.

He waited, but she didn't move, didn't lift the basket to him or make the offer with her eyes or the subtle lift of her chin, and then he knew that this time she wouldn't. All he had to do was . . .

Dylan Kincannon took off his boots and walked barefoot through the melting snow. He let her know that he was certain.

They were married in Reverend Pritchard's church directly beside where the new parsonage was being built. The good preacher insisted Ulysses stay outside, but everyone else was welcome. For weeks it was all most people talked about, not just the impending nuptials but exactly how it had all come about. No one missed an opportunity to retell the story because they didn't know the truth of things. In the fine tradition of Dover Falls they went on as they always had, trusting to their imaginations to supply the details they didn't know.

It only required the passage of one full moon and a closer inspection of Ulysses for the town to finally suppress the rumor that Dylan Kincannon was a lycanthrope and, strangely enough, no one could remember ever thinking seriously that he had murdered his wife up North. He was still a Yankee, though, and they regarded that with enough suspicion until he eased Mr. Kinsey's gout and saw one of Mrs. Fitch's twins through the diphtheria. After Dylan's success with Mrs. Imans's lumbago, Mr. Imans from the bank offered him a loan on a house a quiet block from Main Street that had enough room for an office and a surgery and sufficient living space to raise a family.

When the banker had said this last, Dylan supposed that he, like everyone else, had decided Abby was already carrying his child. She wasn't, but the proof of that would come after the wedding, when the town ticked off the passing months on its collective fingers. He could wait, he decided, just as Abby advised him he should, for them to stumble over the truth. Perhaps the fall would put a nose or two out of joint. Treating those would be a pleasure.

He was thinking that now as he looked above the heads of the gathered congregation and the doors at the back of the church opened. Abby stepped forward on the arm of her Uncle Edward and walked with solemn purpose down the center aisle toward him. Dressed in white, she was an otherworldly creature, more spirit than substance, so in the end it seemed that she approached him on a cushion of air, and that her uncle did not so much provide an escort for her as hold her grounded until Dylan could put his hand in hers.

She smiled when his long fingers curled around hers. His clasp was warm and dry and there was just the faintest tremor in it that made her know he was not as calm as he appeared.

They spoke their vows in tones that never faltered, barely pausing for the reverend's prompts. The promises they made came to them easily, having been made once before in the cabin at Sperry Gap, with a basket of anadama bread between them. The same sweetness was here now, the same magic, and no one who heard the exchange doubted there was a fine hand at work here.

But exactly whose hand was the question they raised.

They could all bear witness to the fact that Abigail

Maddox Winslow delivered her groom a start when she had dutifully repeated her fully given name. They weren't so clear on why the surprise on Dr. Kincannon's face was immediately transformed to wry amusement, or why Abby searched his features with a smile of beatific beauty on her own, but they suspected it had something to do with invoking the Maddox name.

Things like that happened when folks mentioned the Maddoxes. Abby's mother had been one, they all remembered, but her Uncle Tucker had been something else again. They counted it as a good thing that she had grown up with the more settling influences of the Winslow side, and remarked on it to one another as they filed out of the church to see the bride and groom off.

"They're like a swarm of hornets," Dylan whispered, helping Abby onto the buckboard.

She laughed because she was thinking the same thing. "They're talking about Tucker Maddox."

"Uncle Tucker." Dylan thrilled the onlookers by kissing his bride scarlet. "A relationship you failed to mention."

The high color in Abby's cheeks faded slowly, but happiness kept her violet eyes bright. She sought out her aunt and uncle in the crowd and waved to them. "I told you my uncle wanted me to come to you."

"You know I thought you were talking about your Uncle Edward."

She glanced back at him, her smile at once innocent and sly. "Why would you suppose for a moment that I would know what you're thinking?"

Dylan's look was rife with disbelief, his dark brows nearly at his hairline. "Why would I—" He stopped because nothing that made any sense would come of that line of questioning, and besides, the guests at their wedding were preparing to pelt them with rice.

Dylan and Abby instinctively ducked their heads as the crowd's first volley came at them, but what was thrown high into the air weren't tiny white pellets. This shower sparkled blue and green and gold in the high noon sun, drifting down on the newlyweds in a pyrotechnic display of light.

Dylan held out his hand to catch the offering and examine it more closely. He looked at it and then at Abby. Truly, he thought, nothing else would ever surprise him.

"I suppose you know what this is," he said, showing her the bread crumbs in his palm.

She nodded once, serenely. "Fairy dust."

THE MAGIC GARDEN

Hannah Howell

Chapter One

Scotland
Summer 1390

"He willnae hang me. He only wants some food."

Rose Keith repeated those words again as she took the apple tarts she had made out of the stone oven. It had to be the hundreth time she had said those words, but she was not feeling any calmer. She said them again as she dribbled honey over the top of the tarts, but noticed that her hands still shook a little. If she did not calm herself down, she would never make it to the keep. Someone would find her sprawled on the road in a swoon, crushed tarts all around her.

"Why would the laird wish to see me?" she asked the black-and-white cat sprawled on her kitchen table, but he simply opened one eye a little, yawned, and turned onto his back. "A fat lot of good ye are, Sweetling."

She took off her apron and hung it on the hook

by the back door of her cottage. The day had dawned so bright and warm, she had been certain it would be a good day. Then little Peter had arrived with word from the castle that the new laird wished her to bring him some of her fine apple tarts in time for his evening meal. Rose had felt her heart plummet into her feet and it had not returned to its proper place yet, no matter how many comforting things she told herself.

Visiting the old laird had never troubled her so. She had skipped up to the keep several times a week since she had been a small child to deliver food to the old laird. He had been very kind to her, had even grieved with her when her mother had died three years ago. In fact, she was sure it was the old laird who had left the basket of kittens at her door in an attempt to cheer her. But the old laird was dead now, his son now home to take his place.

As she braided her hair, she tried to recall the boy she had once known. Dark, she thought, and smiled faintly. Dark hair, dark gray eyes, and dark skin. He had been so surprisingly tolerant of and kind to the child she had been. It had saddened her when he had left to fight in France almost ten years ago. His visits home had been rare and brief and she had not seen him, so her last clear image of him was as a young man of barely nineteen years. Now he was nearing thirty, his youth given to battle and the last of his family dead. It was no wonder he was dark-humored she thought, then scolded herself for heeding rumor and gossip.

Men grew up. Kind, smiling young men were changed into stern, solemn lairds. It was a sad fact of life that the sweet joy of youth faded. She had been a happy child, sheltered and blissfully innocent. Time and understanding had stolen that cheerful ignorance. Her mother had not been able to mute all the ugly whispers about the Keith women or halt every outbreak of fear and anger. Rose could understand people's fears, for she had felt the touch of them herself from time to time, but she was not sure she would ever understand why their fear made them cruel.

Gently setting the tarts in her basket, she prayed the laird was one of those rare people who felt nothing when eating her food. Or, that he accepted the soothing or lifting of his spirits as simply the result of eating something delicious. Rose had enough trouble in her life without having the new laird cocking a suspicious, fearful eye her way.

"Weel, lads, wish me luck," she said as she donned her cloak.

Rose shook her head when only two of the four cats sprawled around the kitchen deigned to glance at her. It was very sad, she decided as she picked up her basket and headed out the door, when a woman of only one and twenty was reduced to talking to her cats. Even sadder was the fact that, since her mother's death, she rarely had anyone else to talk to.

"Pssst! Rose!"

Then again, she mused, there were times when talking to cats was preferable to talking to some people. She hastily scolded herself for being unkind and smiled at the young girl who stumbled out from amid the tangled shrubbery she had been hidng behind. Meg was at that awkward age of not quite a child, but not quite a woman. Even harder, Meg had a lively mind that was not being kept fed. Unfortunately, that lively mind had become fixed upon Rose, her family, and her garden.

"I fear I cannae visit now, Meg," Rose said, almost smiling at the way the young girl had to

brush her thick dark hair off her face. "I must hie
to the castle."

"I ken it," Meg said as she fell into step beside
Rose. "The laird wants to see ye and test your food
for himself."

Rose frowned slightly. "How did ye hear about
that?"

" 'Tis being whispered all about the village."

"Oh, dear."

"Aye. Seems the old laird kept a journal. 'Tis
said he thought it might help his son settle in as
laird if he kept clear records of all that was said
and done at the castle, in the village, and all about
the lands of Duncairn."

"And the old laird wrote about Rose Cottage,
the Keith women, and the garden."

"He did. He praised your apple tarts, 'tis said."

"Weel, that is kind, but I rather wish he hadnae
done so."

"Why? The young laird lived here nearly a score
of his years. I suspicion he heard all about it."

"True." Rose sighed. "He may have forgotten
it, though."

"Wheesht, even if he had, he would soon have
been told about it all." Meg shook her head, then
had to brush the hair off her thin face again.
"S'truth, Mistress Kerr has nay doubt complained,
as is her wont."

"She has already been to see the new laird?"

"Fast as she could. He *has* been home a fortnight,
ye ken. She was dragging poor Anne up there 'ere
the dust had settled behind his horse. The laird
has no wife, has he?"

Worse and worse, Rose mused, eyeing the stout
walls of Duncairn warily as they appeared before
her. Joan Kerr hated her, had hated her mother,
and was the most vicious and consistent voice

speaking out against the Keith women. She had married a Kerr but returned home once widowed. Rose's mother had often jested that the Kerrs had probably had a grand celebration when the woman had left. Joan was a distant cousin of the old laird and made far more of that connection than it was worth, considering how many of the clan could claim the same. For some reason Joan had always disliked the Keith women. Rose had a feeling her mother had known the reason for that animosity, but she had never shared that information.

"It would be a good match," she murmured, wondering why the thought of the new laird with Anne should irritate her. "Despite her mother, Anne is a sweet woman."

"Too sweet. I think the laird terrified her. That seemed to be what Mistress Kerr was scolding her about as they walked home. Timid, wee mousie, her mother called her. Anne stayed to the shadows and the few times she spoke to the laird, 'twas in a tiny, shaky whisper."

"Ye listened for quite a while, didnae ye?"

Meg nodded, revealing not a glimmer of remorse. "Thought they might catch me at it a time or two."

"Did the laird do something in particular to frighten Anne?"

"Not anything they mentioned." Meg frowned and scratched her slightly pointed chin. "All Anne would say, or could say with her mother moaning on and on about ungrateful bairns, was that he was too big, too dark, and too fierce."

"Too fierce?" Rose's steps slowed even more as she neared the towering gates of Duncairn.

"Och, weel, I wouldnae pay much heed to that. Anne is sweet, as ye say, but she is also a coward.

A wee brown rabbit shows his teeth and she is all aswoon.''

Rose looked away as she swallowed a laugh. It was not well done of her to listen to Meg's gossip, but she was unable to resist the allure. It was also, sadly, often the only news about those she lived among that came her way.

"I begin to understand poor Anne," she muttered, pausing in front of the gates.

"Nay, ye are far braver than her," Meg assured her. "Anne could ne'er live alone, although I suspicion she oftimes dreams of it."

This time Rose could not fully restrain a giggle. "Naughty Meg." She quickly grew serious again and sighed as she stared through the gates at the thick walls of the keep. "I dinnae feel verra brave at the moment." She looked at the basket of tarts she held. "I keep wondering why the mon wants my apple tarts? Is he but wishing to see if he finds them as delicious as his father did? Or is he seeking proof that I am a witch, that I am an evil thing that must be cast out of Duncairn?"

"Wheesht, ye have been thinking on this too long." Meg got behind Rose and gently pushed her along until she was inside the gates. "If naught else, ye cannae run away and hide, can ye? Best to get this o'er with. And, doesnae your food make people happy and at ease, scowls turning into bonny smiles? A calm, smiling laird isnae apt to be hanging ye from the battlements."

"Thank ye." Rose nimbly eluded Meg's pushing and turned to frown at her. "I was recovering weel until ye said that."

"Ah, good, there ye are, Rose," called a lanky young man named Donald as he hurried over to her.

"Aye, *here* she be," said Meg. "Ye are *so* clever to track her down right here in the bailey."

Donald glared at Meg. "This rat's nest of hair on a stick wasnae invited. Hie along home, bairn."

When Meg returned that insult with an impressive one of her own, Rose sighed. Only four years separated Donald and Meg, yet Rose could not think of many times when the two were not arguing or insulting each other. Her mother had found the pair a source of great amusement, even called what the two did a mating dance. Flora Keith had always revealed a great skill at judging such matches, but Rose sometimes wondered if the two would survive it.

Taking a deep breath, Rose squared her shoulders and walked into the keep. Donald and Meg, needed no audience to their strange courtship. Meg was right in saying it was best to get this confrontation over with. Anticipating it, thinking of all that could go wrong, was only agitating her. Rose was almost tempted to eat one of her own apple tarts. Her agitated state might be uncomfortable, but it kept her wary. She felt that was more important than greeting the new laird with a calm heart and a pleasing smile.

She paused in the doorway to the great hall to study the two men seated at the laird's table. With his long gray hair, Robert the steward was easy to recognize. Rose cautiously turned her full attention upon the new laird, Sir Adair Dundas.

The long black hair, the dark gray eyes, and the dark skin told her the man next to Robert had to be the new laird. A closer look revealed the shadows of the old laird in the strong line of Adair's jaw and his long, elegant nose. Fighting for France had added the muscle the boy of nineteen had lacked, although the lean, almost graceful lines of the tall body were still clear. Little else of the boy she had once known remained, however. There was no hint of a smile upon that well-shaped mouth, no sign of softness at all in his finely hewn features. France and its wars had taken the boy she had once known and sent back a stranger.

"Mistress Keith," exclaimed Robert when he finally noticed her. "Come, sit down," he said as he stood up, along with Adair. "Do ye recall Sir Adair?"

"I do. My laird," she murmured and curtsied.

"Where is Donald?" asked Sir Adair. "I sent him to meet ye at the gates."

"Meg was with me, Laird."

"Oh, dear." Robert frowned toward the door even as they all took their seats, obviously wondering if he should go and rescue his son.

"Meg?" Sir Adair frowned for a moment. "Lame Jamie's lass?"

"Aye," replied Robert. "She and my son seem to forget all else when they meet and begin to trade insults." He smiled crookedly at Rose. "I ken that your mother said they would be mates, but I oftimes wonder if they will survive each other long enough to see that truth."

"I, too, wonder. Indeed, I pondered that riddle e'en as I left them hurling insults at each other." She set her basket upon the table. "It does seem more of a battle than a courtship."

As Robert and Rose talked, Adair studied the woman he had last seen as a too thin, slightly untidy child. High full breasts, a tiny waist, and gently rounded hips declared her a woman grown, but he could still see that sweet, beguiling child in her delicate heart-shaped face. Her bright hair had darkened to a rich copper and hung down past her waist in thick, tempting waves. Most of the freckles had faded from her skin, leaving no more than a scattered trail across her small straight nose and soft cheeks. Thick, dark lashes and gently arched brows enhanced her wide, beautiful, sea green eyes. Her full mouth was curved in a smile as she and Robert wondered at the odd behavior of the two young people she had left behind in the bailey. He felt a slight tightening in his body and was not surprised that he would desire her.

There was something missing, however, and it took him a moment to decide what was gone. The child he had known had been a cheerful sprite of a girl, ready with a smile or a laugh. That joy had been dimmed. It pained him to see that, but he was not sure why. He had no time or interest in such foolishness. In truth, such joy and laughter as Rose had once possessed belonged cast aside with her childhood. It was born of the ignorance of blind innocence. At some time during the years he had been away, Rose had finally seen the world as it truly was, a place full of misery, grief, and pain.

He inwardly cursed when he realized that dose of good sense had not completely banished his disappointment. Adair feared he had hoped Rose still had the gift to make him smile as she had so often as a child. Whenever he had thought of Duncairn, he had thought of her, smiling and laughing. It was past time to bury that foolish memory.

"I was sorry to hear about your mother's death," he said when Rose looked his way, then inwardly grimaced over that appalling attempt at conversation.

"Thank ye, Laird," she said. "I still miss her sorely."

"Aye. Father wrote of her death with great sorrow."

"He was always verra kind to us and will be sorely missed as weel."

Adair nodded and touched her basket. "He spoke often of the cooking skills of ye and your mother. Father was verra fond of the apple tarts."

Rose reached for the goblet of wine Robert had poured for her, realized her hands shook, and quickly clasped them tightly together in her lap. Adair had a beautiful voice, deep and slightly rough. Her all-too-vivid imagination could hear it condemning her as a witch and she felt cold. She tried to find comfort in the fact that Robert was so at ease. He certainly did not act as if she was, more or less, on trial.

"When he had them in the dead of winter, he often called them a touch of spring," she said.

"Father also said he found them most comforting, that eating one was sure to pull him free of a dark mood. He talked so often of them, I felt compelled to try some myself. I hope my request didnae inconvenience you."

She managed a smile. "Nay, laird."

When he tugged her basket closer, she tried to remain at least outwardly calm. The boy she had known would have never been a threat to her, but that boy was gone. Rose was a little surprised that she felt so strongly attracted to this dark man but knew that did not mean he was safe. Her mother had taught her that desire, even love, could cloud one's thinking, dull one's instincts. As he chose a tart and moved it toward his mouth, she prayed that, if the food did anything to him, it simply stirred to life the spirit of that kind young man she had once known.

Chapter Two

Sweet, yet tart, Adair mused as he chewed. The blend was perfect. Even the texture of the food was perfect. It seemed strange that such a simple food could be such a delight to the tongue. Adair reached for another one.

Slowly, he relaxed in his chair. A gentle warmth seeped through him, easing the tense readiness of his muscles that seemed to afflict him even in his sleep. Although he had always thought of Duncairn as home, for the first time in far too long, he felt its welcome reach out and touch him. He looked at Rose, noticed she was looking a little pale and was clenching her hands in her lap, and felt an urge to take her into his arms. Adair realized he wanted to kiss and stroke away the fear from which she was suffering.

Adair reached for his tankard and had a deep drink of ale. It did not banish the feelings. Comforting, his father had called the food of the Keith women, and that was exactly what Adair felt. He felt just as he once did when his late mother used to stroke his brow and kiss his cheek. Adair felt he ought to be alarmed by that, but he was not. If it was due to sorcery, as Mistress Kerr suspected, it was certainly a very benign sort.

Then again, he mused, if little Rose could make food that gave comfort to a man who had not known it for far too long, what other trickery could she produce? He studied her lovely face and felt guilty for that suspicion. There was no evil in Rose, no darkness. At worst, she was misguided.

"They are verra good," he said at last, resisting the urge to have another. "I shall save the rest for later, I think."

"As ye wish, m'laird," she murmured.

"Ye grow the apples yourself?"

"Aye. Rose Cottage has a lovely garden."

She inwardly cursed. The last thing she wished for was for his attention to turn to her garden. When people turned a fearful, superstitious eye on Rose Cottage it was mostly set upon the Keith women. Only rarely was it turned upon the garden itself. Rose preferred it that way. The garden was not only her heritage, but it was far more vulnerable than she was. If nothing else, it could not flee the anger and fear of the people.

"Mistress Kerr spoke of your garden when she was here."

"Did she?" This time Rose was grateful for the anger she always felt toward that woman, for it dimmed the fear she could not conquer on her own. "I believe she has intruded upon it once or twice." With torch in hand, Rose added silently.

Adair heard the hint of anger in her voice and noted that her hand no longer trembled when she took up her goblet and had a drink of wine. Mistress Kerr had managed to slip out several disparaging remarks about Rose Keith during her visits. There had even been a few less-than-subtle accusations. His father had written of the long-standing animosity the Widow Kerr had for the Keith women of Rose Cottage, but not the cause of it. It was clear from Rose's reaction to the woman's name that the animosity was still alive and strong.

"Come, I will escort ye home," he said as he stood up.

"That isnae necessary, laird," she said.

The moment he grasped her hand in his to help her to her feet, Rose decided that Sir Adair walking her home was not only unnecessary, it would prove disastrous. That tickle of attraction she had felt while looking at the man was increased tenfold at the touch of his hand. A little stunned by the feelings rampaging through her, Rose somewhat meekly allowed Adair to lead her away.

Her mother had warned her about such feelings. Flora Keith had not believed it wise to keep maidens ignorant of such things as desire. Rose knew she desired Sir Adair, that her affection for the youthful Adair had somehow lingered in her heart and might well be struggling to become something more. She could not allow that. Sir Adair was her laird, a man so beyond her touch it was laughable.

"The Keith women have held Rose Cottage for a long time, aye?" asked Sir Adair, telling himself there was nothing wrong with being so intensely curious about Rose, for she was living on his lands, one of those he was sworn to protect.

"Aye," she replied, "for nearly as long as the laird has been a Dundas." She knew she ought to tug her hand free of his but told herself it was a small, harmless indulgence. "The tale is that the first Keith woman was fleeing a mon and sought shelter in a small copse. The Laird of Duncairn was moved by her troubles and offered her shelter, told her she could make her home upon his lands. She built Rose Cottage with the help of some of the laird's men and started the garden. Keith women have been there ever since. They always keep the name Keith as weel, e'en if they wed. That was done mostly in the beginning. The family grew enough after that, so that if a Keith woman was to marry, another Keith woman would come to tend the garden."

"Your mother remained a Keith."

"Aye, she wed one. My father died when I was a wee bairn, though, and I dinnae recall him."

"And when did the women become so famous for their food?"

"I think it was from the first time the garden gave us enough food to cook with." She sighed. "My mother ne'er told me the why of it all. She may have intended to, but the fever came upon her swiftly. She was ill and then she died, too quickly to settle any of her affairs or tend to matters left undone. I have yet to get through all of her writings. The tale may be in there."

"Do ye read and write as weel?"

"Aye. The Keith women have long been healers. 'Twas thought wise to keep careful notes of herbs and cures. If something new was tried, it was quickly noted, and its success or failure as weel." As they neared her cottage, she tugged her hand free of his. "I thank ye, laird. 'Twas most kind of ye to walk me home."

Adair fought to ignore the sense of loss he felt when she pulled her hand away. "I suppose 'tis too dark to see the garden now."

"Oh, aye. 'Twould appear as no more than shadows." She opened the door to her cottage and grimaced when all four of her cats hurried out to twine themselves around her legs.

"Four cats?"

"Shortly after my mother died someone left a basket of four kittens on my threshold. Your father denied it, but I am sure it was he. Oddly enough, there are three toms and one female."

"Why are ye nay o'erwhelmed with the beasts?" He bent to scratch behind the ears of a large ginger tom and almost smiled at the deep, loud purr that erupted from the animal.

"I have a wee but verra comfortable cage I lock the female in when she is in season." She picked up a sleek gray cat. "Lady accepts her occasional banishment. She has had but one litter, quickly dispersed among the villagers." Rose frowned down at her biggest cat. "Sweetling broke through the door. 'Tis thicker now." Looking back at Adair, she caught the faintest hint of a smile curving his lips.

"Sweetling? Ye named that monster Sweetling?"

"Weel, he was but a wee thing when I got him. The ginger tom is Growler, for he did a lot of that, and the gray-striped tom is Lazy, which he still is."

"All alone as ye are, ye ought to have something more protective than cats."

"Weel, Geordie the blacksmith's son found them a fierce obstacle when he was creeping about here one night. Of course, he couldnae tell people he was sent to heel by four cats, and the tale he told caused me a wee bit of trouble for a while."

Her familiars, the Widow Kerr had called Rose's cats, demons in disguise. Adair suspected Geordie's lies fed that nonsense. Many people feared cats. Even those who kept them to control vermin were often uneasy around the animals. He was sure the rumors about Rose only enhanced the tales whispered about her pets.

Adair was not exactly sure what he felt about magic. Most of the time he did not believe in it. On the rare occasion when he found himself wondering if it did exist, he disliked the idea. Rose had made no mention of it, and he hoped that was because she did not believe in it either.

He told himself it would be necessary for him to spend some time with Rose to search out the truth, ignoring the inner voice that scorned his thin excuse. In his writings, his father had talked of magic and the trouble it often caused the Keith women. Rose's trouble was being brewed by the Widow Kerr, as her mother's had been, and by others like Geordie the blacksmith's son, who wished to turn critical eyes away from his own shameful attempt to attack Rose. He would not allow this superstitious nonsense to exist upon his lands.

When he fixed his attention back on Rose, he found her and her cats staring at him, their heads all cocked at the same angle. Adair could easily imagine how such things could stir superstition in the ignorant. He found it both charming and a little amusing. At the moment, it was not hard to see the beguiling child he had once known. He reached out to brush his knuckles over her soft cheek.

"Mayhap ye havenae changed as much as I thought," he murmured. "Good sleep, Rose."

Rose watched him walk away. With a faintly trembling hand she touched the still warm place upon her cheek. Such a light caress he had given her, yet she had felt it right down to her toes. The man was definitely a threat.

* * *

"Robert, has someone been eating my tarts?" Adair asked his steward.

Once back in his great hall, Adair had made himself comfortable in his chair and poured himself some ale. He had set Rose's basket in front of him, intending to indulge himself. Although he had been greatly distracted by Rose, he was sure that eight tarts had remained when he left to escort her home. There were only six now. He counted them a second time to be certain, then eyed a blushing Robert.

"I had one, laird," Robert confessed. "Your father always allowed me to have one, and I fear I helped myself out of habit."

"Ah, and then it tempted ye to have a second. I understand. They are indeed verra tempting."

"Aye, they are, but I only had one. My son had the other 'ere I could stop him. He was agitated after his confrontation with Meg and, as he ranted and raved, he snatched one up and ate it. I reprimanded him severely, m'laird, and he was verra sorry. Although it did ease his temper."

"Of course it did. No harm done," Adair murmured, then he frowned at the tart he held in his hand. "They are verra good. Rose is an excellent cook."

"As was her mother, laird."

"Do ye think there is magic in her food or in her garden?"

Robert grimaced. "I dinnae wish to use the word *magic*. 'Tis a word that can stir up trouble and talk of evil. I believe the Keith women have a true skill at cooking food that pleases both the mouth and the heart. I think they chose wisely when they chose their land, picking a place with rich soil and ample water that enhances the flavor of all they grow."

Adair smiled faintly. "Weel said. I believe I will still have a close look at that garden."

"Do ye suspect magic, or, weel, witchcraft?" Robert whispered the last word as if merely speaking it stirred his fear.

"Most days I dinnae believe in either. Howbeit, many others do, and the Widow Kerr seems most intent upon stirring up that fear. If I have a good look at that garden, I shall be able to turn aside such fear and superstition with clear, cold fact. I would prefer to tell the widow to close her mouth and cease with her lies, but—"

" 'Twould be easier to make the wind cease to blow or stop the river's flow," muttered Robert.

"Quite probably," replied Adair, faintly amused by this sudden show of temper in the usually sweet-natured Robert. "The game she plays is dangerous, however. She could get that poor lass hurt or killed. I will try to weaken the power of her poison, but if I cannae, I will make her cease. I willnae have that idiocy at Duncairn."

Brave words, he thought later as he lay in his bed and savored the last of Rose's apple tarts. Superstition and fear were difficult enemies to fight. Especially when Rose made food such as these apple tarts, he mused, as he savored the sense of peace and well-being that flowed through him. Any fool knew food, no matter how delicious, should not have such an effect upon one's humors. Adair still resisted calling it magic, but he had to admit it was unusual. If he was not feeling so pleasant, such a reaction to eating an apple tart might even make him uneasy.

Crossing his arms beneath his head, he closed his eyes and was not surprised when visions of Rose

Keith filled his mind. She had grown into an enchantingly beautiful woman. He had wanted her immediately and knew a long celibacy had nothing to do with it. Something about Rose stirred him in more ways than he could count. He wanted to ravish her even as he wanted to shelter her from every harsh word. He wanted her to soundly disavow any taint of magic yet found the mystery surrounding her and her garden intriguing. Just thinking about her made him feel like smiling, yet it had been a very long time since he had seen or felt anything worth smiling about.

Despite his confusion, seeing Rose in his dreams would be far preferable to what usually haunted him. Adair had a suspicion he would not be suffering any of those dark dreams this night. The painful memories and grief that had kept such a tight grip on him for so long were still there, but not so insistent, so overwhelming. He had lost so many friends, bold young men who had gone to France to find glory and riches only to find pain and death. Although he had gained some wealth, it could never buy him back the time he had lost with his family, now all dead and gone.

The grief inside his heart stirred a little, but only a little. It was as if some unseen hand had restrained that demon. He thought for the thousandth time that it was his own pride, his own arrogance, that had kept him in France, that he should have seen more clearly how time was slipping away. A soft voice in his head told him true arrogance was thinking he could forsee God's will. Guilt, yet another demon with which he had long wrestled, raised its head before it, too, was subdued.

Dark, bloody memories of battle and capture were still there. He could see their nightmarish shadows lurking in the back of his mind, eager to scar his dreams and disturb his sleep, but they did not surge forward as they always had before. They were in the past, a voice soothed, one that sounded very much like his late mother's.

That was a little alarming, he thought, yet he did not *feel* alarmed. He felt comforted. Adair could almost feel his mother's touch, her soft kiss, and hear her say, *Aye, my braw, wee laddie, 'twas a sad time, weighted with grief and pain, but 'tis past. Ye are alive, ye are home, and ye have met a bonny wee lass. Let those truths fill your heart and mind and sleep, my laddie, sleep.*

A bonny lass who fed him apple tarts that made him hear his mother's voice in his head, he mused, but could not gather the strength or will to be troubled by that. He would court Rose, he decided. It was time he was wed and set about the business of breeding an heir. Rose was the first woman he had met who had stirred such a thought in his head.

For one brief moment he feared that, too, was caused by her apple tarts, but only for a moment. Adair knew the feelings Rose stirred within him were caused by Rose and Rose alone. The seed had probably been planted years ago by the endearing child she had been. He would have her for his own, but first he would get her to cast aside all this dangerous foolishness about magic.

As sleep crept over him, Adair thought he heard his mother's voice again. She was scolding him for thinking he could take only a piece when true happiness and the prize he sought would only come to him when he could accept the whole. Adair decided he was too tired to understand what that meant.

Chapter Three

"Ye willnae get away with using your witch's tricks on the laird."

Rose sighed, then took several deep breaths to try to smother her anger. Mistress Kerr's voice was enough to stir her anger now. After years of enduring the woman's poison,she simply had no patience left. She knew she had to be careful, however. Every word she said to the woman had to be carefully weighed or it could come back to haunt her. It was not fair, but Rose knew she had to remain calm and courteous. It was her own fault she was going to have to endure this confrontation. She had been so caught up in her thoughts about Sir Adair that she had undoubtedly missed several opportunities to elude the woman.

"Pardon, Mistress?" she asked in a sweet voice as she turned to face the woman.

Mistress Kerr crossed her arms and glared at Rose. "Ye heard me. The mon has barely warmed the laird's seat and ye are trotting up there with some of that cursed food. Aye, and then ye bewitched the lad so that he followed ye home.''

"Ye make our laird sound like some stray pup. And might I ask how ye ken he walked me home?''

"Geordie saw the two of ye walking along hand in hand. Ye have probably already lured him into your bed.''

"Ye insult the laird *and* me. Our laird is a gallant knight and didnae like the idea of my walking home alone. Since Geordie was obviously lurking in the wood again, it appears the laird's protection was needed.''

"If ye hadnae bewitched the poor lad, he would-nae be such a trouble to ye.''

"Mither,'' whispered Anne, shock and a tentative condemnation in her voice.

Rose glanced at Anne, who stood just behind her mother. She was a little embarrassed to realize she had not even noticed the young woman, then told herself she had nothing to feel guilty about. Anne had developed a true skill at hiding whenever her mother was near. The fact that Anne could do so when only a few paces away from the woman was astonishing. It was also, Rose decided, a little sad.

"Geordie is nay bewitched,'' Rose said, surprised at how calm and reasonable she sounded, for she was furious. "He is a rutting swine who sees a lass alone as easy game. I would think he deserves far more watching than I do.''

"Oh, aye, ye would like it if I ceased to watch you,'' snapped Mistress Kerr. "That would leave ye free to ensnare the laird.''

"The mon has survived ten years of fighting in France. I dinnae think he can be brought to his knees by a wee, red-haired lass.''

"Heed me, Rose Keith: I mean for my Anne to become the laird's wife."

"I dinnae want to be," protested Anne, even as she retreated a few steps from her mother.

"Hush, ye stupid lass," snapped Mistress Kerr. "Ye will do as ye are told. And ye can begin by ceasing to fawn o'er that fool Lame Jamie."

"The laird doesnae want to wed me, either."

Mistress Kerr ignored her daughter and returned her glare to Rose. "I mean what I say, Rose Keith. I have plans for the laird and I will be verra angry if ye interfere with them."

Rose watched Mistress Kerr stride away, Anne a few steps behind her. Since Mistress Kerr was always angry with her, Rose idly wondered how much would change if she did interfere. Then she sighed and started to walk home from the village. Even if she fled to a nunnery on the morrow, if Mistress Kerr did not get her daughter wed to the laird, Rose knew the woman would still blame her. She also knew she should take the woman's threats very seriously, but it was a warm, sunny day and she would not spoil it with dark, chilling thoughts of what might happen.

Instead, she fixed her thoughts on what Mistress Kerr had let slip about Anne. Anne wanted Lame Jamie, Meg's father. Rose grimaced, not fond of the name Meg's father had been stuck with. The man had only a slight hesitation to his walk due to a broken leg that had not healed exactly right. Unfortunately, there were half a dozen men named Jamie around Duncairn, and people felt compelled to mark each one with some extra, identifying name, and Meg's father did not seem to mind.

She frowned as she wondered exactly what Mistress Kerr's objections were to Lame Jamie. The man was barely thirty, was a widower, had a fine cottage and only one child. He was not rich, but he was far from poor. And, unlike Mistress Kerr's thin claim of kinship to the old laird, Lame Jamie was second cousin to Sir Adair. Of course he was not the laird, she thought, and felt sorry for poor Anne. Even though Anne was two years older than she, free to choose her own husband, Rose knew the woman lacked the courage to break free of her mother's tight grip.

"Wheesht, if I was a witch, I would brew up a potion to give poor Anne some backbone," she muttered as she started up the path to her cottage.

Suddenly Rose stopped and carefully put down her basket. It took her a moment to understand what had so firmly caught her attention. Her front door was slightly open. That was not an immediate cause for concern, for Sweetling was capable of opening the door. He only did so, however, when something outside strongly caught his attention. She told herself that there was still no need for alarm—a cat's interest could be firmly caught by a falling leaf—but she still looked around very carefully. Geordie was still after her, always lurking in wait.

Her heart skipped with fear when she saw that the gate to her garden was open. Sweetling could not do that. Only human hands could manage to open the heavy iron-banded gate. Picking up one of the stout cudgels she kept in several strategic places, Rose crept into her garden. It was not until she reached her apple orchard that she saw the intruder.

The laird was strolling through her garden. In some ways, he had the right, as she was on Duncairn land despite the hereditary rights granted the Keith women. Nevertheless, she was irritated that he had not waited for a personal invitation. It was that irritation that subdued the urge to laugh at the way her cats trailed behind him, stopping when he stopped and even studying what he studied. It was impossible to completely restrain a brief grin, however, when he crouched to pick up a handful of dirt and her cats joined him in poking and sniffing at the ground.

Sir Adair's years as a warrior were revealed by how quickly he heard her approach, and the speed with which his body tensed and his hand went to his sword. He stood up, brushed the dirt from his hands, and bowed slightly in greeting. When he glanced down at her hand and faintly smiled, she blushed, realizing she still carried the cudgel.

"A stout weapon," he murmured. "Ye hold it as if ye ken how to use it."

"I do." She leaned the cudgel up against the trunk of an apple tree, idly stroking the trunk as she often did, for it was the tree her mother had planted when she was born.

"Did ye have one near at hand when Geordie attacked ye?"

"Aye, but my cats got to him first."

He looked down at the cats flanking him. "I didnae let them out."

"I ken it. Sweetling can open the door." She smiled faintly. "He does so when something catches his interest. I kenned he couldnae open the garden gate, however."

"Ah. I came hoping ye could show me the garden so many talk about, but when ye didnae appear after near half an hour, I decided to meander through it on my own. 'Tis weel laid out, and the wall that encircles it is a fine tall and stout one."

She nodded and started to follow him as he resumed walking. "It took many years. Some was done by the Keith women, some by their husbands,

and some in return for food when harvests were
poor or destroyed.''

''And your harvests have ne'er been poor or your
crop destroyed?'' He paused by some blackberries
growing near the wall and plucked a few ripe ones.

''My harvests have been hurt at times, but my
garden is weel planned, the wall shields it from
damaging winds as weel as from intruders, and I
have plenty of water close at hand. We dinnae have
large fields to protect, and o'er the years we have
done all we can to protect what grows here. Some
of the people have accepted our ways, if their own
gardens are small or in one small area of the larger
fields they plow and plant. At times, the fact that
our garden still grows whilst others falter and fail
has caused us trouble. 'Tis mostly good planning,
its size, and ample water within these walls that
makes it flourish.''

''And what makes it so, weel, comforting?'' Adair
moved so that Rose was standing between him and
the trunk of an apple tree. ''I should like to scorn
its effect upon people, but I cannae. Nor can any
others. 'Tis the one thing they all agree upon.''

That was a question Rose heartily wished he had
not asked. She knew the food from her gardens
did something other food did not, most people
calling it a comforting, a soothing, even saying it
gave them a sense of peace. Her mother had never
truly explained that. Flora Keith had spoken of a
blessing by the fairies and that, some day soon, she
would tell Rose the whole tale. Sadly, death had
stolen her mother's chance to speak. Sir Adair was
not a man who would accept talk of fairies, however.

'' 'Tis just good food, the fruit plump and sweet,
the vegetables and grains hearty and strong. Nay
more,'' she said.

"I think ye believe there is more than that. I think ye believe there is magic in this garden, just as so many others do."

"Ye think a great deal," she muttered. "Mayhap ye need more work to do."

Adair popped a blackberry into his mouth to halt the smile forming on his lips. He savored the softening that happened within, that continued blunting of the sharp edges of his dark memories. It was impossible to deny what food from Rose's garden made him feel, but he did not want to attribute it to magic. Something in the water or even in the soil was causing it. That was his preferred explanation. Adair knew he would not cease to eat anything she allowed him to, for he ached for the calm the food gifted him with, the growing ability to look at the past with more understanding and acceptance.

"For now, my work is to discover why the food from this garden affects what people feel," he said, stepping a little closer and placing his hands on the trunk of the tree to either side of her head.

"Why is that so important? It is what it is. It does what it does. It harms no one."

"It harms you."

"Nay, it—"

"It harms you. It causes talk, dangerous talk. Dark whispers of magic and witchcraft."

"Not everyone thinks such things."

"Not now, but we both ken that, at times, such whispers have gained strength, roused the people, and put the Keith women in danger. I want the whispers stopped. I dislike the thought that I might be dragged from my bed some night because some fools have gotten themselves all asweat with fear and are determined to root out the evil at Rose

Cottage. I mostly dislike the thought that the chances of getting here too late are verra good."

Rose took a deep breath to steady herself only to feel her breasts brush against Adair's broad chest. She knew he had drawn close to her, but not that close. That nearness made it difficult for her to think clearly. She was far too aware of his strength, his size, and her own deep attraction to the man. Rose knew she should move, that he probably would not try to restrain her, but she lacked the will.

"If they come hunting me, I will do my best to nay let it wake you," she said.

"This isnae a game, Rose."

"Do ye think I dinnae ken that? Mayhap better than ye do?" She thought it odd that she could be both tense with unease and tremble with pleasure when he stroked her cheek. "I cannae stop the whispers. I cannae hold back fear and superstition. I am but a wee lass who tries to make a living with what she grows in her garden and, occasionally, with what she can cook. I harm no one and, in truth, have helped many. There is nay more I can do."

"Ah, lass, that isnae good enough and weel ye ken it. Ye must openly deny there is magic here. Ye must show people there are reasons why your food tastes better, why your garden stays healthy nay matter what afflicts the others."

Adair closely watched her face. It was evident she was trying to neither deny nor admit that there was any magic at Rose Cottage. He wanted denial, but he began to suspect he would not get it. That troubled him, for he also wanted Rose.

He fixed his gaze upon her mouth. For now he would help himself to a little of what he wanted.

All the other complications could be dealt with later. Adair almost smiled when her eyes slowly widened as he lowered his mouth to hers. Since she made no attempt to move, push him away, or speak a denial, he deemed that a silent acquiescence and kissed her.

Rose felt his warm, surprisingly soft lips touch hers and felt trapped by her own desire. Heat flowed through her body, softening her, rousing a heady welcome. A tiny part of her was shocked when she wrapped her arms around his neck, but it died when she parted her lips and he began to stroke the inside of her mouth with his tongue. Her whole body shivered with the strength of the delight she felt. This was what she wanted, needed, despite every instinct that warned her against reaching so high. Or for a man who was determined to make her deny the magic that was her heritage.

That thought gave her the strength to pull away when he began to kiss her neck. She met his gaze, saw how passion had darkened and warmed his eyes, and nearly threw herself back into his arms. Taking a deep breath in a vain attempt to calm herself, she stiffened her spine and faced him squarely. Despite her own confusion about magic, whether it even existed and, if it did, where it came from, it was all tangled up with her heritage, with who she was. She had to be wary of a man who scorned it, disliked it, and wished her to do the same.

"That was unwise," she said, silently cursing the huskiness of her voice.

"Aye?" He stroked her cheek and felt her tremble slightly even as she pressed herself back against the tree, away from him. "Ye didnae cry me nay."

"I should have—verra loudly."

"Ah, lass, 'twas but a kiss. The sweetest I have e'er had, and I ken I shall be longing for another taste, but, when all is said and done, 'twas just a kiss. 'Twas no great stain upon your honor."

"I ken it, yet I am a lass who lives alone. I must guard my honor with greater vigilance than some other maid. Since I have no guardian here, if anyone learned ye had kissed me, many would quickly assume there was far more between us. I cannae afford that sort of talk."

He reluctantly let her move away. " 'Tis strange that ye so firmly guard your reputation for virtue yet allow the far more dangerous talk of magic to continue."

"Do ye expect me to stand in the middle of the village and vow I have none of this magic, ne'er deal in it, and dinnae believe in it? And why would anyone heed me? They will believe what they wish."

"But ye feed these beliefs. All the Keith women have. Ye dinnae seem as bad as the others were—"

Rose put her hands on her hips and glared at him. "There have been Keith women here since the first Dundas laird claimed these lands. Did ye ne'er think that alone is enough to stir tales? Few women hold land, and we nay only hold some but have done so for more years than most can count."

"Your mother did naught to still the whispers. In truth, she often spoke or acted as if it was all true."

"Aye, she did, and I willnae dishonor her memory by spitting on all she believed just to make my life easier." She started toward the cottage. "And I am nay sure I dinnae believe it, too. Some days I do; some days I dinnae." She reached her door and turned to glare at him again. "Ye are my laird, but ye dinnae have the right to tell me what I can and cannae think, feel, or believe. Good day," she said as she stepped inside and firmly shut the door behind her.

Chapter Four

Adair stared at the door that had been shut in his face. He was not accustomed to such things, especially not when he was in the middle of a conversation. Rose might think it was done, but he did not. Even as he considered the wisdom of following her into the house, he watched Sweetling stretch up, cleverly work the latch, and open the door. The cat then pushed the door open and walked inside, the other three cats right behind him. Adair shrugged and followed the cats inside. He smiled when Rose turned to stare at him in surprise.

"Your cat let me in," Adair said as he followed her cats right into her kitchen.

Rose scowled at Sweetling as the cat sprawled on the hearth and began to clean himself. "Traitor."

"I wasnae through talking with ye, Rosebud." Adair sprawled in a chair at the table and started to look around.

It annoyed Rose that his use of the name he had given her as a little girl should cause a softening within her. "I was done. Just because I hadnae said what ye wished to hear didnae mean I wasnae done discussing the matter."

"Ye are a stubborn lass. 'Tis a verra fine cottage ye have here. There are nay too many who have such fine fireplaces, yet ye have two. Or more? Upstairs as weel?" Rose nodded. "And good stone floors. More than one room and the same in the loft, I suspect."

"And glass in the windows," she drawled as she began to chop up some leeks for the stew she was making. "Some years have been verra profitable and we could afford such gentling touches to our home. Some things were done by those helped by the Keith women. We ne'er asked for anything, but people have their pride. I also think that, although a mon might be verra glad there is someone ready to help him feed his family, he needs to pay for that in some way. The fact that it was a woman who did so only makes that need greater. And so we find ourselves living in a verra fine cottage indeed."

"Aye, a mon would need to dull the bite of failure e'en if he kenned it was nay his fault."

She nodded. "A few things were done in trade. The mon who put a fireplace in my mother's bedchamber jested that his wife was pinching at him for one. The right stone wasnae easy for him to find, nay on his land. My mother kenned where there was a good supply—right where she wanted to enlarge the garden at the rear of the cottage. The two of us would have needed years to clear that land, but the mon and his sons wouldnae. E'en better, he had the sort of rock that makes a good wall. So we got our garden, a goodly start to the wall, and his wife got a fine fireplace."

"And everyone was satisfied."

"Exactly. And no magic was used."

Adair gave her a narrow-eyed look and helped himself to an apple from a large, elaborately carved wooden bowl on the table. "Lass, ye ken 'tis verra dangerous to let talk of magic continue." He took a bite of the apple and was no longer startled by how it made him feel. "The way the food makes a person feel—"

"I ne'er feel anything different or unusual," she said, staring down at the carrot she had begun to chop, for she found she was unable to directly meet his gaze while telling such a big lie.

"Ye ne'er were a verra good liar, Rosebud."

She scowled at him, annoyed when that only made him smile faintly. "I feel something, but nay so verra much. My mother said that is because I am mostly content, with myself and with my life, and I have few scars upon my heart. When my mother was sad because she so badly missed my father, she said she was comforted by the food, could feel the spirit of the love he had for her. Since my mother died, I have often felt the same, only 'tis her I feel."

He nodded. "I felt as if my mother soothed me. I e'en thought I heard her voice in my head."

"Ah, ye are a troubled soul, so ye feel it more strongly. Most people feel, weel, soothed." After her outburst in the garden, she decided it was foolish to continue speaking as if there was nothing odd about her garden.

"And why should it do that?"

"I told ye, I dinnae ken. In truth, I am nay sure I would have fully believed whate'er tale my mother may have told me if she had lived long enough." She shook her head. "Mayhap 'tis just the water," she muttered as she tossed the chopped vegetables into the stew pot hung over the kitchen fire. "No matter what I do or dinnae believe, it doesnae change things. Again, as I have said, it is what it is and does what it does. I am but the farmer and the harvester.''

"Weel, I dinnae think it is so verra simple."

"Ye are welcome to your opinion."

"Kind of ye." He sniffed the air as she stirred the stew. "Smells good."

"I am sure your cook has begun to prepare a verra fine meal for ye," she said sweetly as she sat down and poured them each a tankard of sweet, cool cider.

"I wouldnae be so sure. Did ye ken that Old Helga died?"

"Oh, aye. So who cooks for ye?"

"Meghan, Old Helga's niece." He almost laughed at the grimace she could not fully suppress. "The lass was taught by Old Helga for near to ten years, but 'tis verra clear she ne'er heard a word."

"I have heard that said about her." Rose felt sorry for the people at Duncairn, for Meghan was said to be able to ruin a raw carrot. "Ye cannae keep her as the cook. I ken 'tis an important position, but mayhap ye can find one for her that is nearly as important. Then ye might watch to see which men rarely come to the meals. 'Twould mean they are being fed elsewhere. Ye might find a new cook there."

"A good plan." He smiled faintly. "And ye are-nae going to invite me to eat with ye, are ye?"

"I cannae. By the time the food is ready and ye have eaten your fill 'twill be verra late and ye will have been here, with me, for a verra long time. 'Twill start whispers ye may find as upsetting as the ones about the magic of the garden."

Adair finished off his cider and stood up. "I

would nay be too sure of that," he murmured and started out of the kitchen.

Rose followed him and inwardly cursed herself for a soft fool even as she said, "Send Donald here in an hour. I will send ye enough stew and a few other things to make ye, Robert, and Donald a meal. Just be sure to watch the food carefully around Donald. The lad's stomach doesnae seem to have any bottom."

"Roused your pity, did I?" he drawled as he paused in the doorway and looked at her.

"Weel, aye. And now I ken why Donald wanders by here more often than he e'er did before, and always near to the time I might be sitting down to a meal."

"Clever lad." He grasped her by the chin and held her face steady as she leaned down. "A fare-weel kiss, lass."

"Someone might be watching," she whispered just before he brushed his lips over hers.

"Ye worry too much for a bonny wee lass."

He pulled her into his arms and gave her a kiss that left her weak in the knees. Rose slumped against her door and watched him stride away as she fought to regain both her wits and her breath. It annoyed her a little that he did not seem to be equally affected, if that confident stride was any indication.

"Weel, that looked heated."

Rose clasped her hand to her chest as her heart briefly leapt into her throat, then glared at Meg, who now stood directly in front of her. "Where did ye pop up from?"

"Weel, I was just about to rap on your door when the laird stepped out," replied Meg. "So I slipped into the shadows just off to the side here."

"Couldnae ye have just said a cheerful greeting and joined us?"

"I could have, but then I wondered why he was here. Then I remembered that ye were a wee bit scared when ye went to the keep. That started me thinking ye might have been right to be afraid and that matters had grown verra dire indeed. Thought ye might need rescuing."

"Weel, as ye could see, I didnae."

"I am nay so sure of that," murmured Meg.

"And might I ask why ye are out at such a late hour?"

"Ah, weel, my father has gone off to a fairing to sell his bowls and the like. He will be gone two days, mayhap a little longer if the weather doesnae hold fine. I told him I could stay with you."

Rose shook her head and almost laughed. "Ye are a wretched brat, but come on in. In truth, I shall be glad of the company. Something Mistress Kerr said today revealed that that cursed Geordie is lurking about again."

Meg cursed as she stepped inside and set her bag down on a chair. "Someone should do something about that swine."

"They should, but it willnae be you."

"Weel, I might be able—"

"Nay. If the fool grabs me again, weel, much as I hate to do it, I will speak to the laird."

"Good idea," Meg said as she followed Rose into the kitchen and sat down at the table. "He certainly wouldnae like anyone mucking about with his woman."

Rose sighed, collected a good-sized basket, and started to fill it with things that Adair and the others might like for their dinner. "I am nay the laird's woman."

"He was kissing you."

"I ken it. That doesnae have to mean much at all, Meg. Men like to kiss women. To be honest, I rather liked kissing him. That is all it was, though— a kiss. E'en if I felt like it was more, it wouldnae matter. He is the laird and I am nay much more than a crofter on his lands."

Meg snorted and shook her head. "The laird doesnae go about kissing just any lass. Fact is, he has been home a fortnight and hasnae e'en bedded a lass despite all the offers. Nay, ye can think what ye will and I willnae be telling anyone about all of this, but I think 'tis more than *just a kiss.*"

"Mayhap he has decided he needs a leman to pass the time whilst he looks for a wife," she said, hating to even speak the sudden suspicion infecting her heart.

"And I think the smell of those leeks ye put in the stew have addled your brain. The Keith women may not be lairds' daughters, but they have all been better born than some crofter's lass. The laird wouldnae choose ye for a leman. Ye can claim kinship with enough of the high-born Keiths to make ye a dangerous choice. But I am just a wee, skinny lass. I suspect ye will need someone older and wiser to talk sense into ye."

"Do ye think 'tis the food that makes him want to kiss me?"

"If your food made people feel amorous, we would be tripping o'er rutting fools in the road."

"Meg!" Rose tried to look shocked and stern but quickly gave in to the urge to laugh. "Ah, weel, I am just confused. Save for that fool Geordie who keeps trying to grab me, no mon has shown much interest in me. For the laird himself to be the first seems most strange."

"Most of the men at Duncairn ken ye are a wee bit above their touch, and I think ye scare them a little. Nay because of the magic, but because ye can read and write and ye have these fine lands. I think the laird is a mon who cannae or willnae believe in anything he cannae see, touch, or feel, and he, more or less, owns these fine lands. What makes the other lads timid just isnae important to him."

"Aye, that could be it."

"Why are ye packing that basket with food?"

"Oh, it seems the cook at Duncairn is Old Helga's niece Meghan."

Meg grimaced. "I am surprised any of them are still alive up there."

Rose grinned. "I ken it. I was moved to pity for the laird and told him to send Donald here to collect enough food for him, Robert, and Donald to have a fine meal. Dinnae frown; there will be enough for the two of us to eat as weel."

"I wasnae frowning about that. I was frowning because that rutting boy is coming here."

"Rutting boy?"

"He has been tumbling about in the hay with Grizel the alewife's daughter."

That explained some of the intensity that had lately been behind Meg's insults, Rose mused. The girl was jealous, although Rose doubted Meg knew it or would admit to it if she did. It had to be hard for Meg, as she was too old to ignore it and too young to understand why it troubled her so. And if she did understand, she was too young to challenge Grizel in any way for Donald's lusty attentions.

"Weel, all lads feel the need to test themselves in that way. I believe Grizel has been the testing ground for quite a few." She grinned when Meg laughed. " 'Tis unfair, but I doubt many men come to their marriage bed as innocent as they demand their wives to. I sometimes wonder if they feel the need more. And the first time for them doesnae hurt, though I suspect it may be embarrassing now and then.''

''And they dinnae need to fret that they may get with bairn.''

''Verra true. Grizel willnae. She takes a potion, ye ken. 'Tis nay one of mine. I dinnae like to deal in such things except when asked by some wedded woman who needs a wee rest from the birthing bed. But I have studied what Grizel takes and I cannae like it. Told her so, but she wouldnae heed me. I fear she may ne'er have a child; probably doesnae need to take the potion at all now.''

''Oh. She has hurt herself.''

''Aye.'' Rose spooned out a large quantity of her stew into a pail and then covered it. ''So, if Donald has reached the age to test his monly wings, so to speak, at least he willnae leave a trail of bastards behind him. And mayhap 'tis nay such a bad thing that the lads put themselves to the test a few times 'ere they wed. It cannae hurt to have at least one of the newly wedded couple kenning what to do.'' She shared a giggle with Meg, pleased to see that the shadow of hurt had left the girl's eyes.

''That must be Donald,'' Meg said when there was a rap at the door.

''Ye stay here. I dinnae wish an argument to start between the two of ye, for the food will get cold.'' As she hurried to the door with the food she had packed, Rose admitted that it really was going to be nice to have Meg visit for a few days.

It was late by the time Rose sought her bed. She closed her eyes and cursed when her mind filled with thoughts of Adair. Just thinking of his kisses had her lips aching for a return of his. It had helped a little to speak of her fears with Meg, but the girl was right—she really needed someone older to discuss it all with. There was no one, however, so she was doomed to try and sort out her confusion all by herself. Rose found herself very afraid that she might allow her heart to lead her into a great deal of trouble.

Chapter Five

"Rose? Where are ye?"

Rose was tempted not to answer, but curiosity got a hard grip on her when she realized it was Anne Kerr who was looking for her. She suspected she had not immediately recognized the woman's voice because she had never heard Anne speak much above a whisper. Anne actually had a pleasant, clear voice when she chose to use it.

"O'er here, Anne," she called. "I am sitting under an apple tree."

Enjoying a moment of peace, she mused, then scolded herself for being selfish. Not too long ago she had bemoaned the lack of company or someone to talk to. It was foolish to complain now that she had some simply because it did not appear at her convenience. Anne rarely spoke to her, or to anyone, for that matter. The woman had never come to visit, although Rose suspected that was not an intentional avoidance. In truth, Rose could not recall ever seeing Anne unless her mother was there.

"Ah, there ye are." Anne hurried over. "God's mercy, 'tis rather warm."

"Sit in the shade, Anne, and have a drink of cider." When Anne sat down, Rose handed her the wineskin she had filled with cider. "Ye will feel cooler in a moment or two."

After she had a drink of cider, Anne stared at the wineskin. "Oh, dear. I just had some of your food."

"Dinnae fret. Ye willnae turn into a newt." It was difficult to hide her astonishment when Anne giggled.

"I ne'er thought it would do that. Nay, I just feared it would change my humor enough so that my mother might notice the change."

"Nay, that willnae happen."

" 'Tis so pleasant here. So cool and shaded. And 'tis surprising when the walls are so high, but there is also a pleasing breeze."

Rose prayed Anne would not ask why that was, for she really had no explanation.

Anne clasped her hands in her lap and looked straight into Rose's eyes. "I had meant to be here earlier so that I wasnae just asking ye for something and then hurrying away, but I had to wait for Meg to leave. I would like a love potion."

"A what?" Rose sat up straighter.

"A love potion."

"Ah. Anne, I am nay sure there is such a thing." She briefly wished she could brew one right up when she saw the way Anne slumped with disappointment.

"I had heard that all the Keith women left behind writings and receipt books. I thought one of them might have known of such a thing." Anne took another drink of cider and appeared to relax a little. "Are ye verra sure there are no such things?"

"Anne, I can make ye a potion to ease the pain of your woman's time. I can e'en make ones to loosen tight bowels and tighten loose ones. I cannae make a potion to make someone fall in love with ye or ye with him. And 'twould be a false love, too, wouldnae it?"

"Oh, I hadnae considered that. But I am sure they sell love potions at some of the fairings."

"False brews, naught but trickery and lies, and some could even be dangerous. At best they might give ye something to make ye or the mon feel amorous for a wee while. Love must come from the heart, Anne, or it willnae last."

"Ye havenae asked who I want it for," Anne said quietly.

" 'Tis for Lame Jamie. I heard your mother scold ye about it two days ago." She smiled faintly when Anne blushed. "Ye are three and twenty, Anne. Ye dinnae need your mother's approval to wed."

"I ken it. I need to ken if he wants me, however. I have loved the mon for years. Yet I am ne'er without my mother close at hand, and as soon as she kenned where my heart lay, she made her disapproval verra clear."

"How did ye get free of her today?"

"She thinks I am with the priest."

"Oh, dear." Rose fought the urge to look around for an enraged Joan Kerr.

"I ken it: I am a selfish woman, for I may have caused ye a great deal of trouble. Yet I am desperate. As ye say, I am three and twenty. I have wanted Jamie for near as long as I can recall. Yet year after year passes and naught changes. I am stuck at mother's side and cannae e'en speak to the mon." She shook her head. "I sometimes wake in the night all asweat with the fear that I shall live and die in the shadow of my mother. Or, mayhap worse, I shall see the mon I love wed another."

"Anne, only ye can stop that fate. Ye are the one who must break free. Many can tell ye to do so, but only ye can actually do it."

"I ken it. I sometimes weep o'er what a wretched coward I am. When my mother's scold told ye my deep secret, I wanted to come here immediately to see if ye could help, but it still took me two days to work up the courage." She frowned at the wineskin. "I was feeling almost sick with fear."

Rose smiled faintly. "Cool cider can be verra calming."

"Of course," Anne murmured, but gave Rose a look that told her that she did not believe a word of that explanation. "I am certain that, if I could get some sign from Jamie that my love is returned, I could walk away from my mother. To do so 'ere I have that is what holds me where I am. After all, if I take the chance and he doesnae care for me, I shudder to think of the scorn and ridicule my mother will pile upon my shoulders when I must return to her."

"Ah, aye. I think that would make me hesitant as weel. Start small."

"What?"

"Start small. When ye are verra sure your mother isnae watching and ye see Jamie, give him a smile."

Anne looked both horrified and intrigued. "That would be so brazen."

"Nay, 'tis just a smile. 'Tis just enough to tell him ye find him pleasant to look upon. How he responds to that smile can tell ye a little about how he might feel about you. Dinnae take it to heart if he acts confused or e'en startled. Just try again. A smile doesnae cost ye anything and 'tis nay

enough to make ye look some lovesick fool." When
she saw how Anne still hesitated, she said, "Ye must
do something, Anne, or ye will fulfill those chilling
dreams ye spoke of."

Anne nodded. "Ye are right. I must take the first
step, tiny though it is. And I think I must also try
to take a small step away from my mother from
time to time."

"Slowly ease the choking hold of her apron
strings?"

"Aye." Anne sighed, as she started to twist her
hands together, and hastily took another drink of
cider. "My mother is a verra strong woman and, I
fear, nay verra kind. I have spent my whole life
enduring that until I am nay sure I ken how to
stop. But I will be four and twenty all too soon,
and I suddenly realized I might ne'er be free. She
talks of me wedding the laird, but that willnae
happen. Aye, I might be coward enough to march
to the altar despite loving another, but the laird
has no interest in me, thank ye God."

"At least that worry is off your shoulders."

"True. I want bairns, Rose. I want a family. I
want to love and be loved. I ken that I must find
the courage to reach for it, but I am nay sure I
have it."

Rose reached out to pat Anne's hand. "Just keep
your eye on what ye want. Ask yourself from time
to time if Jamie isnae worth it all. He is a good
mon, a kind mon. If he can return your love, I
think ye would be verra happy, e'en if your mother
continued to disapprove. Try to let the love ye feel
for him give ye the courage ye seek."

"That might work." Anne suddenly turned pale
and leapt to her feet. "Oh, nay."

The look of horror on Anne's face told Rose

who was walking her way. She sighed and looked in the direction Anne was. Mistress Kerr looked as angry as Rose had ever seen her.

"How dare ye lure my child into this garden of sin," Mistress Kerr snapped as she grabbed Anne's hand and yanked her daughter behind her.

Rose did not even bother to rise. "Anne sought a moment of respite from the heat."

"She didnae need to come here for that." She glared at her daughter. "And ye lied to me. Ye ne'er went to the priest." She looked back at Rose. "Ye have already begun to poison her heart and mind, teaching her the sin of disobedience." She looked at the wineskin and gasped. "And ye have been feeding her that witch's brew!"

"Och, 'tis far too hot to deal with your nonsense today," Rose said, her voice still calm but her temper beyond her control. "Ye have found your daughter; now go. Anne was welcome here. Ye are not."

"Ye heard her," snapped Meg as she appeared from behind the apple tree and sat down next to Rose.

"Ye heed me, Rose Keith," hissed Joan. "I willnae forget or forgive this. Ye have tried to steal my child from me. That cannae be tolerated."

"Mither," Anne protested.

"Silence," Joan snapped. "Ye and I will talk on this when we are safe at home."

Rose watched the woman drag poor Anne away, sighed, and closed her eyes. She wished she could do something for Anne, but the strength to change her life had to come from within Anne. She had to break her mother's tight grip herself or she would never be completely free. She opened her eyes a little and looked at Meg.

"Where did ye come from?"

"I saw that vicious crone march into your garden and slipped 'round her, staying in the shadows. She wasnae hard to elude, for her eyes were set on ye and Anne. What was Anne doing here?"

"Seeking answers."

"Such as what sort of poison might silence that fool of a mother she is cursed with?"

Rose laughed softly, then grew serious. "Anne is a verra unhappy woman, Meg. She is a coward and she kens it weel, but her mother made her one, has shaped her into what she is from the day she came into this world. It willnae be easy for her to change. Yet she lied to her mother and came here. A small step, but a step away, nonetheless."

"But what did she think ye could do?"

For a moment she studied Meg, then decided the girl could be trusted with a confidence. "I will tell ye, but only if ye swear ye will say nothing to anyone."

"I swear."

"Anne is in love." She frowned when that news appeared to worry Meg.

"With who?"

"She loves your father, Meg."

Meg breathed a hearty sigh of relief and helped herself to a drink of cider. "I was worried for a moment."

"Ye dinnae mind?"

"Och, nay. I have begun to think my father might have a soft place in his heart for Anne. He always mentions seeing her, e'en talks of how bonny she looked. I doubt they have passed two words between them because of the tight guard Mistress Kerr keeps on Anne, and my father is a shy mon."

"Then there is hope."

"How can there be if she willnae leave her

mother and my father is too shy to brave approaching Anne?"

"If Anne does as I say, she will soon be giving your father a wee hint that she favors him. I told her to slip him a smile whene'er she can do so without her mother seeing. Anne needs some hope to give her strength. If your father smiles back, weel, mayhap she can find some."

Meg nodded. "I will try to stay close to him when he returns."

"I dinnae think ye should interfere too much."

"Och, nay. I willnae. I will, however, make sure he is looking the right way when Anne gets a chance to smile, and mayhap pinch him into responding. I ken he likes her and, weel, he is lonely. He is but thirty and I think he needs a wife."

Rose was surprised at Meg's wisdom. "I am sure he values your company."

"Oh, aye, but 'tis nay the same, is it? And he would sore like to have more children, but he needs a wife for that. I ken there are one or two other things he would like a wife for, too, though one doesnae always like to think of one's father doing such things. Has to, to beget children, though, and I wouldnae mind a few brothers and sisters."

"Ye are a good-hearted lass, Meg."

"I just want him to be happy, and he always seems so when he speaks of Anne. I think I might take a few of your apples, if ye dinnae mind. Mayhap I can slip one to Anne now and then. They might help her. If she feels softened, she might ease the grip of some of that fear that keeps her tied to her mother."

"Just dinnae get caught." Rose closed her eyes. "I believe I need a wee rest. Solving troubles and battling crones can make a body verra weary."

Meg giggled. "I will go and see if any of the gardens are sprouting a weed."

Rose murmured her thanks and listened to Meg move away. She hoped Anne and Jamie could find their way to each other. They would be good for each other. Rose suspected her mother would have approved the match. Mistress Kerr was a formidable obstacle, however.

And pure trouble, she mused. The warnings were gaining in number and force. If Anne and Jamie wed, Rose knew Mistress Kerr would blame her. It was something she had best be prepared for. If Meg had decided her father and Anne should be wed, Rose suspected it would happen. Meg was almost dangerously clever at times.

There was really nothing she could do to stop the trouble coming her way, she realized. There was no reasoning with a woman like Joan Kerr. The woman looked at things with a twisted heart. It seemed beyond comprehending that she could not see where her child's happiness lay, or, if she did, simply did not care.

Thinking on the things Anne had said, Rose realized that Anne felt her mother had no real love for her. Anne had said that she wanted to love and *be loved*. That rather strongly implied that she had never felt loved. Mistress Kerr was in danger of losing her only child and did not seem to see it.

And I will be blamed for that as well, she thought with a sigh. She put her hand on the trunk of the apple tree she sat under, the one that had been planted when her mother had been born. It was at times like these that she sorely missed her mother. Flora Keith had understood these things far better than she could.

A part of her wished Anne had never come to see her, pulling her into the midst of her troubles, but she told herself not to be selfish. It would make at least three people happy if Anne and Jamie were wed. That was a gain worth any trouble Mistress Kerr wished to hurl at her.

Chapter Six

"Weel met, Iain, ye handsome fool."

Iain stared at the woman who greeted him with a smile. "Mary? Mary Keith?"

"Aye." Mary winked. "Come, I havenae changed so verra much, have I?"

"Och, nay." He stepped closer to the fence that enclosed this part of his fields and wiped his face on the sleeve of his shirt. "What are ye doing here?"

"Weel, I felt the need to come. Is someone courting my niece?"

"Ah, weel, there are a few rumors that the laird may be interested in her."

" 'Tis that, then. I woke in the middle of the night a fortnight ago and kenned it was time to get myself to Rose Cottage. I couldnae head right out, for my son was to be wed in a few days. But as soon as he was wed and I recovered from the grand celebration, I packed my wee pony and set out."

"Your husband?"

"Dead for near to six years. Your wife?"

"Dead for near to eight."

"Ah, a shame; Fiona was a good woman. Cannae say the same for the fool I wed, but he did give me three fine lads."

"No lasses?"

"Nay." Mary sighed and leaned against Iain's fence. "I have been set a quest as weel. There have been few Keith women born in the last generation or two, and e'en fewer left. Me, Rose, and one other, a cousin. I fear I cannae find the cousin."

"But why should ye need to?"

"I am nay sure yet, but it must be done. 'Twill come to me." She smiled at Iain. "Ye havenae changed all that much, ye great hairy brute."

Iain laughed. "Older. Nearing five and forty years. Got me five sons, though, and they help their old mon. I was surprised when ye didnae come after Flora died."

"Nothing called to me. Why? Has there been trouble for Rose?"

Iain nodded at the woman marching down the road. "There is the trouble."

"Curse it, is that that wretched Joan Kerr?"

" 'Tis, and she is still a vile-tongued wretch. Since Flora died Mistress Kerr has turned her attention to young Rose."

"Who is that poor girl she is dragging along behind her?"

"Her daughter Anne. And, since they are coming from Rose Cottage way, I have the ill feeling that the girl slipped away to visit Rose. That could cause a storm or two. The woman keeps a verra tight grip on that lass and intends her to be the laird's bride." He shook his head. "She has seen ye."

"What are ye doing here?" demanded Joan Kerr as she stopped in front of Mary. Her eyes widened when she noticed the full packs on the pony. "Sweet Jesu, ye arenae moving into Rose Cottage, are ye?"

"Aye, I am," replied Mary, and then she smiled at Anne. "And ye must be Anne. I am Mary Keith, Rose's aunt."

"And more trouble for Duncairn," snapped Joan before Anne could do more than nod in greeting. "Weel, I willnae stand for it."

"Then sit." Mary winked at Anne when the young woman started to smile, but quickly banished the expression when her mother glanced her way.

"Ye were always the worst of the Keith women," said Joan. "Enjoy your wee visit with your niece."

" 'Tis nay a visit. I intend to stay."

"What ye intend and what ye will be allowed to do are two verra different things. I wouldnae become too friendly with this woman, Master Iain. She willnae be here long."

Mary shook her head as she watched Joan stride away, still dragging her daughter along. "Wheesht, that woman still has a thistle stuck up her boney arse, doesnae she?" She grinned at Iain when he laughed.

"Just be wary, Mary. She managed to stir up a fair crowd against poor Flora once. The old laird stopped it, but it was unpleasant. She could stir them up again."

"I ken it." She bent closer and gave him a kiss on the cheek. "Dinnae be a stranger, Iain."

"Ne'er that, Mary." He watched her walk off toward Rose Cottage for a while, then straightened up only to find himself surrounded by his five sons. "Nay any work to do?"

"Who was that woman?" asked Nairn, his eldest.

"Weel, ye ken that I loved your mother and was

ne'er false to her." All his sons nodded. "If I had met that woman e'en a day or two 'ere I wed Fiona, there is a verra good chance ye would be calling her mother."

"Ah. A fine-looking woman. Ye still havenae said who she is."

"Mary Keith, Rose Keith's aunt."

"Wheesht, no wonder Mistress Kerr left here with fire in her eyes." Nairn grinned and nudged his father. "So, are ye going courting?"

"Ye dinnae mind?"

"Nay," Nairn said and his brothers all mumbled in agreement. "I think she was giving ye the invite to do so, too."

"Then, aye, your old father is going courting, and all of us are going to keep a verra close eye on the Keith women."

"Trouble is brewing?"

"It is, and I dinnae want it to disturb my courting." He grinned when his sons laughed and, after one last glance toward Rose Cottage, he returned to work.

"That bitch wore ye out, did she?"

Rose frowned, certain she recognized that sweet, husky voice. "Aunt Mary?" she asked even as she slowly opened her eyes.

"Aye. I have come to stay." Mary laughed when Rose leapt to her feet and fiercely embraced her. "Ye have grown into a bonny woman, lass," she said as she held Rose a little away from her; then she noticed Meg moving to stand at Rose's side. "And who is this?"

Rose introduced her aunt to Meg and took a moment to steady herself. Her aunt looked so much like her mother, with her sea green eyes and bright red hair, that it was both a pain and a pleasure to see her. The woman's arrival seemed a little too much like the answer to her prayers, as well.

With Meg's help she got her aunt settled in her mother's old bedchamber, moving Meg in with herself. As Mary enjoyed her bath, Rose and Meg prepared a meal. Rose was looking forward to talking with her aunt. Perhaps Mary could give her the answers to a few questions.

It was late before Rose found herself alone with her aunt. She suddenly was both eager to talk and yet unsure of what to say. Although she had a lot of questions, she was not sure how much she wanted to tell Mary.

"Come, child, let us go for a walk in the garden," said Mary, taking Rose by the hand and leading her outside. "I will start by saying I am sorry I didnae come to visit after coming for your mother's burial. I fear I have no real excuse, except that all three of my sons found their loves and got wed one after the other. 'Ere I kenned it, three years were gone."

"No need to apologize, Aunt Mary," Rose said. "Ye had a family and your own home." She looked around the garden as they began to walk through it. "Believe me, I can weel understand how fast the days go by."

"Weel, I am here now. I was called, ye might say. Had a dream that told me to get that last boy wed and settled and get myself to Rose Cottage."

"Why would ye be, er, called?"

"Because ye are soon to mate."

"Pardon?" Rose asked in a choked voice as she stopped and stared at her aunt.

"Ye heard me. Ye will soon be wed. I spoke to an old friend on the road here, and he told me the laird has been sniffing about your skirts. 'Tis true?"

"Aunt, he is the laird. Far and above my touch."

"Pah. Ye have good blood in your veins, lass. Near as good as his. Ye are clever, learned, and beautiful. Ye would make him a fine wife and I suspect ye would like it just fine."

Rose sighed. "I would, but I am nay sure why he seems to seek me out. I fear that somehow the food has made him—"

"Nay," Mary said firmly. "I refuse to believe that."

"He doesnae like the talk of magic, doesnae believe in magic, and doesnae want me to."

"Now that is a real problem. Lass, did poor Flora e'er tell ye about the garden?"

"Nay. She said a few things, hints and pieces of the truth, but ne'er actually sat me down and told me the tale."

"This garden is fairy blessed, lass. The first Keith woman to come here saved the lives of several fairies, hiding them from some mortal fools. In return they asked her if she wished for anything. She told them she wanted a garden, a garden that gave people peace, that would soothe them in times of trouble and ease their heart's wounds. I think she was just asking for a pretty garden and one that would produce weel. They took her at her word. After they had her walk the borders of the land the laird had given her, they put their blessing on it all. She still had no real idea of what they had given her, but she invited them to make their home on her lands. She promised that, as long as a Keith woman was able, one would be here to guard this place, to tend it and keep it from harm."

"And, again, they took her at her word?"

"They did. Have ye ne'er seen them?"

Rose sighed and crossed her arms over her chest. "Aye," she reluctantly admitted. "I have seen them. Some nights more clearly than others. I can see some now, their glow all 'round the apple trees."

"Aye, your mother said they seem to love the trees most of all. Ye cannae deny that heritage, lass. E'en if ye tried, the truth would come out. The magic is in ye, as weel as in this land and all that grows from it. 'Tis in all the Keith women descended from that first one. The fairies need the guardians of the garden to remain aware of them, to believe in them, so each guardian is kissed with magic. 'Tis nay always an easy gift, or a pleasant burden, but 'tis our fate and we must accept it."

"I ken it," she muttered and went to stroke the trunk of her mother's tree. "Do we linger here, Aunt? At times I swear I can feel my mother's presence in this place."

"Oh, aye, all of them are here in a small way, e'en the first one. 'Tis why a tree is always planted when a Keith woman is born. That is your mother's"—Mary touched the one opposite it—"and this is mine. Yours is o'er there, aye."

"Aye." She touched the tree on the other side of her mother's. "And this belonged to a Margaret Keith. Mother was afraid she had died, for she seemed to disappear. I am nay sure who this young one belongs to." She touched the tree her mother had planted thirteen years ago. "Mother simply said she had to plant it. Something told her to plant this tree. Ye dinnae look surprised."

"Nay. I am nay only here to be guardian after ye wed, but to find the one who must follow me."

"Oh. I willnae have a daughter?"

"I forsee a lot of braw laddies for ye, and only one lass, but she will have a different destiny. Nay, this tree is the one belonging to the guardian who will follow me. I just hope I am nay forced to search too far and wide. Most Keith women ken when it is time to come here, but this could be a lass left untold about her heritage, ignorant of what her dreams might try to tell her.''

Rose sat down on a stone bench within a group of trees and smiled faintly when her aunt sat beside her. '' 'Tis not such a bad place to linger.''

"Och, nay. Ye have been having trouble with Joan Kerr?''

"Oh, aye. Her daughter slipped her leash and came to visit me. Wanted a love potion.'' She smiled when her aunt laughed. "She loves a mon her mother willnae let her marry. Her mother wants her to be the laird's wife. Anne wants Meg's father. Anne is old enough to do as she pleases, but—'' Rose shrugged.

"She has been too long under Joan's boot heel.''

"Exactly.'' She told her aunt what she had advised Anne to do and what Meg planned to do.

"Good advice, lass. Aye, and the wee lass Meg will do her part weel. She is a canny one. And though she has a tongue as sharp as mine, she has a soft, loving heart. All that is good, but nay for ye.''

"Och, nay. With the laird showing me what Mistress Kerr sees as interest and now Anne easing free of her grip, I have become the verra worst of enemies. I wish I kenned exactly what the laird is about, besides stealing kisses and trying to prove there is no magic here. Most times I dinnae think the food has stirred his interest in me, and I am almost always sure he isnae after naught more than a quick rutting, but I just dinnae ken.''

Mary put her arm around her niece and kissed her on the cheek. "When 'tis a mon's feelings ye must judge the worth of, it can take a while to get to the truth. I offer ye but one piece of advice: Dinnae let him make ye deny what ye are. That road leads to misery. He must accept ye as all ye are or leave ye be."

"I ken it. I didnae want to, but I do ken it. I may nay be sure of anything else, but of that I am. I realized it during one of our arguments. I felt that, if naught else, 'twould be like spitting upon my mother's memory, e'en on that of all the ones before her, if I denied magic. I can still waver in my belief, or mayhap 'tis more a waver in my wanting to believe. Life would be so much easier without such complications."

"Ah, but nay so interesting."

Rose laughed. "True. Do ye have any thoughts on how to deal with Mistress Kerr?"

"Aside from sewing her mouth shut, nay." She grinned when Rose giggled. "We must prepare ourselves. She will try to hurt us in some way. Her daughter will have that mon she seeks and that will cause her to fair foam at the mouth."

"So, Anne will be with Jamie?"

"I believe so." Mary frowned. " 'Tis a little hard for me to say it with certainty, for I got such a sense of conflict and fear from the girl when I met her on the road here. But Meg is right. Her father is a shy mon, and if Anne is brave enough to give him a hint of interest, it would be best if someone is there to be sure he responds."

Rose nodded, then quickly placed her hand over her mouth to hide a wide yawn. "I didnae do a great deal today, yet I feel verra tired."

"Ye suffered through a lot of turmoil and were afflicted by Joan's bitterness and anger. Emotions can weary a person as easily as hard work." She stood up, took Rose by the hand, and led her back to the house. "I hope your young lad comes round soon, for I am eager to have a good look at him."

"Oh, dear."

Mary laughed. "It willnae be so bad. Mayhap I will charm the fool."

"Oh, ye can be verra charming when ye wish to be, but ye are also verra open about, weel, magic. That is why I said, 'Oh, dear.'"

"He has to face it, lass. No one is asking him to become a believer, just to cease refusing ye the right to believe."

"He is verra concerned about the trouble it could bring me."

"A good sign. Yet the trouble coming our way has a verra clear source—Joan Kerr. In truth, most of the occasional trouble visited upon the Keith women has come from but one person. Sad to say, 'tis most often a jealous woman. We Keith women are simply too beautiful and charming for some women to accept."

Rose laughed and kissed her aunt's cheek. "I am glad ye have come. Meg is clever and good company, but just lately I seem to have been besieged by problems I wished to speak to another woman about."

"I understand. Ye ken that ye can talk to me about anything."

"Och, aye. Even mother used to laugh and say ye were a blunt-tongued wretch who ne'er seemed to be embarrassed by anything."

"Aye, she was verra fond of me." Once they were inside the cottage, Mary secured the door as Rose moved to bank the fire. " 'Tis a verra fine place," Mary said as she looked around. " 'Twill be easy to call it home. Weel, I am to bed. See ye in the morning, lass."

Rose wished her aunt a good sleep and, after

securing the house, made her way to her own bed. Her aunt was lively, loving, and sometimes far too outspoken, but it was good to have her at Rose Cottage. Although a part of her was delighted by her aunt's prediction that she and Adair would be wed, Rose forced herself not to put too much faith in that. There was a lot she was yet unsure of, and there was also his aversion to magic. Neither obstacle was a small one.

Chapter Seven

Adair dismounted in front of Rose Cottage. He felt embarrassingly eager to see Rose. It had been a full week since he had last seen her. Even though the week had been full of hard work, his mind had often been filled with thoughts of her. Once he had often awakened in the night asweat with fears caused by nightmares. Now he often woke all asweat with desire for Rose. She had faithfully sent an evening meal to him, Robert, and Donald for the whole week. Even though he was not sure he wanted to give them up, he had taken her advice, followed the men who had consistently missed the meal in the great hall, and found himself a new cook. He knew it was only right to tell Rose she no longer needed to do all that extra cooking. It also provided an excellent reason to visit her.

Just as he was ready to rap on her door, he noticed her four cats arranged in various indecent positions on the top of the sun-drenched garden wall. A neatly stacked collection of kegs and barrels revealed how they had gotten up so high. He had known some men who treated their hunting dogs better than they did their children, but Rose took the spoiling of her animals to new lengths. The woman had far too soft a heart.

Then he heard a soft familiar voice drifting up from behind the wall. Strolling over to the garden gate, he found Rose in the middle of one of her raised plots just beneath the wall the cats were sprawled on. He grinned as he entered the garden and moved up behind her. Her skirts were tucked up, exposing a fine pair of slender legs to just above the knee. When he realized what she was saying, he had to bite back the urge to laugh.

"This is your last warning, Sweetling," Rose muttered as she used her small garden spade, a hand-sized one the annoying Geordie's father had once made for her, to remove a clump of dirt from the garden. "Ye are to cease using my gardens as a privy. Aye, 'tis fine, soft dirt and ye ne'er hurt the plants, but I dinnae like finding it. Have I nay set ye aside a fine, large plot of dirt in the garden behind the cottage? Use that, ye wretch." She tipped fresh dirt into the small hole she had made.

"I dinnae think he is listening to ye," Adair said.

Rose gave a soft screech and stumbled as she tried to turn. Adair moved quickly to catch her around the waist and lift her out of the garden. He set her down on her feet, keeping his hands on her waist, and grinned. Rose's face was smudged with dirt. Long strands of hair had escaped the loose braid she had forced it into to tangle around her face. There was even the faint gleam of sweat upon her face and neck.

"I didnae mean to startle ye," he said.

"Ye shouldnae creep up on people that way."

"I didnae try to be stealthy. Ye didnae hear me because ye were too busy scolding your cat."

It was not easy, but Rose suppressed the urge to curse. She had a very good idea of how poorly she looked, dirty and disheveled. That was embarrassing enough. To realize he had heard her talking to her cat was almost more than she could bear. She tugged free of his grasp and went to the well in the heart of the garden. If she cleaned herself up a bit, she might be able to regain some small scrap of dignity.

"Just why are ye here?" she asked as she pulled a soft rag from a pocket in her skirts and used the water from the well's bucket to wash her face.

"Would ye believe me if I said I missed ye?" He smiled at the way she rolled her eyes. "I did. Howbeit, I also felt ye should ken that Duncairn has a new cook. Ye were right. When I took the time to notice who didnae eat in the great hall, then followed them, I found a cook. 'Tis Sorcha, Colin the shepherd's eldest daughter. She and her family consider it quite an honor I have given her."

"Oh, aye, it is." Leaning against the side of the well, Rose idly wiped her hands and neck with the wet cloth.

"Her sister will help." He stepped closer, placing a hand on the rim of the well to either side of her and lightly caging her. "I offered Meghan several other places, but she didnae want them. Didnae seem to care that she had been replaced, either."

"Does she think she can just live at Duncairn and nay work at all?"

"Nay. She has gone to work at the alehouse." He slowly smiled at her shock. "It seems Meghan does have one skill. As Sorcha told me, the lass spends more time on her back than a dead beetle." He grinned when she laughed. "Sorcha feels

Meghan intends to gain a few coins now for what she oft gave away for little or naught."

"Oh, dear. Grizel willnae be pleased. So, ye came to tell me my plan worked and that I dinnae need to cook your meals again." Her last word ended on a gasp as he moved closer until their bodies touched and began to kiss her throat. "Adair."

" 'Tis but a wee kiss I seek. One to show ye how verra grateful I am that ye didnae let me starve."

Even as she opened her mouth to inform him that a simple thank ye would do, he kissed her. Rose rapidly lost the will to object, as well as the ability to think of any of the very many reasons why she should push him away. She wrapped her arms around his neck and returned his kiss.

"Weel, this must be the new laird then."

The sound of her aunt's cheerful voice startled Rose so much that she suspected she would have tumbled back into the well if Adair had not kept such a tight grip on her. She quickly eluded his grasp to stand beside him. As she lowered her skirts and brushed them off, she introduced Adair to her aunt.

" 'Tis good that Rose is nay longer alone in the cottage," Adair said, idly deciding that the Keith women aged well, for Mary Keith was still a fine figure of a woman.

"Oh, Rose was ne'er really alone here," murmured Mary.

Adair decided to ignore that and looked at Meg, who stood next to Mary. "I met your father in the village, lass, and since I was coming here, he asked me to tell ye to come along home now. He is sorry he was away longer than he had planned, but he is weel." He smiled faintly as Meg babbled out her gratitude for everything to the two Keith women, then raced off.

"She was beginning to fret o'er him," said Rose.

"He feared she might have. He also wished me to convey his deep thanks for watching o'er her whilst he was gone."

"She was far more help than hindrance."

Mary nodded. "She has a true feeling for the garden."

" 'Tis one of the best gardens I have e'er seen," Adair said. "Holding both beauty and purpose."

"And ever so much more. Cannae ye feel none of it, laddie?"

Rose sighed, realizing that her aunt intended to bludgeon Adair with all manner of talk about magic. It was, perhaps, not such a bad thing to be blunt, to speak the truth as one saw it, be it good or bad. She just wished her aunt had warned her that she was going for the throat. Since she was still reeling from the effects of Adair's kiss, Rose did not particularly feel like getting into an argument. She was not sure her aunt ought to be calling the laird *laddie,* either.

" 'Tis a verra peaceful place to visit." Adair began to suspect that Rose's aunt was about to make Rose look like a complete nonbeliever.

"Stubborn, stubborn lad. Your fither ne'er cared one way or t'other. But, ye do, dinnae ye?"

"My father wasnae so verra fond of the trouble it all caused."

"He kenned full weel that the trouble didnae come from Rose Cottage."

Adair glanced at Rose and caught her watching him with the glint of sadness in her fine eyes. If he had made any progress at all with Rose in getting her to cast aside all this foolishness about magic, Mary Keith would steal it all away. That made him angry. He decided he should leave, but not before he got this stubborn woman to see the risks she was taking, that she was endangering herself and her niece.

"Where the trouble has started doesnae make a great deal of difference when it kicks in your door," he snapped.

" 'Tis good that ye worry on the lass's weel-being."

Rose's aunt was one of those women who could make a man crave the oblivion of drunkenness, Adair decided. "Ye refuse to see reason."

"Oh, I often see reason." Mary smiled faintly. "Too often, 'tis said. The trouble here is that ye refuse to accept that there are some things that defy reason, things that one cannae always explain. I dare ye to tell me that ye dinnae feel the wonder of this place or taste it in the food. 'Tis a magic place, my braw laddie, and ye can scowl, mutter, curse, and growl all ye like, it willnae change that fact."

"To speak of magic and fact together is foolishness. 'Tis also foolish to speak of magic at all. It stirs fears, Mistress Keith. Dark, violent fears. If ye continue to spit in the eye of that truth, it could cost ye verra dearly."

"The Keith women of Rose Cottage have faced trouble before and won."

"Weel enough, then. Ye keep talking and bring that trouble down upon your heads. Just dinnae expect me to put out the fire after they set the kindling about your wee feet."

As she watched Adair stride out of the garden, his anger clearly visible in every lean line of his body, Rose had to bite her tongue to stop herself from calling him back. She realized how dangerously close she was to giving up her heritage, a large part of herself, just to make him happy. It was not good or wise to want a man so much that she was willing to consider changing all she was. When she caught her aunt watching her with concern and sympathy, Rose suspected she looked as if she was about to burst into tears at any moment. She certainly felt inclined to do so.

"Weel, that rather settles that, doesnae it?" she murmured.

"Nay, child, that was just an argument," said Mary.

"He was verra angry, Aunt."

"Aye, and I suspect he will get angry a few more times 'ere he comes to his senses. That is a stubborn mon. He kens the food from this garden has helped heal his heart and loosen the grip of the dark memories he brought back from France, but he willnae call it magic."

"How did ye ken about his troubled soul?"

"The scars are still there to see, lass. 'Twill be a while 'ere he is completely free, but he can sleep now, I suspect. And he can do that because of the food from this garden and he kens it weel."

"But doesnae wish it to be magic."

"He will, lass. He will."

"Mayhap. As ye say, he is a verra stubborn mon." She sighed. "I think I will go for a walk."

"A walk can be verra good for hard thinking. Where do ye go?"

"Down to the river that marks the eastern boundary. I think I might e'en walk into it."

"What?"

Rose smiled faintly and shook her head. "Nay for any dark reasons, but because 'tis a hot day and I am dirty."

"Ah, of course." Mary followed her out of the garden. "Dinnae be gone too long or I shall worry."

"Duncairn is a peaceful place, Aunt. I shall be safe."

Mary shrugged. "E'en peaceful places have their dangers."

It was not until she had been walking for a few moments that Rose began to wonder if her aunt had sensed something to prompt that subtle warning. She shook her head and continued on. It might not be something her aunt had ever done at her home, but Rose had often walked alone throughout Duncairn and had never come to harm. Duncairn was, she suddenly realized, unusually peaceful. Mayhap the fairies had something to do with that, too, she mused with a smile.

She grimaced when she had to admit that she truly did believe in all the magic of Rose Cottage. Despite her moments of trying to ignore it all because she so badly wished to be just like everyone else, she had always believed. As a child she had even danced in the garden with the fairy lights.

Of course, she had had few children to play with, Rose thought. The mothers of Duncairn were reluctant to let their children get too close to the ladies of Rose Cottage. She inwardly cursed. That thought tasted of resentment, and she had to admit that such feelings had gained strength in her over the years. It was true that the garden was a burden at times, a weighty responsibility, but it was also a blessing, and one the Keith women had willingly shared with the people of Duncairn. If she was going to resent anything, she decided, it should be the ignorance and ungratefulness of those in Duncairn.

It felt better to have faced that truth about herself, but Rose doubted anything could make her feel better about the problems between herself and Adair. Even if she tossed aside all other doubts about their relationship, there was still the magic to contend with. Adair's angry response to her aunt's talk of the garden and its wonders told Rose that Adair's uneasiness about that magic went deeper than a simple concern for her safety.

Once at the river, she sat down to take off her shoes. Rose stood up, tucked up her skirts, and cautiously dipped her toes into the water. It was a lot colder than she had anticipated, but she decided a little wade would probably feel very nice.

She had barely gotten her feet wet when someone grabbed her braid and yanked her back so forcefully, she felt as if she was about to be snatched bald. Her first reaction was to reach for the braid to try and free it or, at least, grab enough of it to try and ease the pain in her scalp. As she stumbled around, she came face-to-face with her attacker.

Rose decided that, in a strange way, being found alone by Geordie was almost to be expected. The day had begun badly and was about to end very badly indeed. Despite the tears slipping from her eyes due to the pain he had caused her, she glared at him.

"Do ye ne'er stay at home to help your poor father?" she snapped, and almost smiled at his shock, for he could not have expected her to simply scold him for sloth.

"I kenned that, if I waited long enough, I would find ye alone," he said.

"How verra clever ye are. Tell me, my clever brute, just how do ye intend to explain rape? Dinnae think I willnae cry this crime to the verra rooftops."

"Wheesht, do ye think that will gain ye anything? I will just say that ye bewitched me, that I was caught in some spell. Mistress Kerr will hasten to support me."

There was a chilling truth to that, but Rose fought to ignore it. It could make her lose some of her strength. She kicked out at him and nearly caught him square in the groin. He yowled and then cursed her as he tossed her to the ground. Rose managed to get out of his way when he tried to pin her down with his brawny body, but she did not escape completely.

As she wrestled with Geordie, Rose found herself thinking of Adair. She did wish he would ride to the rescue, like some gallant knight in a minstrel's tale, but knew the chances of that were very slim. Rose also thought of how, if Geordie got what he was after, she would have only a horror to recall concerning her first time with a man and not the loving interlude she might have enjoyed with Adair.

Chapter Eight

Reining in several yards before the gates of Duncairn, Adair sighed. His anger had faded. He had not handled himself well in the confrontation with Rose's aunt. The woman had believed in the tales of the garden her whole life, as had Rose. It was not reasonable of him to expect such long-held beliefs, wrongheaded as they were, to be cast aside just because he said they should be. Weaning Rose away from the grip of those tales and fancies was going to take time and patience. He had shown very little of the latter in the garden.

Adair decided an apology was in order. He turned his mount and started to ride back to Rose Cottage. If nothing else, he had intended to spend some time with Rose, and he would not let an argument with her stubborn aunt rob him of that.

As he rode up to the cottage, he was surprised to find Iain of Syke Farm standing by the garden gate talking to Mary. "Greetings, Iain. I hadnae expected to find ye here."

"Came to fetch some herbs," the man replied.

"Ah." Adair bowed slightly to Mary. "I apologize for my earlier display of anger."

"Nay need, laddie," Mary said. "I have been kenned to stir up a temper or two."

Although he was sure Iain was suppressing a laugh, Adair was more interested in seeing Rose than trying to discern what was or was not going on between her aunt and Iain. "I was hoping to speak to Rose."

"She went for a walk down to the river."

"Alone?"

"Aye. She told me she often does it and that 'tis safe."

"No place is that safe," muttered Adair as he turned his mount and rode off to the river.

"That lad is verra concerned about my Rose," murmured Mary as she watched Adair ride away.

"Aye," agreed Iain. "He may nay ken it, but I am thinking there will be a wedding atween those two."

"There will be. And why did ye tell him ye were here for some herbs? Ye arenae ashamed of kenning me, are ye?"

"Nay. I just had me the sudden thought that, for a wee while, it might serve us weel if people dinnae ken that ye have an ally here and there."

"Ah, ye may be right." She took one last look in the direction Adair had gone, then shrugged. "They will be fine. I must try nay to poke my nose in there too much. He has to sort out his concerns on his own."

"Aye. 'Tis always best to let a mon think he got to the place ye wanted him to be all on his own." Iain grinned when Mary just laughed.

* * *

Adair heard the trouble before he saw it. A feminine screech of fury and fear firmly caught his attention. What roused his concern and fear was that it had come from the river, where Rose had gone. He kicked his mount into a slightly faster speed, searching the area as he rode. There was no sign of any other people than the two he could now hear, so that meant that this was a private squabble.

When he cleared a line of trees and saw what was happening, he drew to a halt. Shock and a rapidly building rage held him still for the barest moment as he struggled to bring both feelings under control. Then Geordie got Rose pinned firmly beneath him, and Adair decided he would be showing more than enough control by not drawing his sword and killing the man on the spot.

He dismounted, walked over to the pair, and grabbed Geordie under the arms. He had a brief glimpse of Rose's eyes, looking huge in her pale face, as he tossed Geordie to the side. Even as he reached out a hand to Rose, she was already scrambling to her feet.

"Ye are unhurt?" he asked Rose.

She nodded, annoyed at her sudden attack of mute shock. There was such fury evident in Adair's face, however, she was not surprised at the tickle of fear she felt. When Geordie groaned, Adair turned and moved toward the man. Rose took several long, deep breaths, fighting to gain control over her confused emotions. There was a good chance she would need all her wits about her to stop a killing.

"Ye dare to attack a woman on my lands?" Adair asked as a white-faced Geordie struggled to his feet.

"She bewitched me!" Geordie said, his voice cracking with fear. "I couldnae help myself, laird."

Adair felt Rose move nearer and knew he had to restrain himself. Taking a deep breath, he punched Geordie in the mouth, sending the burly man back to the ground. He really wanted to beat the man within an inch of his life but had never believed in such violence. Now, however, he had a better understanding of the feelings that might cause a man to act so brutally.

"Take yourself home. I will deal with ye later. 'Tis best if I dinnae do so now. I dinnae think it for the best if I go about killing my own people, nay matter how much one or two of them might deserve it," he added in a calm voice and watched Geordie stumble off toward the village.

"I wouldnae have thought Geordie could move so fast," Rose murmured, then tensed when Adair turned to face her. He still looked angry.

"Do ye have no sense at all?" he snapped. "Ye shouldnae walk about all alone. Nay, especially not when ye have suffered an attack by that swine once already. Duncairn is a lot safer than many another place, but nowhere is truly safe for a lass wandering about on her own."

The whole time he scolded her, he gently moved her closer to the stream. He knelt, tugged her down beside him, and tugging off his shirt, used it to bathe her face and hands. Rose suspected she ought to protest being spoken to and treated like a terrified child, but she was finding it a little difficult to think straight. She could not tear her eyes from that broad, dark chest. Adair was all smooth skin and taut muscle.

She gave in to the urge to touch him and, reaching out, ran her fingers over a jagged scar on his right side. "Ye didnae come home from France completely untouched, did ye?"

"Nay." He felt himself tremble beneath her touch and grabbed her hand. "I gained several scars. Nay all of them are from battle. I was caught once by the enemy. They were nay kind. Lost two friends there to torture 'ere I and three others escaped."

"How sad. 'Tis sad enough to have young men die in battle, but to have a precious life lost to men whom ye are nay e'en able to fight is verra sad indeed."

Adair was astonished that he had told her all of that. He had been forced to relate a few tales about his years in France, but the time he and five others had spent eight months in a dark hole, their days filled with pain and humiliation, was one tale he had not told anyone. Yet, suddenly, he blurted it out to Rose. It was odd behavior on his part and he was not comfortable with it.

"Are ye certain he didnae hurt ye?" he asked.

"Aye. There will be a few bruises, and I feared he was going to pull all my hair out, but naught else," she replied.

"I must think of how to deal with the fool, but I think I need to wait a wee while 'ere I do. I am still of a mind to just kill him."

"For a few moments there, if I had had a knife, I would have done it myself." She leaned forward and kissed his chest.

"Rosebud?"

She smiled against his skin, for he had come perilously close to squeaking. "Do ye ken what I thought when I realized that I could nay win a fight with the fool?"

He pulled her into his arms. "Nay. What did ye think?"

"That he was going to make my first time with a mon something out of a nightmare, and I dearly wished I had done it with ye first."

"Oh, hell."

Rose found herself on her back on the ground again, but this time the position pleased her. In that moment of fearing that Geordie would succeed in raping her, she had come to a decision. She might not fully trust the passion Adair felt for her, occasionally questioning its cause, but she knew he wanted her. And she wanted him. Now that she knew how easily she could become the victim of a man, could have lust forced upon her, she chose to take control. There was no doubt in her mind that making love with Adair would pleasure her.

When he kissed her, she wrapped her arms around his neck and fully returned his kiss. Heat pulsed through her body. Hunger for his touch made her shift beneath his weight. Rose blushed as he removed her clothes but did nothing to stop him.

"Ah, Rosebud, ye are so cursed beautiful," he muttered as he tossed aside the last of her clothes and looked her over from head to toe.

"I am a wee lass," she whispered, her eyes widening as he began to tear off his clothes. There was an awful lot of Adair Dundas.

"Wee but perfect."

She gasped with pleasure when he returned to her arms, their flesh touching. That delight was quickly surpassed by the feel of his hands and lips against her skin. Rose lost all concern about Adair's size. She tried to return as many of his caresses as she could and soon had only one clear thought. She wanted him, needed him.

"I will try nay to hurt ye," he rasped as he shifted his body and prepared to possess her.

"I ken it must hurt some the first time. Ah, but the ache I feel now must be nearly as bad."

"There will be nay turning back, my love."

"Hush." She kissed him. "I am yours. Here. Now. Do ye really wish to pause and discuss the rights and wrongs of it all?"

"Nay."

Rose bit back a cry when he joined their bodies. The pain was sharp but fleeting. For a little while she allowed Adair to soothe her with soft words and stirring caresses, but then her need grew too strong for play. She wrapped her legs around his slim hips and arched her body, shuddering with delight as he went deeper within her. Then he began to move, each graceful thrust of his body enflaming her, but she quickly decided she did not want grace and gentleness.

Adair groaned as Rose moved her slim, long-fingered hands over his body. He was fighting to go slowly, to not frighten her with the ferocity of his desire and need. Then she caressed his backside, grasped it in her tiny hands, and made it very clear that she was feeling no less fierce than he was. He released his control, giving in to the wild passion thrumming through his veins. When Rose cried out in release, her movements becoming somewhat wild, he held her close and let her take him with her.

It was a long time before Adair found the strength or will to move out of Rose's arms. He wet his shirt in the river and cleaned them both off. Her blushes amused him even as her silence began to worry him.

His own silence was probably not helping to ease the awkwardness of the situation. There was so much he wanted to say, yet there was still a lot standing between them. He wanted her as his wife, at his side night and day. He needed that. Yet he did not want magic at Duncairn, and Rose showed no sign of giving it up. Adair feared that, if he spoke of their future now, before they had settled that problem, he was telling her that it was already settled. The last thing he wanted was misunderstandings following them to the altar.

"Rosebud . . ." he began as she stood up and finished dressing.

"Ye dinnae need to give me sweet lies and promises, Adair," she murmured.

When he had not spoken of love or a future for them after the haze of passion faded, Rose had decided she would offer no hint of her feelings either. Since she had felt so profoundly moved by their lovemaking, knew that he was the mate of her body, heart, and soul, it was painful not to hear or see that he felt the same. It was, however, a sad fact of life that men did not have to feel much emotion at all to indulge in lovemaking. She had her pride and she would not chance humbling herself before a man who saw it all as little more than a moment of delight on a fine summer's day.

He stood up and went to put his shirt away in his saddle pack. "I have ne'er been good with sweet words, lass," he admitted as he walked back to her side, leading his horse.

"I begin to think many a mon isnae."

"Weel, ye need nay worry about sweet words from any other mon," he grumbled as she started to walk toward Rose Cottage and he fell into step at her side.

"Nay, I suppose not. I have reached the age of one and twenty and ne'er heard one. I doubt there will be a sudden swarming of men ready and eager to whisper flatteries in my ears in the next few weeks."

"Rose, ye are mine."

"Am I? Is that how ye see it?"

"Aye."

This was going all wrong, he thought. Yet even hearing her speak of unknown and yet unseen men wooing her stirred his jealousy until it was difficult to think. One thing he was sure of, and that was that Rose was his. When she gave herself to him by the river, that merely sealed the bond between them. It annoyed him that she did not seem to feel that way.

"I see. And are ye mine?"

"Aye." That much, at least, he could confess to. Whatever else passed between them, he was hers, did not want any other woman, and, he suspected, never would.

"Fair enough." Rose took him by the hand. "We seem to have trouble agreeing on so many things, 'tis nice to ken we think alike in this matter."

"I would like to think we could agree on many another thing if we but set our minds to it."

"Mayhap. It shall depend upon how much of the matter concerned is one of reason or one of emotion." She frowned as she realized Meg had returned and was standing in front of the cottage talking excitedly to Mary and Master Iain. "I hope naught has happened to Lame Jamie." She had barely finished speaking when she had to nearly run, for Adair had begun to trot toward her home.

"Oh, Rose," Meg cried as she ran forward to hug her. "Ye will ne'er guess what has happened. I ran home to see my father and Anne was standing at the door."

"Anne was?"

"Aye, I think her mother may have said one thing too many when she was scolding her. Weel, she looked at me and I looked at her, and I gave her some of the blackberries I had brought home for my father. Then I told her to cease standing there like a post and do something 'ere her mother chased her down."

Rose heard Iain and Adair choke back a laugh. "That is what ye think is helpful?"

"It worked. So did the blackberries. She ceased to tremble, looked me in the eye, and said I needed a mother's guidance. I said that might be true, and was I looking at one who thought she could do the job? Then she got a wee bit cowardly again." Meg shook her head.

"But ye set her aright, did ye?" asked Adair.

"I did, laird. Told her the best thing to do was just say what she had to say, because this was the second time she had slipped her mother's noose and it was sure to be tightened after this until she couldnae say a word. Almost had to rap on the door for her."

"Anne did finally rap on the door, did she?" asked Rose.

"Aye, after a few more blackberries," replied Meg. "Then she stared at my father and my father stared at her, and I was getting sorely bored. So I told Anne that if she didnae have the wit to speak, why didnae she just kiss him? Thought she might swoon right there, but my father had more wit. He kissed her. I left them alone for a wee while."

"Verra wise," murmured Adair, but everyone except a grinning Iain ignored him.

"Weel, they eventually recalled that there was a child standing about outside. I think the singing told them." She grinned when Iain and Adair laughed aloud. "So 'tis settled. Ye are all invited to a wedding. 'Twill be in two days' time. My father feels that is about as long as he will be able to deal with Mistress Kerr trying to get her daughter back."

"Anne didnae go home?" asked Rose.

"Nay. She didnae want to, and I think my father is verra happy that she is staying away from her mother." Meg winked at Rose. "Especially since there is only my bed and his bed, and Anne isnae sleeping with me. So, will ye come?"

"Aye," said Mary and kissed Meg's cheek. "And we shall bring as much food as we can carry."

"And some of our mead for the bride and groom," said Rose.

"Tell your father me and my lads will be there," said Iain.

"And I shall be certain to tell everyone at Duncairn. I will contribute the ale." Adair covertly patted Rose on the backside, then mounted his horse and held out his hand to Meg. "Come with me, lass. I will take ye home."

"I have ne'er ridden a horse before," said Meg as she nimbly swung up behind him. "I will see ye at the wedding," she called as Adair nudged his horse into a slow trot.

By the time Rose got over the shock of Adair's rather intimate touch and turned to face her aunt, Iain was already gone. "I ne'er thought Anne would act so quickly."

"I think Meg has the right of it. That fool Joan said one nasty thing too many. Since the thought of leaving was already in the lass's head, the poison didnae pass o'er her as it used to. I wouldnae be surprised if it was something unkind about Meg's father." Meg suddenly looked closely at her niece. "Ye are looking a bit rough, lass."

As she and her aunt went into the cottage, Rose told her about Geordie's attack. A part of her ached to share the news that she and Adair had become lovers. It would be good to be able to discuss it with an older woman, one who had known a man.

For the moment, however, Rose realized she
wished to hold the secret close. When she did
finally talk about it, all the doubts and questions
she had would undoubtedly come out. For a little
while she wanted to remember that moment on
the soft grass by the river through the haze of desire
and love, untarnished by reality. The time to face
the consequences of it all would come soon
enough.

Chapter Nine

"A fine wedding," Mary said as she and Rose stepped into the cottage.

"I cannae believe Mistress Kerr would be so cruel as to refuse to attend her own daughter's wedding," muttered Rose as she moved to light the fire. "Ye would think she would be happy for Anne. 'Tis nay as if Jamie is some poor, ragged stable lad."

"He isnae the laird." Mary poured each of them a goblet of sweet cider and, after handing Rose hers, sat down in a chair in front of the fire. "But Joan wasnae far away. Nay, nor was that fool Geordie. He is verra lucky his punishment was so light."

Rose grimaced as she sat down in the other chair set before the fire. Geordie had gotten fifteen lashes, and the whip had been readily wielded by his enraged father. Considering the rage Adair had been in, it was a merciful punishment. She had just never liked whippings.

"Where was Mistress Kerr?" asked Rose.

"Near."

"Aunt?"

"Have it your way. She was but 'round the corner, sitting in front of the alehouse with Geordie. In truth, by the time we left there was near a dozen people with them."

"Oh, dear. She has blamed all of this on me, hasnae she?"

"Loudly and repeatedly. 'Tis why I decided we should leave sooner than I might have wished to."

"I noticed ye were having a fine time with Master Iain." Rose almost laughed when her aunt blushed.

"He is a fine figure of a mon and I am nay in my grave yet."

"Far from it, I pray." Rose frowned, felt the tickle of fear, and took a long drink of cider to quell it. "Do ye think there may be trouble?"

"I cannae be sure, lass. This cursed gift of mine can be an uncertain thing. I feel as if there will be, but mixed in those feelings of warnings are ones of happiness. All I can think is that mayhap there will be trouble, but it willnae cost us so verra much. And somewhere in the mess, a few problems will be solved or hurts eased."

"I think it might be wise to prepare for trouble. Ye heard Mistress Kerr spouting her poison and saw a fair crowd gathering to listen. 'Tis a strong warning right there. I would rather be ready for trouble and have the threat fade away than nay be ready and have the threat catch us unprepared."

Mary nodded. "Wise. As soon as we have finished our cider, we will go out and set the water buckets around."

"Aye." Rose shook her head. "Someone should sew that woman's lips together." She managed a tired smile when her aunt laughed. "Anne did look bonny, didnae she?"

"Aye, and Jamie looked verra happy, too. Meg is happy because her father is, and I think she likes Anne. It will be fine. She will soon have all the brothers and sisters she could want."

"I ken how Meg feels. I often wished for brothers or sisters. My mother wanted no other mon after my father died, however."

"Some people love only the once. Like ye. Like that stubborn lad Adair."

"Ye do ken he is the laird, dinnae ye?" Rose drawled.

Mary grinned and winked as she stood up. "I ken it. I tease the lad, 'tis all, and I ken he really doesnae mind. Nay sure he e'en realizes I do it." She took Rose by the hand and tugged her to her feet. "Come. We will set the buckets around and then we can get some sleep. It has been a long busy day."

Rose set the last of her buckets, brimming with water, next to her mother's apple tree. She grimaced as she stood up and tried to rub away a pinch of pain in her back. It was more work than she had wanted to do after tiring herself out at the wedding, and with all the cooking she had done in the days before it. She tried to ease her temper by telling herself that, if no trouble came their way this night, watering the garden in the morning would be a great deal easier, as the water had already been drawn from the well. Then she tensed, a sound she dreaded cutting through the quiet of the night.

"Ah, me, here the fools come," muttered Mary as she joined Rose. "Let us meet them at the gate."

Following her aunt, Rose winced at the sound of the angry voices. She stood beside her aunt just inside the gate and sadly watched two dozen people stride up. Mistress Kerr marched at the fore like

some conquering hero. Rose idly wished she was
a more violent person, for there was a woman she
would sorely like to beat into the mud, Then she
caught sight of Geordie at her cottage door.

"Ye get away from my house, ye bastard," she
yelled.

"Aye, lass, there be the way. Keep a firm grip on
your temper," drawled Mary, but she grinned when
Rose sent her a look of apology. "In truth, say and
do as ye please, lass. 'Twill make no difference to
this lot of fools. Most of them are weel soaked in
ale and wouldnae ken reason if it fell on them."

"Witch!" screamed Joan Kerr. "Ye ensorcelled
my only child and turned her against me."

"Do ye really think one needs magic to turn
anyone against ye, ye nasty old woman?" snapped
Mary.

"Verra calm, Aunt," murmured Rose, but she
fixed her gaze on Mistress Kerr. "Ye wouldnae let
her choose the mon she wanted. If Anne has left
ye, 'tis nay anyone's fault but your own."

"She should heed what I say, nay ye, nay him,
and nay her," Joan said, pointing at Mary. "And
I ken weel that ye poisoned her mind and heart
against me with the food ye grow in there. Weel,
we have let the tools of the devil sit secure inside
those walls for far too long."

Even as several men came forward to pound at
her gates, Rose saw three of her cats come racing
out of her house. Fear for her pets distracted her
enough that the gates were pushed open, nearly
knocking her to the ground. Her aunt pounded
on the two men who tried to get inside the garden
with a thick cudgel, but one boy holding a torch
slipped by her.

Cursing, Rose hurried after the boy, catching
him just as he tried to set her mother's tree alight.

She used the bucket of water there to dampen down both him and the tree. Grabbing him by the ear, she dragged him back to the gates, where her aunt stood, cudgel in hand. Rose pushed the boy back outside, wondering how long it would take Mistress Kerr's drunken followers to realize that, even though she and her aunt could give a lot of them some hard bruises, they could not stop them from pushing their way in.

"Oh, dear," murmured Mary. "Some of them look like they might actually be trying to think."

"Now that could cause us trouble," agreed Rose, then frowned as three of her cats ran into the garden and under her and her aunt's skirts.

"If they do rush us and get by, just set your mind to putting out any fires they may start. Me and the others will take care of pounding some sense into these heads."

Before Rose could ask what others, Joan Kerr glared at her. "That witch stole my child as surely as if she had dragged her to an altar to sacrifice her. Are ye all going to just leave her safe here until she comes after your children?"

"I fear that may have been a good prod on that bitch's part," grumbled Mary.

"Are ye saying I should prepare for the real fight?"

Mary took Rose's hand in hers and held her cudgel more firmly in the other. "Aye. Ye might try your hand at a wee bit of praying as weel."

"Laird!"

Adair looked toward Donald as the youth stumbled into the hall, yelling for him. He had come home from Jamie's wedding feeling a little sorry for himself. There was a woman he had chosen for his wife, but fate and nonsense seemed to want to keep them apart. All he asked was that she cease all this talk of magic. He did not see that that was so very much to ask. Since his mind could not seem to cease chewing over the problem until his head ached, Adair almost welcomed this alarum of Donald's. It might keep him too busy to think, at least for a while.

"Wheesht, are we being raided, lad?" he asked, as Donald's father, Robert, halted the youth before he stumbled right into Adair.

"Och, nay. I dinnae think that would worry me as much as this does."

"What has happened?"

"Mistress Kerr spent her daughter's wedding stirring people into a frenzy. She kept saying the Keith women had ensorcelled her daughter, stolen her away with their magic."

"The woman got married. Most all the village was there. Are there really any fools who would heed her?"

"With their heads clouded with ale fumes, aye," Robert replied.

"Mayhap ye should have let the Keith women bring the ale as weel as the food," said Donald.

"And what good would that have done?" demanded Adair.

"Weel, their ale mixed together with their food, and there wouldnae have been anyone Mistress Kerr could stir up with her talk. I mean, their food makes people happy, aye?"

"Aye," Adair agreed a little reluctantly. "So, I suppose I best hie to the village and try to beat some sense into a few fools."

"They are nay there."

Adair felt a chill seep over him. "Be quick about it, lad. Where are they?"

"Headed to Rose Cottage. I tried to stop them, e'en gave away a few tarts I had saved for later, but that only stopped a few. So I felt I best come here and tell ye about it. They were carrying torches, and Mistress Kerr was saying it was time to be rid of that witch's source of power. I just dinnae understand it. The women and their food dinnae hurt anyone. If 'tis magic, 'tis a verra peaceful sort."

"I should have done something sooner to shut that bitch's mouth," snapped Adair as he stood up and marched out of the hall. "I will be taking six men with me, Robert. Ye and Donald must see to their replacement at their posts."

"Aye, laird," said Robert.

"I will get your horse," Donald said, even as he raced toward the stables.

"Though it would be more pleasant about Duncairn, I think it wouldnae be wise to kill Mistress Kerr," drawled Robert after Adair bellowed orders to the six men he had chosen to go with him.

It surprised Adair that he could do so, but he laughed briefly, and was sure that was what Robert had intended. That moment of lightness had eased the murderous strength of his fury. The very fact that, even for a brief instance, he had considered killing a woman, made him even angrier with Joan Kerr, for she drove him to such dark thoughts. If there was any evil in Duncairn, it rested in Joan Kerr's heart and mind.

"I willnae kill the woman," Adair said. "It was but a brief, pleasing thought. Nay more. I would like to banish her from my lands, but that might hurt Anne, and she is a good lass. Howbeit, I think I do have a way to steal the sting from that adder's tongue."

"Ye do?"

"I do. It, too, will hurt Anne, so I may nay use

the weapon. 'Twill depend upon how hard that woman pushes me.''

"She will probably push ye verra hard." Robert held out an apple. " 'Tis one from the garden that fool woman seeks to destroy. I doubt it will still your anger for 'tis a righteous one, but it may help ye gain some control o'er it."

Adair took the apple and stared at it. It would help. He could not deny that truth. The food from the garden had eased his nightmares, soothed his pain, and taken away his guilt. It had even roused the spirit of his gentle mother in his mind and heart. What grew in the gardens at Rose Cottage was not just unusual, not simply a product of rich soil and good water; it was magic. He had fought that truth because he did not understand it, and that troubled him, made him uneasy. Well, he mused, Mary Keith was right—sometimes there were things that could not be explained and one just had to accept that.

He took a bite of the apple even as he mounted the horse Donald brought him and felt a sense of calm seep through his veins. It did not banish his fury, but it gave him the strength to think clearly despite it. That only confirmed his growing conviction that he had been wrong, that, in a small way, he, too, had given in to the fear of the unknown. The food did not change him in any way. Something in it simply reached out to soothe a person's pain or sorrow, to calm agitation and fear. Strange as that was, there was no harm or evil bewitchment in it.

Seeing that his men were ready, Adair rode out of Duncairn. He had to reach Rose before she could be hurt or her cherished gardens destroyed. The fear he felt over her safety brought him to yet another realization. He loved her, loved her with all his heart, soul and mind. Now he understood what his mother's voice had whispered in his mind the night he had decided he would have Rose. As long as he decried the magic at Rose Cottage and demanded she turn her back on it, he would never really have her. He was asking her to give up something that was a very large part of her, something that had helped to make her the woman he loved.

Suddenly he did not care about what the magic was or where it had come from. He did not even care if Rose brought it into the heart of Duncairn, so long as she came to him. Spurring his horse to a greater speed, he prayed he would find her unharmed so that he could tell her of the changes in his heart and mind.

The moment Rose Cottage came into view, Adair signaled his men to halt and dismount. It was tempting to just ride into the midst of the torch-bearing crowd and scatter them like rats, but he knew that would not really solve the problem. A confrontation was long overdue. As he strode toward the garden gate, he saw the crowd begin to move forward, and hoped he could control his temper long enough to make the fools see sense.

Chapter Ten

"Hold!"

Rose clasped her aunt's hand and thanked God as the tall form of Adair pushed through the crowd. Half a dozen of his men followed, turned, and stood between their laird and the crowd, their hands resting on their swords. She gave Adair a weak smile as he stepped close and looked her over.

"Ye are weel? Unhurt?" he asked, briefly glancing at her aunt. "Both of ye?"

"Aye, Adair," Rose replied. "They were trying to burn the garden. I ken Aunt and I wouldnae have been able to stop them. Nay alone."

Adair looked over the crowd. He was pleased to see that several people already looked uneasy, even embarrassed. Even as he prepared to speak, he saw Lame Jamie, Anne, and young Meg hurry up, cudgels in hand, to push their way through the crowd.

"Nay alone, my bonny Rose," Adair said.

"Are ye hurt?" demanded Meg, running over to Rose and then turning to glare at the crowd. "Fither, ye can start knocking heads now," she said to Lame Jamie, who lingered near the battered gate to the garden, Anne at his side.

Reaching out to give Meg's tossled hair a light tug, Adair said, "I will deal with this, brat." He bowed to Lame Jamie. "I commend your father for the speed with which he came to the aid of the women, however. 'Tis good to ken that nay everyone has had all their wits addled by the rattling tongue of a bitter woman." He did not need the way everyone looked at Joan Kerr to tell him she was the one behind this madness. She stood to the fore of the crowd, as stiff and fierce as any commander, unaware that the loyalty of her troops was already beginning to fade.

"Those women bewitched my daughter, setting her against me," Joan Kerr snapped. "Anne has ne'er disobeyed me, yet one visit to this accursed cottage and Anne thwarts all my wishes."

"How old is Anne?" asked Adair.

"Three and twenty."

"Far past the age for her to cut free of your apron strings."

"She married against my will! She walked out of my house and went to that man!" Joan Kerr pointed at Lame Jamie.

"I should think that, when the lass is three and twenty, ye would be glad she has found herself a husband. Lame Jamie has a fine cottage, a good living, and is my second cousin. Most mothers would be dancing with joy o'er such a fine match." He lightly poked Meg when she stuck out her tongue at Joan Kerr, but the soft chuckles the girl's impertinence stirred told Adair he had muted that accusation.

An eerie howl drew everyone's attention. Geordie was walking toward the crowd holding a writhing, hissing Sweetling by the scruff of the neck. Rose moved to help her cat, but Adair grasped her by the arm and held her back. Lame Jamie was already striding over to the youth, cudgel in hand.

"I got one of the witch's familiars," Geordie said, then cursed and dropped the cat when Jamie rapped him on the back of the head with the cudgel. "The beastie got away! Didnae ye hear the evil noises he made and how fierce he was?"

"Ye were near to strangling the poor animal, ye half-wit," snapped Jamie. "He was fighting for his life. Where did he go?" Jamie looked around. "Is he hurt?"

"He is weel, Jamie," Rose replied, feeling her cat trembling against her leg.

Adair looked down and saw Sweetling's rump and tail sticking out from beneath Rose's skirts. "Wheesht, such a fierce demon." He heard a ripple of laughter go through the crowd and quickly looked up to grin at them, drawing their attention and hoping no one else saw that yellow paw slip out from beneath Rose's skirts to nudge Sweetling's backside underneath.

"How do ye explain this garden?" demanded Joan Kerr, her voice shrill as she realized her allies were rapidly deserting her.

"Rich soil and plenty of water," Adair replied.

"It takes more than that to make it grow e'en when others fail."

"Iain," Adair called to a burly, hirsute man he strongly suspected was an ally of Mary's, and the man quickly stepped forward. "Ye are considered a skilled farmer, aye?"

"I believe so, m'laird," the man replied.

"Rose, get a handful of earth to show the mon," Adair said and frowned when she shook her head.

"I cannae move," she said. "Sweetling and Growler are wrapped about my ankles. Lady and Lazy cower under Aunt's skirts."

"I will get it, m'laird," offered Meg.

"Take some from the bed where the peas grow," instructed Rose as Meg hurried off.

A moment later Meg held out a handful of dirt for Iain. The man took it into his own hand, inspecting it closely, even sniffing it. Adair was not sure what some of the things the man did tell him, but Iain's eyes grew wider and wider.

"Wheesht, ye could grow anything with ease in dirt this fine." He looked at Rose. "Do ye add things to it? I think I can smell fish."

"Come round in the morn, Master Iain," said Mary, "and we shall be verra glad to tell ye what little we ken."

"The water," began Joan Kerr.

"Here ye are, Master Iain," said Meg, who had already fetched the man a small bowl of water.

Iain sipped the water, swished it about in his mouth, then spat it out. He sniffed it, swirled it in the bowl, and stared at it as he trickled a little over his fingers. Finally, he drank the whole bowl full.

"Sweet, clear, and I dinnae feel any change coming o'er me," said Iain. "I am nay growing a tail, am I?" he asked and winked at Rose.

That brought a few crude jests from the others. Iain strode back to his laughing sons and gently clapped each of them offside the head. Joan Kerr stared at the crowd and clenched her fists. No one stood near her now.

"Fools! Cannae ye see how she has bewitched your laird?" she shrieked.

"Mither," protested Anne, but words failed her, and she shook her head.

Adair saw a few people waver in their retreat and frown at him. They had come here to root out evil at the behest of a distraught woman. It was obvious they hoped for some hint that they had not been made complete fools of.

"Ah, weel, mayhap there is some truth in that," he said, and winked at the men before taking Rose's chin in his hand and turning her face up to his. "How could any mon look upon this bonny face and nay feel a wee bit bewitched. Eyes the color of the sea and skin like rich, sweet cream." He grabbed a handful of her hair, held it up, and slowly released the strands. "And I challenge any mon here to tell me this bounty isnae enough to steal a mon's wits. I willnae praise all her beauty, for I dinnae wish all ye fools leering at my bride." He put his arm around Rose's slim shoulders and kissed her cheek before returning his gaze to the crowd.

"Aye, mayhap there is a wee touch of magic here, mayhap the land is blessed in some way. 'Twas certainly blessed to fall into the tender care of the Keith women. I challenge any of ye here to tell me of someone hurt by a Keith woman. They have been here for as long as a Dundas has been laird, yet ye cannae tell me of any evil done by any one of them, can ye?" He nodded when many of the people shook their heads. "But ye can tell me of a hand always extended to help, of no one being allowed to ken the cramp of hunger as long as there was e'en one leek left in this garden ye sought to destroy.

"Go home and I will try to forget that ye endangered the lives of the lass I love and her kinswoman." He felt Rose start beneath his arm but kept his gaze upon the crowd. "I will also try to forget that ye let the poisonous lies of a bitter woman turn ye against women who have been naught but kind and generous."

"Lies? I but tried to—" protested Joan Kerr.

Adair knew he was not concealing the cold fury he felt at the woman very well, for she paled when he fixed his gaze upon her. "Nay more, woman. Ye almost succeeded this night in destroying one of the few almost continuous sources of food at Duncairn, and ye didnae care if two innocent women were hurt or killed in the doing of it. 'Tis past time the truth was told. I was curious about your enduring animosity toward Rose and her late mother, so I went searching for answers.

"What I discovered was that 'tis nay righteousness that stirs your poisonous whispers and accusations but jealousy, mayhap e'en envy. Ye wed a strutting vain cock, a faithless swine, and he turned his lecherous eye upon Flora Keith. 'Tis nay such a surprise. She was a beautiful woman. She would have naught to do with the fool, scorned him openly, but ye had to blame someone for his wandering eye. So ye blamed Flora Keith. And mayhap ye were a wee bit angry that she could so clearly see what the mon was and ye didnae.

"Ye e'en held on to that anger and let it brew after ye left Duncairn with him. When ye returned ye started to spew it out, e'en carrying it on to the daughter when Flora was nay longer in your reach. I suggest ye take yourself to a priest, Mistress Kerr. Mayhap a little confession and penance will release some of that bile." When the woman stormed away, Adair looked at Anne. "Sorry, lass. She wouldnae relent, and I needed to take some of the sting out of her words."

"No need to beg my pardon, laird," Anne said.

" 'Twas a truth that should have been told long ago."

After watching Anne leave with Lame Jamie's strong arm wrapped comfortingly around her slender shoulders, Rose realized that most everyone else was gone as well, and she looked at Adair. "Did ye mean it? I will understand if ye just said such things to—"

Adair silenced her with a brief, hard kiss. "I meant it all. I want ye as my bride, I love ye, and, whether 'tis magic, fairies, God's blessing, or just skilled farming, I dinnae care."

"Are ye sure 'tis nay the food that has made ye feel this way?" she asked, unable to completely still that fear.

"Nay, 'tis nae the food. In truth, I decided I wanted ye 'ere I had taken my first bite of anything from this garden."

"Oh, Adair."

"When I heard that ye were in danger, I realized none of it mattered save that I love ye. That first night ye gave me those apple tarts, I swear I could hear my mother's soothing voice helping me to still my nightmares. As I went to sleep, I decided I would have ye for my bride, but that I would get ye to deny all this magic first. In my head I heard my mother scold me for a fool, telling me that I would ne'er hold the prize I sought unless I accepted the whole. I didnae understand until now. I love ye for *all* that ye are. All I ask is that, if ye decide to dance naked under a full moon, ye let me watch." He grinned when she scowled at him even as she blushed. "So, lass, will ye have me?"

"Oh, aye, Adair." She brushed her fingers over his cheek. "I do love ye so. I think I have since I was a wee child."

He held her tightly, briefly overcome with emotion. "Ye willnae be sorry, lass." He stepped back and held both her hands in his. "And I willnae keep ye from your garden. I ken how much a part of ye all this is."

Rose looked around and felt a brief sadness. For every day of her life the garden had been the center of her world, and she would miss that in many ways. It would not be a complete loss, for she could visit the garden whenever she wished to, and renew her ties to this land that had nurtured generations of Keith women whenever she felt the need. She smiled at Adair.

" 'Tis a part of me and I shall always need to come here, but only for a visit," she said. "My time here is o'er. 'Tis my aunt's turn now. She kenned this time was near and that is why she came," she added in a soft voice, so that his men did not hear. Adair and others might be able to accept the magic of the garden, but her aunt's *feelings* were another matter entirely.

"Ah, I see. Then come, lass. We will go to Duncairn and"—he winked at her—"talk on our future."

A blush stinging her cheeks, Rose looked at her aunt. "I think I best stay here. We are nay wed yet, ye ken."

"Go, lass," said Mary, smiling widely. "The lad told near all the village that ye are his bride and that he loves ye. Go, and I will come to see you on the morrow to help ye plan the wedding. I think it should be a grand celebration."

"Aye, verra grand," agreed Adair, but when he tugged on Rose's hand, she did not follow him. "Rosebud?"

Releasing his hand, Rose lifted her skirts a little to reveal two of her cats. "I am still shackled by Sweetling and Growler."

Adair rolled his eyes and, ignoring the laughter of his men, coaxed the two cats out. The amusement of his men was increased when the other two cats stuck their heads out from beneath Mary's skirts and cautiously looked around before emerging. That laughter was good, however. These men would never be able to see these animals as *familiars*, as evil lurking in disguise. He picked up Sweetling, who quickly draped himself over his shoulder. Rose picked up Growler and cradled him in her arms.

"Come, love, we will take these wretched, spoiled beasties back to Duncairn," he said as he wrapped his arm around her shoulders.

Rose went only a few steps before glancing behind her, stopping when she realized her other cats were not following. "Lady? Lazy?" She looked at her aunt when the cats did not move. "They willnae leave?"

"Not yet, lass." Mary smiled at the two cats and then winked at Rose. "Nay until Lady has her litter and she and the proud fither are sure their bairns are weaned, strong, and hale. Then they will come to you, leaving the young to take their place here."

"Lazy is the father?"

" 'Tis clear he can bestir himself now and then," murmured Adair. He kissed Rose's cheek and whispered, "Come, my love. I am eager to show ye how verra much I love ye."

"I suddenly find I am most eager to show *ye* how much I love *ye* as weel."

Mary watched the two lovers walk away. Her eyes widened when Sweetling lifted his head from Adair's broad shoulder and winked at her. She giggled and winked back, before stepping out of the garden and shutting the battered gate. Leaning her arms on the gate, she stared into the garden that would now be her responsibility.

" 'Twas close this time, Mary," said Iain as he moved to stand beside her. "Thought I might have to knock open a few heads."

She smiled at the man she would soon marry. "Aye, but good came of it. Few will heed Joan Kerr's poison now, and it made the laird open his eyes and see what was truly important."

"And ye put on a fine show, Master Iain," said Meg as she moved to stand next to Mary.

"Dinnae trouble yourself, Iain," Mary said when the man attempted to stutter out some denial of trickery. "Our Meg is a canny one." She looked at the girl. "I thought ye went home."

"Nay. Anne was sad and hurt and my father will need to soothe her. Felt they should be alone for a while. Thought to visit Rose, but she and the laird will be busy saying all they were too timid or foolish to say before. So ye get me."

"And ye are most welcome to stay for a while. In a wee while we can all go in and have some blackberry tarts."

"So, ye now take o'er here," Iain said, "holding it for Rose's lass."

"Oh, Rose will have a lass along with her eight sons, but that lass's destiny lies elsewhere," said Mary.

"But if ye have no daughters and Rose's lass willnae take guardianship, is it to be an end to the Keith women of Rose Cottage?"

"Nay, one will appear. I feel it, though I cannae say from where or when."

"Oh, Mistress Mary, look at all the dancing lights," cried Meg. "Do ye think the garden is happy for our Rose?"

After exchanging a wide-eyed look with Iain, Mary stared at Meg. "Ye see dancing lights?"

"Aye," replied Meg. "Cannae ye?"

"*I* can and *Rose* can." Mary gently grasped Meg by the chin and turned her face up to hers. When she found herself staring into a distinctive pair of sea green eyes, she inwardly cursed her own stupidity for not seeing it sooner. "Did ye ken your mother, lass?"

"Nay; she died when I was born near thirteen years ago."

"Always a sad thing, but I meant do ye ken her name?"

"Oh, aye. She was a Margaret, too. Margaret Keith. I always like to think I might be a cousin to Rose."

Mary laughed, gave a grinning Iain an exuberant embrace, then grasped Meg by the shoulders. "Ye *are* her cousin. Your mother was my first cousin. I cannae believe I ne'er thought to look for her here when she disappeared so long ago."

"Ye mean I am a Keith woman?"

"Aye, lass, ye are, and ye will be the next to take o'er guardianship of this garden. Ye already have an apple tree planted for ye, planted by Flora on the day ye were born, though she wasnae sure who she was planting it for at the time."

"But, Rose—"

"Believe me, lass, ye willnae be stealing another's place. 'Tis ye I have been looking for. Now, tell me what ye see in the garden, and dinnae fear to speak before Master Iain. He kens all."

Meg stared into the garden, and slowly her eyes grew very wide. "The lights! They are more than lights!" She looked at Mary. " 'Tis true, then, all true. The garden is fairy blessed. 'Tis really magic here."

Wrapping an arm around Meg's thin shoulders, Mary nodded. "Aye, it is, and I will soon tell ye the tale of how that came to be. I will also teach ye what is needed to keep the magic alive."

"I think I ken what it is. 'Tis love, isnae it?"

"Aye, my canny brat, 'tis love, for love is a strange, sweet magic, too. Love is the strongest magic there is. Ye will do weel, lass. Verra weel indeed."

THE ORANGE TREE

Linda Madl

Chapter One

As he studied the few glossy leaves remaining on the stunted orange tree, Sir Hugh became aware of the approaching footfalls of his steward on the flagstone path. Fulk stopped a few feet from him and waited to be recognized. Hugh chose to ignore the man and continued to examine the sickly tree.

The other five specimens he had brought back from Sicily nearly two years earlier had grown and been fruitful, bearing shiny, plump, sweet-smelling fruit. This poor tree, however, damaged during the long overland journey, looked no better than it had the day of its arrival on the shores of Sully. Despite his best efforts it remained barren save for the few leaves that clung to its straggly branches, refusing to decide whether to live or die. Oddly, he understood that sentiment.

With a sigh of frustration, Hugh straightened. "What is it, Fulk?"

"My lord, there is a herald at the gate." The steward's tone was tentative. As he spoke he shuffled his soft leather boots on the flagstones. Strange. Fulk was a calm, even-tempered man. It was unlike him to be anxious.

One by one his gardeners began to desert the arbor. Hugh paid little heed to their sudden retreat to the farthest reaches of the orchard. He knew he was a difficult man to work with. It did not trouble him particularly that his men knew when to withdraw. They had at least learned when to avoid him, which suited him well.

"I heard the trumpet." He stepped away from the small tree. Tilting his head back, he looked up at the sailcloth stretched across the ribs of the arbor as protection against the cold and frost. He took a deep breath, trying to ignore the irritation that Fulk's announcement caused him. He hated visitors. Everyone knew that. Still, once or twice a year some fool thought they had some cause to sell or to introduce to the Lord of Sully. "I assume you informed the herald that we do not offer hospitality at Castle Sully."

"I did, my lord," the steward said, wringing his hands, a gesture Hugh had never seen him do. "However," Fulk continued, "it seems the visitor has a letter of introduction." After a significant pause, he added, "From the Bishop of Somerfield."

"God's teeth!" Hugh muttered, turning to Fulk. His irritation was growing into full-blown annoyance. Disillusioned, inhospitable, and unsocial as he had become since his return from the Crusades, he still held respect for the Church. Despite all that he had seen, deep in his heart he still believed in its tenets. It was not in him to deny a visitor sponsored by a clergyman, especially a visitor from the kindly Bishop of Somerfield.

"Did you see the document? Is it legitimate?" he demanded.

"Yes, my lord." The younger man nodded emphatically. "It does indeed bear the bishop's seal."

Hugh muttered another curse. Turning away visitors was a deed that seldom troubled him. What need had he of outsiders? He had his gardens and his gardeners. There was Father Paul to act as his scribe, tend to his soul, and offer him a good game of chess. And he had the captain of his men at arms to train with when he so desired. Dame Gilda from the dockside tavern took care of his other desires when necessary. That was all the company he required or cared to have. Even the troubadours had learned not to cross the water to the Isle of Scully. There was no welcome for them here.

"What does he want, this fool?" Hugh demanded.

"I do not know, my lord," Fulk said, backing away a step in the face of Hugh's displeasure. "And *he* is a she. Lady Emmalyn of Trentworth, to be precise."

"A woman?" he nearly shouted in surprise.

"Yes, my lord, Lady Emmalyn, her maid, her steward, her herald, their palfreys, and two pack-horses," Fulk said. "She requests an audience at your convenience."

"God's teeth, she brought her entire bloody household," Hugh said, throwing his hands up in the air. His morning's work was to be interrupted, and the castle was unprepared for guests.

"By reputation, my lord, I believe Trentworth is a sizable holding," Fulk said.

"Yes, I know." Hugh waved away what he knew to be the truth. Lady Emmalyn doubtless was the widow of the wealthy Terence of Trentworth who had gotten himself killed by a wild boar, or some such misfortune. Her wealth would explain the bishop's sponsorship. She was probably traveling very simply—by her standards.

What in heaven's name did she want on Sully? His mind raced through several unlikely reasons and several excuses not to see her. There must be some way to send her on her way quickly—but nothing came to mind that would not offend the bishop.

"One other thing you should know, my lord," Fulk said, pursing his lips in uncertainty and backing away several more steps.

"Yes?"

"The boat to the mainland has already set sail."

"Damnation!"

Hugh strode through the lower castle passages toward the great hall. "The ship never should have been allowed to sail before it was known whether or not I would receive the lady."

"I gather the crossing was rather rough, my lord," Fulk replied, striding along in Hugh's wake. "The lady was indisposed for some time upon disembarking."

Hugh snorted. "Seasick. That should have forewarned her."

"Shall I see to the readying of rooms, my lord?" Fulk asked, breathless now from his attempts to keep up with his master.

"What choice do we have?" Hugh halted at the foot of the stairs. "None of the fishing boats are large enough to take the horses. The mainland boat does not return for a fortnight."

"I shall see to it immediately." Fulk backed away, clearly eager to escape to other regions of the castle.

"Show her into the great hall as soon as possible," Hugh said, starting up the spiral stairs to the floor above.

Fulk hesitated. "But . . . do you not wish to wash first?"

"No."

"Perhaps Lady Emmalyn will wish to—"

"She will have an audience with me as I am and as she is or none at all," Hugh called back to his steward. By the time he reached the dark shuttered great hall, he was in an exceptionally black humor. He went straight to his large chair by the cold hearth and sat down.

As he sat there with his fingers steepled beneath his chin, servants scurried into the hall and began to throw open the shutters, brush the cobwebs from the tall candlesticks, and sprinkle fresh herbs on the rush-covered floor. No one had been received in the great hall since his return from the Crusades. He and his retainers took their informal meals in the kitchen or in the kitchen yard.

"Fulk is greeting the guests," a servant told Hugh. "Shall I light a fire, my lord?"

"I think not," Hugh said, watching sunshine wash the darkness from the hall. He became suddenly conscious of the herbs sweetening the stale air—the scent brought long-forgotten memories of the hall. Bright colorful images flashed through his mind of strutting lords and laughing ladies in a place filled with light, music, and warmth.

His mother had died soon after the birth of his brother, Edward, who lived on the mainland now—

and would stay there if he knew what was good for him. Their father had never remarried, but he had always welcomed guests to Sully. He liked crowds in the hall and always treated generously guests and troubadours who were willing to make the day-long voyage and who could make him laugh.

Hugh frowned at the recollection of those innocent times and gripped the arms of his chair. His father was gone now, and this was his hall to do with as he pleased. And it pleased him to keep to himself and the great hall empty. "No fire," he added with unnecessary gruffness. "It is the warmest day yet of the new year. No need to waste good wood."

"Will you be wanting food and drink, my lord?" Walter asked, ambling heavily into the hall from the kitchen, where it was always warm. He stopped in front of Hugh's chair. The sleeves of his tunic had not been tied into place, thus leaving his ample arms bare. A clean apron spanned his generous belly. A linen towel lay over his shoulder. His double chin shook as he talked. "I have some cool ale and bread, made fresh this morning. And there is cheese, fresh butter, dried fruit, and honey."

"Well enough, Cook," Hugh said, growing more resentful by the minute. He was not hungry, and he was losing good working daylight to a visit from some lady of leisure. "I suppose feeding a friend of the bishop is a must."

"Aye, you know it is, especially a lady," Walter said, his hands on his hips. The man had cooked for kings and bishops, knights and men at arms, merchants and tradesmen. He was the closest thing to a civilizing influence that existed in the castle full of men. Walter had come to Hugh in Italy, looking for return passage to England. His previous lord had died of his wounds. Needing a cook, Hugh took him on. Walter proved to be resourceful and efficient and had seemed satisfied to remain in Hugh's service. "I shall see to the food."

"While you are in the larder consider that we may have this guest with us for some time," Hugh said. How in heaven's name was he to entertain an old churchly lady at Castle Sully for a fortnight?

"Is that so, now?" Walter said, his face brightening at the prospect of having someone other than the men to cook for. "I will see what we have."

"And send an invitation to Father Paul for supper tonight," Hugh called to the cook as an afterthought. The priest would surely make a better conversationalist than he would.

Suddenly the tall oaken double doors into the great hall swung open and Fulk stood in the doorway. Servants quickly finished their tasks and stepped back against the walls to watch.

"My lord, Lady Emmalyn, widow of Terence of Trentworth, and head gardener to the Bishop of Somerfield," Fulk announced in a loud but dignified voice Hugh had never heard before. And she was head gardener to the bishop? Interesting.

The steward barely managed to step aside in time for a tall, willowy lady in creamy white to sweep into the hall. With her entrance a charge of energy swirled through the chamber, almost ruffling Hugh's hair and sending a strange tingle through him—mind and body.

With a sure step, the lady approached him. The rich fabric of her cloak, veil, and gown billowed gently and swayed gracefully with her quick, purposeful step. An engaging smile lit her face. A mature and intelligent—but not old—face.

Speechless, Hugh stared at her. He had forgotten what a feast for the eyes a beautiful woman could be. His grip on the arms of his chair had gone slack, and he was aware of his mouth hanging open.

"Sir Hugh, it is so good of you to set aside your solitude to see a humble widow," she said, stopping before him and dropping a dignified curtsy. "I apologize for not sending word ahead of my arrival, but alas, time grew too short."

Belatedly Hugh shut his mouth and rose, feeling rude and oafish, though he did not understand why. He should have washed, changed from his work clothes into something more refined, and combed his hair before receiving her. But, then again, she was the one imposing on him. She was just younger and lovelier than anything he had expected, and she was doing the imposing so very graciously.

"Lady Emmalyn, any friend of the Bishop of Somerfield's is a friend of the Isle of Sully's," he said, remembering enough of his manners to accept the hand she offered and to bow over it. Her long delicate fingers were warm and firm against his palm. Her nails were clean, neat but short. Though indeed small in his palm, hers was not a soft and pampered hand.

"Is the bishop not a dear man?" she said, smiling at him, her cheeks rosy with good health, her teeth even and white, and her velvet brown eyes bright and lively with curiosity and interest. If she had been seasick earlier, she did not appear to be in the least indisposed now. There was something contagious about her vitality that inclined him to tarry in her company, for a while at least. There was nothing all that pressing to be done in the garden.

"He is indeed," Hugh agreed, his memory of a host's proper responsibilities coming back to him little by little. "Please, sit. You must be exhausted from your journey."

"Only a bit," she said, accepting the enormous fireside chair across from him. She was so slender she barely needed half of it. "His grace told me the isle was lovely, but it is even more beautiful than I imagined. Just when you see nothing but sea off the bow, the isle rises from the water, the golden limestone cliffs and the green lush vegetation and so promising, just like your colors, Sir Hugh. No wonder you prefer to maintain your seclusion here. A best-kept secret."

"Yes, one could say that." Hugh settled in his chair once more, wary of her flattery and enthusiasm, yet fascinated by her energy and her grace. He wondered how old she was, and why she had not remarried after her husband's death. She was far too striking to have escaped suitors. There must be something wrong with her that escaped notice upon first meeting.

Walter appeared with a tray of food and ale despite the fact that serving was a task he never stooped to. As he placed the tray on the table between them, his open-mouthed gaze never left their guest. Hugh noticed that the cook's sleeves had been tied into place and his apron had been removed.

Hugh nodded his gratitude to Walter and gestured toward the tray laden with ale, bread, fruit, and cheese. "Please refresh yourself, Lady Emmalyn, and tell me, how is the bishop these days?"

She helped herself to the bread and cheese, all the while discussing the bishop's health, which seemed to have improved since Hugh had last heard news from Somerfield. The bishop had once spent a summer on Sully when Hugh was a boy, and he had always liked the clergyman.

"Will you not join me, my lord?" she asked, leaning across the distance between them to offer him a slice of bread and cheese with a smile. It was not a coy smile, nor flirtatious, just a friendly invitation that was difficult to disregard.

Hugh accepted the offering so as not to appear ungracious. "That is good news. I am glad to hear that his grace is feeling better. And I noted when my steward announced you that you are the bishop's gardener. Is that what brings you to the Isle of Sully, Lady Emmalyn?"

She regarded him for a moment, her smile losing some of its warmth, but a wary remnant remained on her lips. "I admire a man who is direct, my lord."

"Forthrightness is something that I also admire, Lady Emmalyn," he said.

"Then let me get straight to it," she said, shifting slightly in her chair to face him more squarely. She seemed to have lost interest in the food. "Yes, you are correct that my work with the bishop's garden is part of the reason that I am here. However, the more important reason is that my daughter is about to marry."

"What does that have to do with me?" Hugh asked, his eyes narrowing as he reassessed her. She was no maid; but she hardly appeared old enough to have a daughter of marriageable age. Then again, there were times when he forgot that he himself was old enough to have a son of an age to wed. Fortune had not smiled on him, though. Long ago, his wife had died in childbirth, and his infant son had died shortly afterward. The deaths had been a painful ordeal for him, an ordeal that began the end of his belief in the beauty of life.

"It has come to the bishop's attention, and mine, that you have orange trees here," she said, speaking slowly and softly.

Hugh nodded. "A few."

"And you were generous enough last winter to share some of the fruit with the children of an orphanage on the mainland when they became ill with scurvy."

"It was a small thing I could do," he said. "The medicinal benefits of oranges are well known, and it was hardly a great sacrifice."

"But a generous deed," she said, that friendly, touching smile returning to her lips. After a moment, she continued. "As you know, in addition to their medicinal benefits, oranges have other qualities, too."

Ah, here was her purpose, Hugh thought. "If you want some to make a beauty aid with, I am afraid I have none to spare. Nor do I have any cuttings I can allocate to the bishop at this time. I am struggling myself to make the trees survive in this clime."

She studied him for a moment, her smile bemused. "No, I do not wish the fruit for a beauty aid. Some think oranges make a fine cleanser, and sometimes I believe they are used in embalming. I assure you the bishop is quite content to allow you to experiment with the trees as much as you like. No, I have come to ask for some oranges for something far more important than a beauty aid."

"And what would that be?" Hugh asked, his impatience beginning to return.

"My daughter's happiness," Lady Emmalyn said, leaning forward in her chair and holding his gaze. "Her future is of great concern to me, my lord. I ask for the oranges on her behalf. I wish to give her and her betrothed, Stephen, the fruit as an assurance of the success of their union and the binding of their hearts, their souls, and their bodies. I wish to give them oranges as an aphrodisiac.''

Chapter Two

Sir Hugh's expression became even harsher, if that was possible. A furrow formed between his straight brows, his eyes narrowed, and the frown on his sensuous mouth deepened.

"Where are your orange trees, Sir Hugh?" Emmalyn asked lightly, refusing to allow his appearance to alarm her. She had never expected that obtaining the oranges for Julianna would be easy. The fruit was too rare, too precious. And this crusading knight turned hermit was known to be difficult, yet that was no reason to despair. If he did not grant her request immediately, for the moment, the important thing became to keep him from refusing outright. "As one gardener to another," she said, peering into his face with a smile, "I would so like to see the plant from which this wonderful fruit comes."

He studied her with a resentful gaze—and the most startling green eyes she had ever seen a man possess. He also had the most beautiful hair she had seen on a man, falling below his shoulder blades, rich brown straight hair tied back with a strip of leather. He seemed to wish to say something more. Perhaps he was even thinking of denying her the sight of his precious trees.

Instead, though, he said, "I was just examining the trees myself when I heard your herald's horn." He rose from his chair and offered his hand. "I would be pleased to show them to you."

"That is most kind of you, Sir Hugh," she said, relieved and pleased. Whatever thought had deepened the frown on his handsome face, with its straight aristocratic nose and strong stubborn chin, was not going to prevent him from sharing his garden with her.

She placed her hand in his, unsurprised to find it strong, dry, and rough from outdoor work, and rose from her chair. She was pleased to discover that he was one of the few men she had met who was taller than she. Politely, he placed her hand on his arm. Beneath the plain green wool of his tunic, his forearm was firm and powerful.

"This way, Lady Emmalyn," he said, starting toward the door.

Smiling, she allowed him to lead the way out of the great hall.

The Castle Sully garden was the strangest she had ever seen—at least the arbor was strange. Every garden had a grape arbor for winemaking, and the bishop's garden had more than its share. Yet she had never seen one like this. It stole her attention from the apple orchard, the herb garden, the flowerbeds, the beehives, and the berry bushes— she barely heard the call of the peacock—because of the oddness of the arbor. It stood toward the northern wall, where its vines would soak up the sunlight most all day. At the moment, however, the arbor was entirely covered with coarse cloth stretched from the ground on one side to the ground on the other, creating a long, tentlike structure with cloth flaps to seal either end.

"Fulk, strip the sails away," Sir Hugh ordered as they approached the structure. His man shouted the orders, and the throng of gardeners began to pull the covering from the arbor arches.

As a panel was removed, she saw the first tree, slightly taller than Sir Hugh himself. It stood in a large terra-cotta pot on the flagstone path between the arches. Glossy green leaves glistened in the sunlight, blossoms shone a delicate white, and the oranges, about half the size of her fist, glowed a vibrant color as rich and as bright as a butterfly's wings.

The fragrance that greeted her was the unique one she had first experienced in the bishop's court. A basketful of the fruit had been presented to the churchman as a gift from a traveler from the East years ago. She had never forgotten that scent, clean and rich. She had never forgotten the cheerful color or the flavor, sweet and tangy. Ever since then oranges and their lore had fascinated her.

Before her stood the first orange trees she had ever seen, their branches drooping with the weight of the luscious-looking fruit.

"I understand what you have done," she said as she watched the gardeners peel away the canvas. "You covered them to keep them warm during the winter."

"It is necessary in the coldest months," Sir Hugh said, keeping a critical eye on the gardeners. "The trees like sunlight, about five hours a day, and they prefer the warm temperatures of the summer. But with the sail covering the arbor and the warmth of braziers on the coldest nights we can protect them from frost damage."

"But you must be very vigilant during the winter," she said, impressed by the amount of work and care he had put into the survival of the trees. "There are four, five of them—no, I see six. What happened to this one?"

The gardeners were nearly finished removing the canvas. She walked into the arbor to scrutinize the stunted tree at the end of the row.

"It suffered a mishap during the journey home," Sir Hugh said.

"Mishap?" she repeated, touching one of the few glossy leaves with care.

After a pause he added, "On the cross-country leg through France, one of the pack horses ate part of it."

"Oh, my, a little equine retribution for carrying it all that way." Amused, she smiled.

"Perhaps," he said, apparently unable to find any humor in the thought. "It has continued to live but has not blossomed and borne fruit. With the others, however, I have had more success."

She turned to the five remaining trees, which loomed over the sickly one, proud and content. Fruit hung from the branches, and the white blossoms basked in the sunlight.

"When the grapevines leaf out, we will move the trees out into the direct sun," he said.

"But this is a most unusual thing," she said, studying the trees more closely now that her first wonderment had passed. "There are blossoms opening beside the fruit. Is that the way of oranges?"

"Indeed, oranges are not like the other fruit trees we are accustomed to in England," he said. "They do not drop their leaves like apple trees do.

The fruit takes many months to ripen. It is not unusual to have blossoms on the tree with ripening fruit.''

"How wondrously strange," she said, admiring the line of orange trees once more. Then she could not resist touching her nose to the soft white petal of one of the lower blossoms and inhaling the sweet scent. "Wonderful."

"The bees like it," Sir Hugh said.

"Were there more trees that did not make the journey?" she asked.

"No," Sir Hugh said, his hands clasped behind him as he studied the trees over her head.

His voice was even and his face bland, but he did not need to tell her that it had been an unpleasant trip. Still, she knew instinctively that this was not the time to ask about it. "I was actually looking for grapevines to bring home, and I did bring some," he explained. "But the oranges were in bloom when I arrived in Sicily."

"You could not resist them," she concluded. "Though I would have thought a Crusader knight would have been more interested in the spoils of war than the plants and trees of a garden."

"No," he said with little emotion. "I was impressed with the orange's medicinal powers. I selected six hardy-looking young trees and arranged for the pack animals to make the trip north."

"I admire your determination, Sir Hugh," she said, smiling at him again.

"I have not regretted it," he said, surveying the results of his work. "Except for the injured tree, they have proven hardy enough. Provided with sunlight, water, and warmth, they yield waxy green leaves year-round, blossoms, and a beneficial fruit."

"And the fruit yields seeds?" she asked.

"In the two years since my return, I have managed to start some seedlings. However, none of them are large enough to bear fruit for your daughter's imminent nuptials."

"Fair enough, my lord," she said, turning away to stroll down the length of the arbor to admire each of the trees. So their conversation had come full circle and they were back to her original request.

"The healthy trees appear to have been fruitful," she said.

"Indeed, they have been," he said. "And the fruit keeps for a surprisingly long time when stored in a cool dry place."

"Is that so?" she said, continuing to stroll through the arbor casually. "My daughter means a great deal to me, my lord. I am prepared to be very generous should you find that you could spare me two or three dozen oranges."

"Remuneration is not the issue, my lady," he said, staring straight ahead as he walked along at her side, his hands still clasped behind him and his shadow engulfing hers.

"Then what is it?" she asked, stopping to examine the blossoms on another orange tree.

"I went to the trouble of bringing oranges back to England because their health benefits are well known," he said. "To see sick children get well, to see the roses return to their cheeks in the dead of winter when all seems lost, is of great value. However, the claim that oranges benefit anyone's love life is dubious, if not vain, and of far less value."

She turned to him. "And how do *you* know this?"

He was silent, the earlier annoyance she had sensed in him returning.

"Have you ever seen oranges tested regarding their ability as an aphrodisiac?" she asked.

"No," he admitted, and after a pause he added rather challengingly, "Have you?"

"No, I have not," she said, looking up into his face and blinking against the brightness of the sun. "Perhaps it is something that needs to be done."

He snorted and shifted his weight from one foot to the other. "And how would you propose to do that?"

"To be perfectly honest, I am not sure," she said, glancing at the trees again. "I have little knowledge of such things."

"Nor have I," he said, shifting his weight again. And was that a note of relief in his voice? She resisted smiling.

"But that does not mean that such things as aphrodisiacs or love potions do not exist," she continued, pleased to expound on an area to which she had given much thought and had researched—academically, of course. "Love potions are fleeting in their influence and sometimes have strange caveats affecting those who take them. You have heard tell of those potions that make the recipients fall in love with the first person they set eyes upon after taking the brew?"

"Yes," he said, "and aphrodisiacs create lust in their imbibers. All nonsense."

"But surely you agree that through lust more than one heart has found the way to true love," she prodded.

"I suppose," he said, though his tone was full of skepticism.

"Perhaps we should find out," she said.

"*We?*" His voice cracked on the single word; he cleared his throat and frowned. "Surely you are not suggesting that you and I put the theory to the test?"

"And why not?" she asked, repressing her own laughter and wondering if he had been born without a sense of humor or had lost it somewhere in his travels. When the challenge had fallen from her lips, she had not been serious, but apparently he thought she was.

She stopped strolling and faced him, but he merely continued to stare at her, speechless. She decided to boldly carry on. It was an audacious proposal, but Julianna's future was at stake. "We are two adults who know our minds," she said. "I am a widow with no man in my life. I assume your situation is similar."

He gave a barely perceptible nod.

"If we share in an orange every day for, let us say the next fortnight—I understand there is not another boat to the mainland until then—and if nothing moves us to share our bodies, then we will know that you are quite right. Oranges are not aphrodisiacs. But should we develop an attraction for one another, you must give me some oranges to ensure my daughter's future happiness. Is that not fair?"

He continued to stare at her as if she were mad. "I am not one to put faith in aphrodisiacs."

"Then, my lord, what have you to fear?" she asked, stepping away from him and holding her hands away from her body as if to prove she was unarmed. She knew how nunlike she looked. More than one stranger to the bishop's court had mistaken her for an abbess. "Do I look like a seductress?"

He swallowed and shook his head, his eyes dark and intent.

"You are known to be a most principled man,"

she said, offering him a smile of encouragement. "An honorable knight. The bishop speaks highly of you. I have no fear of engaging with you in such an experiment. What say you?"

Hugh's first reaction was to seize her arm and march her straight down to the quay, where he would order the first provisioned fishing boat he found to sail her back to the mainland. Her proposal was outlandish. It was provoking. It was disruptive.

It was also strangely irresistible, this challenge of hers to his manhood and his honor. Suddenly sending Lady Emmalyn home empty-handed seemed too easy, too dissatisfying. Disproving her notion that oranges could stimulate a lover's ardor was a much more demanding means to an end.

He had no personal knowledge of all the traditional aphrodisiacs, but he had heard of them: mandrake root, Spanish fly, oysters, ground horn of unicorn. And he knew that every village had a wise woman who offered her own brew for capturing a beloved's heart or enhancing male performance. What did oranges have in common with any of these substances? Still, if his gardeners ever learned that oranges were considered an aphrodisiac, he would never be able to keep them from stealing every single orange from his trees.

His eyes narrowed as he studied the woman before him, waiting, cool and calm, for his response. At this time in his life, a piece of fruit could hardly make him do what he did not want to do—fall into lust or love with a woman, however appealing she might be.

And this woman could be appealing; he had little doubt of that. Still, when the experiment was done in two weeks, when he could smile at her politely and say that as kind to the eyes as her person was, he had no desire for her, he would have made his point. He would have dispatched any obligation to the bishop and ultimately saved his oranges for important, worthy uses. He could send her on her way without guilt or having to deal with that particular mistaken myth about oranges again.

"What say I, Lady Emmalyn? I say that you are a daring, unconventional woman." He took her arm and guided her out of the arbor so they could talk without being overheard. He could feel her eyes on him as he led them away from the gardeners and toward an apple tree. The gardeners were watching, too. "I will agree to your experiment on two conditions."

"And what are those, my lord?" she asked, her voice breathy with anticipation.

"Both of us must fall under the spell of the aphrodisiac," he said, watching her for the smallest sign of disagreement. "You must want me as much as I want you. We must declare our desire to each other and agree that it is so."

She nodded. "That only stands to reason, my lord. Of what use is passion if it is one-sided?"

"The second condition is that you will not tell anyone—nary a soul—about what we are doing. I will not have my crop of oranges endangered by an absurd rumor."

"But, of course, Sir Hugh," she said, her eyes still on him as she easily matched her steps to his. "I agree to your conditions. There is no reason why anyone else need know—unless our passion becomes so obvious that everyone sees it. Which brings me to a third condition."

"And that would be?" he asked.

"Should passion for one another grow between

us," she said, "consummation is not required for proof of the success. A simple declaration of desire will be adequate."

Hugh snorted. "We will deal with that if it happens, which seems very unlikely."

She did not acknowledge his skepticism. "Then, if we are to do this, my lord, I will need access to your kitchen."

"Why?" Hugh demanded, already wondering what kind of fool he was to agree to her nonsense. He drew to a halt and turned to face her, trying to dismiss the uneasy feeling that beneath the somber expression on her face, she was amused. "What need have you of the kitchen?"

"How else am I to see to the tasty preparation of the fruit?" she asked, her eyes wide and innocent. "If we feast on an orange prepared differently in each day's meal simply as host and guest, who would know what we are attempting beyond experimenting with new recipes?"

"Experimenting, indeed?" he echoed, gazing into her soft brown eyes and wondering what color her hair was. It was impossible to tell with the cap, veil, and gorget that she wore. How tempting could a woman be when she was covered from head to toe like this? He could surely resist such a female for two weeks. "I will speak to Walter about allowing you to work in the kitchen. I will tell him that . . . what? That you have a special interest in food preparation and wish to indulge it while you have oranges at hand, which are not usually available to you."

"That will do nicely," she agreed.

"Then that is all there is to it? We share a meal that somehow includes an orange and otherwise behave as host and guest?"

"I have no other suggestion to make for the

experiment," she said. "However, if I may be so bold, if I may confess, I envy you this beautiful isle. I would be pleased to use the days to inspect your gardens. I see things here in your southern clime that I wonder if I might be able to adapt to the bishop's garden. Perhaps we will find something that I might send you from my garden or the bishop's. And what was it you were telling me about the grapevines?"

Hugh liked the notion of talking about something besides oranges. Grapevines were of great interest to him also. If she were indeed as knowledgeable as she seemed to be and as her position as the bishop's head gardener implied, perhaps the next two weeks would not be a complete waste.

He had not said no. Emmalyn smiled to herself as she surveyed Castle Sully's busy kitchen and waited for the cook, Walter, to speak with her. One counted one's victories however small and moved on. Sir Hugh had not said no. That was good. Still, she had no idea whether her proposed experiment would work or not. Though she had made a small study of herbs and their uses and believed wholeheartedly in their medicinal properties, she was more skeptical about such things as love potions and aphrodisiacs.

When her husband Terence had dosed himself with such things, he had only become more selfish in his lovemaking. Their matings had been uncomfortable at best and painful at worst. Nothing she had ever done had changed that. Yet their couplings had brought them the children. No, she had no regrets about the children, though only Julianna, the first of the four, had survived beyond the age of five.

Still, what if she and Terence had started off differently somehow—had known each other better before their wedding or had possessed a better understanding of passion—perhaps their marriage bed would have been more pleasurable. Perhaps their union would have been happier. Perhaps love would have grown between them. But she could not change history. Terence was gone, and God forgive her, she had only felt relief when she buried him.

Nor had she any intention of lying with a man ever again. She liked widowhood. Over the past six years, despite the interest of several lords, she had managed to maintain her widowhood with subtly placed gifts to the king and the influence of her friend the Bishop of Somerfield. Her experiment with Sir Hugh need not put her into bed with him. She sought only to discover if passion might be roused. For she would do all in her power to make the marriage bed better for Julianna.

Walter hurried toward her and bowed as he wiped his hands on his apron. His kitchen was neat and orderly. Skimmers, spoons, shovels, scoops, pincers, and skewers hung along the front of the chimney. Goblets, saltcellars, bowls and trenchers of wood, pottery, and pewter filled the shelves of the open cupboards along the walls. Bunches of herbs hung from the rafters above, drying in the warm kitchen air.

"My lady," the cook said without a smile on his face or the willingness to meet her gaze. "In the two years I have cooked for Sir Hugh there has never been the need for a woman in my kitchen. However, his lordship told me that I am to assist you in any way that you require regarding the meals and . . . the oranges?"

"Yes, Walter," she said. "I do not wish to disrupt

your kitchen, but I have an abiding interest in cooking, and Sir Hugh and I are curious about the variety of ways oranges might be used in food."

"That is a good question, my lady," Walter said, raising his guarded gaze to search her face. He was wary. He ruled here in the kitchen. She knew that her presence and influence was not especially welcome. "It is my experience that his lordship has simple tastes," he added.

"No doubt he does." She gave a nod of understanding. "And I have no doubt that you know his tastes best and will continue to serve them well. I only ask that each day we confer about a single dish to be served to Sir Hugh and myself using an orange."

"Yes, my lady," Walter said, ducking his head again.

"I do not wish to interfere with your well-run kitchen," she continued. "For the most part, the preparation is yours to see to. I only ask for your help. I have some ideas for dishes or uses for oranges. I would be most interested in any ideas that you have. We need to work together on this challenge."

Walter met her gaze hesitantly. "I will gladly help you, my lady, if it pleases Sir Hugh, and it seems it does."

"Good, then," she said, wishing for more enthusiasm from the cook but content with his reluctant willingness for now. "You have a supply of oranges, I understand. May I see it?"

"Yes, a small one, my lady, in a special place," he said, gesturing to the far side of the kitchen. "This way to the larder."

She followed him to the lower level, beneath the kitchen, where he lit a candle. They passed several doors that he explained were the buttery, the wine cellar, and the pantry. While she held the taper, he took a key from the ring that hung from his belt and unlocked a storage room. The door swung open, revealing an area that was little more than a closet. There on shelves from floor to ceiling she saw at least a dozen small round willow baskets of oranges.

"My heavens, Sir Hugh has been successful with his orange trees," she said, stepping into the closet and raising the candle to get a better look. Their citrus scent greeted her.

"There are about a dozen oranges in each basket," Walter said, gesturing toward a lower shelf in the storage area. "The oldest are here. We need to use from this basket, then the one next to it. So there be enough oranges to use one for every supper for a fortnight, if that is what you are asking."

"Yes, I see that." She smiled to herself. So Sir Hugh had oranges to spare if he chose to do so.

"But, my lady, I do not know how you intend to use them," Walter said. "They smell good, particularly when sliced or grated, but on the whole they are a bitter little fruit more fit for a remedy than cooking. Hardly as useful or tasty as apples or plums."

"Yes, that may be true," she said. A remedy? All she had to do was feed Sir Hugh oranges in some form other than medicinal and convince him that he had come to find her desirable. And some of the oranges in the baskets would be hers.

Emmalyn's brow creased in a small frown. The desirable part might be difficult. How long had it been since she had flirted with a man? She had been a faithful wife and had never flirted much. What little she had done had been long ago. Too long. Did she even remember how to tantalize the opposite sex? How to make desire overrule good sense? Where should she begin?

How much help would the oranges be?

She sighed. If the fruit was not of help to her, it would be of little use to Julianna. That is what she—and Sir Hugh—would learn in the next two weeks. If the oranges failed her, she had nothing more to offer her daughter but the wisdom to be strong and love her new husband as best she could.

"Cook?" she said, deciding at last where to begin.

"Yes, my lady?"

"Does your larder have a supply of honey? I suspect I may need it."

Chapter Three

"How is it that you are the head gardener for the Bishop of Somerfield?" Father Paul asked, his silver wine goblet in his hand and a smile of genuine interest on his lips as he gazed into Lady Emmalyn's face.

Hugh, who seldom took interest in formalities, had seated himself on the lady's right while the Isle of Sully's only priest was seated on her left at the hastily set up and laid high table in the great hall. Hugh marveled that Walter had managed to bring out Sully's best silver and table linens with so little forewarning.

He was also having second thoughts about the wisdom of inviting the priest for the evening meal. It had seemed a good idea—a relief that he would not have to carry alone the dinner table conversation with his guest. Father Paul had arrived obviously pleased to be included and, again, Hugh had congratulated himself on his foresight.

Then Lady Emmalyn, dressed for supper, had

appeared in the doorway of the great hall. He had begun to have doubts—about several things.

As before, the lady wore fine creamy white wool, but for the occasion she had obviously donned her best. Her gown was fashioned with full pointed sleeves and a trailing skirt, the throat and the hem deeply edged with gold silk embroidery. Her low-slung belt of silk braid revealed a figure with full breasts, a narrow waist flaring out to just the right amount of womanly fullness about the hips.

This evening she wore no cap, gorget, or veil. His question was answered. Her hair was honey gold. Finely spun. Like a golden veil glistening in the candlelight, it hung down her back almost to her hips. Only a narrow gold fillet across her brow confined her tresses.

Hugh could not keep himself from staring at her. This was no nun seated before them. It was even difficult to think of her as some man's widow. She appeared more like a queenly maid.

The heat that had hit his loins when she had appeared for dinner was still there—and rising. Uncomfortably, he shifted on the bench, thankful that he had allowed Fulk to talk him into wearing his best long tunic. What was that she had said about not being a seductress? No bawdy game of Dame Gilda's ever had elicited such a swift, potent reaction from him.

And if the lady's presence struck him like a blow to the nether regions, Hugh had to wonder what she was doing to the priest.

He glanced at Father Paul and saw that he, too, was staring.

The churchman and he were of an age. During the last two years, as they had shared evenings over the chessboard, they had become friends. Father Paul was an honest, loyal man who took his religious vows seriously. He sat through the night with the sick and dying. He comforted the bereaved. He worried over confessions he could not share with Hugh. He counseled faithless husbands and restless wives. As far as Hugh knew, the priest was chaste. However, Hugh had discovered that the priest, like himself, was a man. Father Paul was not immune to the attraction of a comely face or a shapely leg.

"How did I become the bishop's head gardener?" Lady Emmalyn repeated, turning to the priest to answer his question. "His grace had often admired the grounds of Trentworth. After Terence died, he asked me if I would help him with restoring the grounds of Somerfield. The abbey gardens had been neglected somewhat. I did what I could. His grace was pleased with the results. He asked me to continue. And so I have."

"You must be very good at it," Father Paul said, his eyes glowing with admiration.

"I find the work gratifying," Lady Emmalyn said. "Over the years we have made the grounds lovelier, I hope, and the gardens more productive. In recent years, we have endeavored to restore the ancient Roman vineyards with some success."

"And now Sir Hugh's orange trees have brought you to Sully," the priest said. "How did you learn of them?"

She explained about the oranges Hugh had sent to the orphanage.

"Yes, now I remember." The priest never bothered to glance in his host's direction.

Hugh noted that the churchman was hanging on every word the lady said. If he found her attractive, how intriguing must she be to the priest? Hugh frowned to himself, his annoyance growing with the way his friend and chess opponent had not taken his eyes from Lady Emmalyn since the moment she had walked into the hall. The man was obviously willing to prattle on about anything as long as he could hold the lady's attention. The situation was becoming considerably more complicated than he had ever imagined it might.

"How fortunate for all of us that Sir Hugh is so generous," Father Paul said. "And what is your interest in the fruit?"

"Sir Hugh has graciously agreed to help me learn more about oranges and their uses," Lady Emmalyn said.

"Is that so?" Father Paul said, looking in Hugh's direction for the first time since they had been seated at the table. "I have heard tales that oranges are good for the skin."

"No, we are not going to consider frivolous uses," Lady Emmalyn said, her expression credibly sober now. "Our search is for beneficial uses of the fruit in diet and medicine. I have consulted with Walter, and he and I have devised a dish for our meal tonight that will set us on the path to greater understanding of the fruit's properties."

"What is being served this evening?" Father Paul asked.

"Roasted duck with oranges in the sauce," she replied without hesitation. "Walter told me Sir Hugh fancies duck."

"That is one of my favorites as well," the priest said.

Lady Emmalyn's smile faltered. She cast Hugh a troubled look. He felt her hand on his arm, squeezing it firmly—almost with desperation.

"Father, would you excuse us while we have a word in private?" Lady Emmalyn said, urging Hugh off the bench.

"Of course, my lady," Father Paul said with a puzzled smile.

Dutifully Hugh led her out of the hall, past the castle retainers who were gathering to sup at the lower tables. Outside the doors, she swung around to face him.

"Heavens," she said. "I never thought about a clergyman supping with us this evening."

Hugh shook his head in confusion. "I invited him. He is a frequent guest."

"But not when you are experimenting with the aphrodisiacal powers of oranges," she whispered, glancing around as if she was concerned that they would be overheard. "The man took vows of chastity. I would not want to be responsible for imperiling his vows," she added. "You see my concern?"

"I do." He shared her concern about Father Paul's vulnerability all right, but that concern had little to do with what they were feeding the priest. He was disturbed about the effect of her company on the man—and himself. If Father Paul's vows of chastity could not protect him from the lady's charms—and those vows did not appear to be doing so—how was he to defend himself? Hugh wondered.

"We cannot refuse Father Paul food from our menu," she said, frowning, as she reflected on the problem. "I do not recall oranges bringing any sudden romance into the bishop's life. Though that was long ago, and I was not so observant then. Still, what are we to do, Sir Hugh? The food preparation is complete."

Hugh was suddenly sorry that he had agreed to this ridiculous experiment. For an instant he considered withdrawing from it. As he gazed into her face, his second thought startled and troubled him. He could not back down—he had given his word.

Nor could he bring himself to disappoint her. Why?

Because she had not proposed this experiment for herself. She asked for her daughter. He would learn why in time. But he had come near enough to being a father to understand what lengths one will go to for a child's future.

"We simply must see to it that Father Paul gets as little of the orange as possible," Hugh said, patting her hand on his arm.

"Yes, we could do that," she said, nodding, her gaze directed beyond him in distraction. "The orange is in the sauce."

"There you are," Hugh said, relieved to have the matter settled. He turned them toward the door of the great hall once more.

Suddenly she hung back, frowning at him as she peered into his face intently. Uncertainty glimmered in her eyes. What now?

"You are not having second thoughts about our experiment are you, my lord?" she asked in a small voice.

"No, of course not," Hugh lied with a heartiness and confidence that astounded him. By the saints, how did this woman manage to sense his deepest thoughts when he hardly knew them himself? "We see to it that Father Paul gets very little sauce. And that he is *not* invited to supper again for the next fortnight—until I have proven my point."

"Or I have proven mine," she countered, her smile slowly renewing. "Yes, that would probably be wise—not to invite Father Paul to sup with us again."

"Done." Hugh said, leading her back into the great hall and thinking of the old Adam and Eve story. Was it possible the apple that had been Adam's undoing had really been an orange?

Emmalyn rose early the next morning, before Prime, crawling out of her curtained bed and pulling on her work clothes without disturbing her maid, who was just waking. She combed and bound her hair beneath a veil, snatched up her cloak, and left her chamber. With only the early light of dawn she found her way through the twisting castle passages to the gardens. She wanted to examine the stunted orange tree she had seen the day before.

She was pleased thus far with her stay on the isle. It was a lovely, prosperous-appearing place with well-tended fields, trim fishing boats, fat sheep and cattle, and friendly residents—except for their lord. Sir Hugh's reputation as a hermit seemed well earned. Still, the supper with Father Paul had been a success—after a faltering start, Emmalyn admitted to herself.

For a moment, when Sir Hugh had seemed to be having second thoughts, she had feared that he was about to withdraw his agreement to their experiment. Yet it seemed that his only concern had been for his friend, the priest. She smiled to herself. Truly, she had been touched that he was so concerned for Father Paul.

A cool gust of wind caught at the edges of her cloak as she stepped out of the castle and into the garden. She gathered the folds around herself and made her way toward the arbor. From overhead came the cry of the gulls, and she sniffed the scent of the sea on the wind. A unique scent to her—Trentworth was too far inland to smell the ocean from there. Yellow daffodil heads bobbed and budded apple tree branches swayed in the southerly wind. As she walked, she became aware of the gardeners already moving about the grounds, pruning and turning earth to start planting. She wondered if Sir Hugh joined his men this early.

The sky was clear and the sun just rising out of the sea behind her as she made her way along the north wall toward the arbor. Already the deep green leaves of the orange trees were glistening in the morning light. Emmalyn could not resist smiling at them, the proud trees, their branches stretched toward the sun and their toes thrust deep into their terra-cotta pots. Their joy in growing almost made her want to laugh out loud.

She strolled along the length of the row of trees, admiring them. "Good morning, my beauties," she said. "It promises to be another lovely day for you to sun yourselves and grow your fruit and make more of your lovely blossoms."

When she reached the end of the row, where the stunted tree stood, she stopped and regarded it with pursed lips.

"And just what ails you, small one?" she asked, studying the tree from top to bottom. She leaned closer. Its leaves were healthy and its trunk was undamaged. "You survived the nibbling of a hungry horse and the journey overland and across the Channel into a new land. Hardships, true, but you have shown you have the strength. Why do you not thrive like your fellows?"

She heard the sound of boots on the arbor flagstones behind her.

"Good morrow, Lady Emmalyn," Sir Hugh said, stopping at her side. "Are you always such an early riser?"

"But of course." She straightened and turned to smile at him. He, too, was dressed in work clothes, a short plain tunic of an earthy rust color and hose similar to the ones he had worn when he had first greeted her. She liked the sight of him in a short tunic.

The long brocade one of a dark green rivaling a midnight forest that he had worn the night before covered too much leg. And his legs were fine to look upon. Still, she had to admit to herself, with his height and proud carriage in the formal dress, he had appeared more a prince than a mere knight, and the regal look suited him, too. This morning, though, he was a gardener again.

"No need to waste the light of the day," she added. "I hope you do not mind that I am drawn to your orange trees again. They made such an impression on me that I saw them in my dreams."

"I do not mind," he said.

"They seem to have survived well during their first night uncovered in the spring air," she said, still clutching her cloak about her for warmth.

"By mid-morn the sun will be high in the sky, and you will be tossing your cloak aside," Sir Hugh said. "There is little likelihood that we need cover them against the cold again until late fall."

"Your clime here is marvelous," she said. Then, tilting her head slightly, she inquired, "Did Father Paul enjoy himself last night? After I retired, did you notice any sign that might indicate that he was affected by the duck in orange sauce?"

"He did not stay long after you pleaded exhaustion and excused yourself," Sir Hugh said. "He was gone by Compline. Nor did he comment upon the manner in which you soaked the sauce off your shared trencher with your bread."

"Ah, a gallant man, your priest," she said, recalling the look of shock Father Paul had tried to cover when she had first helped herself to the duck sauce from his portion. "I did my best to keep him from imbibing anything orange."

"A valiant effort, Lady Emmalyn," Sir Hugh said without a smile. "I am not worried about oranges corrupting the poor man."

"It was the least I could do for your friend," she said, "and my host. How do you feel this morning after your first dose of orange aphrodisiac?"

"I liked the duck well enough." He shrugged. "But I feel no different than I do any other morning."

She nodded. "Nor do I. I think it is much too soon for the fruit to have any affect, do you not agree?"

"I most certainly agree, assuming there is anything to the tale," he said. "To be honest, Lady Emmalyn, as a mother determined to win the oranges for her daughter's betrothal, I would have expected that you would know more about the power of the fruit."

"I do not have personal knowledge about oranges, my lord," she said, untroubled by his comment. "And as for other potions of which I do have personal knowledge—through observation and reading only, mind you—they have shown themselves to be inconsistent at best."

"But why do you feel any kind of love concoction is necessary for your daughter's betrothal?" he asked.

"I want to ensure her happiness," Emmalyn replied. "She is but fifteen, so young. She is sweet and sensitive. She deserves a husband who will be gentle. Who will love and cherish her, who will be faithful and will share freely as only a lover will. Someone with whom she can build a life, sharing dreams as well as life's disappointments. She hardly knows the young man the king has chosen for her to wed."

"How well did you know your husband when you were betrothed?" he asked.

"We had met once in a crowded hall, and I knew then that a marriage to him would be arranged," she said, trying not to recall awkward and painful memories that had blessedly faded over time. "I want a happier future for my daughter."

"You wish for romance," he said in a dismissive tone, as if she had spoken of something fabled.

"I wish her love," she said, surprised with how deeply his cynicism annoyed her. "I understand you had a wife once, Sir Hugh. Did you love her?"

"My marriage was arranged much like yours, when I was but fourteen," he said. "At our station in life, whose marriage is not arranged? And I had the highest regard for my wife. Adela was also young, but I have no reason to believe she was unhappy. Neither of us was. Not about our marriage."

She hesitated, but was finally compelled to ask, "About what, then?"

"Nothing of importance now."

"But it was of importance then?" she pressed.

"Merely a boy's dreams." Sir Hugh shrugged. When she stared at him in silent expectation, he continued. "I longed to go to the Crusades, King Richard's Crusades, and my father would not permit it. He wanted me to stay and fulfill my duties as a husband and heir."

"Did you share this dream with your wife?"

"Why should I? It was my foolish dream, not hers."

Emmalyn considered this insight into the life of the man at her side. "But then, you did respond to Pope Innocent's call to arms in Twelve-aught-two.''

"Thirteen years later. By then Adela had died in childbirth," Sir Hugh said, turning away from her. "And my brother Edward had wedded and provided heirs. I was my own man. Father could not prevent me from taking the Crusader's vow and joining my mother's French family in the march to the Holy Land."

"I see," she said, aware that he had not answered her question about loving his wife. And she was also aware that she had tread into sensitive territory.

"So what think you concerning the sickly tree, Lady Emmalyn?" he asked, plainly wishing to change the subject. "Have you any advice for how we might heal it? There were so few leaves on it by the time we pulled the horse away that I almost left it behind. I had no idea whether it would survive or not."

"Then it has regained its leaves," she said. "I can suggest nothing more except perhaps giving it more love."

"Love?"

"Yes, love," she replied sweetly. "We are back to that topic again. Clearly, you have loved all your orange trees, and they have returned the favor by thriving, but perhaps this injured one needs a bit extra."

"You have listened to too many troubadours' songs, my lady." Sir Hugh folded his arms across his broad chest. His tone was nearly amused, but when she glanced at him, she saw no smile on his face. She had not seen one since she arrived.

"They are but trees, my lady. Plants that need sun, water, and good soil. I will grant that attention is important, but love has little to do with it."

"I beg to differ, my lord." She had no intention

of being drawn into a disagreement on the subject. "Love has everything to do with survival."

Any argument he might have tried to offer was forestalled by the tolling of the Prime bells, calling them to mass.

"After chapel I have something for breaking your fast, my lord," she said, taking the arm he offered her.

He gave a resigned sigh. "Something made of oranges, no doubt."

"Indeed, that is the object of this experiment, is it not?" she said, allowing him to lead the way toward the chapel. She smiled, but truly it was an effort not to be discouraged. His gardens were full of love, yet he did not know it. He was closed. He had chosen to withdraw from the world and to give all of himself to his gardens—to the flowers and vegetables, shrubs and trees. Clearly, he had little interest in living things of a more animate nature, things that walked and talked like himself: like human beings—

Emmalyn was beginning to think she had about as much chance of winning him over as she had of bringing blooms to that poor stunted orange tree.

Chapter Four

When Sir Hugh ushered Lady Emmalyn into the kitchen after mass, Walter was already busy with the day's food preparation at the worktable standing in the center of the room. The kitchen was filled with the bustle and clatter of churning, baking, chopping, and slicing. A fire roared in the enormous hearth, and cauldrons simmered on their trivets over the flames. Delicious smells permeated the air.

Hugh led them toward a small alcove where a table with benches sat beneath a wide window overlooking the kitchen garden. The lady seemed to like gardens well enough. He figured all he had to do for the next two weeks was keep her entertained with the plans and work he had done, avoid the subject of love whenever possible, and try not to appear bored with orange-flavored food.

If Lady Emmalyn was uncertain about the power of the oranges, then he should be able to convince her that the tales she had heard were false. Victory would be his. He had little doubt of it.

"In cold weather I usually break my fast in here and leave the men to eat wherever they find a place." He motioned to Walter at the same time he offered her a place on the bench nearer the fire than the window. He preferred the window view, but the chapel had been as cold as the outdoors. She was shivering and needed the warmth of the kitchen. "Bread and hot cider," he ordered as Walter approached.

Walter nodded. "And the honey we made yesterday, right, my lady?"

"Yes, bring the orange honey," she said, smiling at the cook as she took off her cloak and laid it over the bench. "Perhaps this will be more to your taste, my lord."

"We will see." Hugh settled himself across the table from her as Walter carried a basket of bread, a plate of fresh butter, and a small earthenware pot of honey to the table. He had liked last night's duck and orange sauce well enough, but it had been no better than any number of other ways Walter had prepared duck for him. And he had slept soundly enough, untroubled by romantic dreams or amorous urges. One dreamless night had strengthened his confidence and resolve that no piece of fruit could seduce him to mindless lust if he did not wish it.

Two tankards of hot cider soon followed the food Walter brought.

Lady Emmalyn seized her steaming drink immediately, warming her hands around it and then raising the tankard to her lips. "Hmmm." She drank at length. "That is good."

Hugh watched her, fascinated by her obvious pleasure in a simple tankard of cider. When she set it down, her eyes were bright with satisfaction, her cheeks pink with warmth, and her lips glistening from the cider. She licked them and smiled at him.

Hugh's loins reacted.

"Please, my lord," she said, looking at him curiously. "You must try the honey with oranges."

He struggled to ignore his body's response to the gleam on her lips and glanced at the earthenware pot she had gestured toward. When a movement caught his eye, he realized that Walter was also hovering nearby, anticipating his reaction to the new concoction.

"Walter and I wondered what to do about the bitterness in the fruit," she said, reaching to take her knife from her belt. "Oranges smell so good when they are peeled and grated, but sometimes the fruit is bitter."

"You like ground orange mixed with your butter, my lord," Walter said, stepping forward.

"Yes, that is how I like it," Hugh said uneasily. So she had won over his cook, too. "A touch of flavor to the butter."

"So we have ground up an orange to mix into your honey as well," Walter said, grinning at him.

"Indeed." Lady Emmalyn smiled. She picked up a piece of bread, spread the golden orange substance from the honey pot on it, and offered it to Hugh. "Here, try this, my lord."

He accepted the bread, his fingers brushing against hers, his body leaping again. Shifting on the bench, he stuffed the bite into his mouth, feeling like a fool as his cook and his guest stared at him and held their breath.

Careful to keep his expression bland, he glanced up at the two eager faces studying him as the sweetness spread through his mouth. He noted the fruity flavor first, followed by the honey sweetness, then the bitter—not bitter like bark tea, but a fruity bitterness that was almost a scent as well as a flavor. For a moment he forgot about the thrill of Emmalyn's touch. The combination of taste sensations was pleasing in an indescribable way. Remarkable. In truth, it was the best thing he had tasted in a long time. He licked his lips and almost reached for another piece of bread, and then thought better of it. He did not want to appear to like it very well. They would make more of it than it deserved.

"What do you think, my lord?" she asked, leaning toward him. "Do you fancy it?"

Walter leaned closer, too.

"It tastes well enough." Hugh nodded slowly, then shrugged to resist the urge to lick his lips again. Then he drank from the tankard of cider to resist snatching up another piece of bread and slathering orange honey on it.

Lady Emmalyn and Walter glanced at each other.

"I had hoped for a little more enthusiasm," she said with a small frown. "I would not have you tolerating food you do not like just to please me, my lord. Walter, take away the orange and honey and bring us some of that ham I saw yesterday."

"Aye, my lady." Walter reached for the honey pot.

Hugh put down the tankard and snatched the pot out of the cook's hand. "I like it well enough, I said."

Walter stepped back, surprised.

Lady Emmalyn stared in openmouthed astonishment.

"Fetch us the ham as the lady bid." Hugh dropped the pot back on the table, reached for his knife this time, speared a chunk of bread, and began to cover it in orange honey.

"Aye, my lord," Walter said, hurrying away.

When Hugh finished the bread, he looked up to see Lady Emmalyn watching him, her frown replaced by a small smile.

"I have always liked honey," he said, lest she think she had stumbled onto some great discovery.

"I am glad Walter and I thought to try orange in it then," she said, also helping herself to the bread and honey.

"I would not mind having this to break my fast often," he offered as casually as he could manage.

"Excellent," she said without looking at him or broadening her smile. Clearly the lady knew when not to press her victories. "I will tell Walter. He will be pleased with our experiment with the oranges."

Hugh looked at her, startled. "You have not told him about . . ."

"No, of course, not," she said. "He seems to think of oranges as medicinal. Now he is intrigued by the challenge of making them tastier."

"Yes, the challenge," Hugh muttered, reaching for more bread, doing his best to ignore her gaze as he heaped orange honey on the crust. Indeed, a challenge was what their experiment had become.

For the next several mornings when it was still barely light enough to see, he found Lady Emmalyn huddled in her cloak, standing by the sick tree, talking to it, caressing its glossy leaves, and probing its soil to determine whether or not it needed a drink. She treated the blessed thing as if it were a beloved pet. If she had thought of some way to relieve its suffering, she had not shared the remedy with him.

Otherwise she made herself an amenable companion as women went, taking a sensible interest in the gardens. She approved of his marling efforts, discussing the merits of the clay in the garden soil. She also approved of the manure spreading. When he gave her a tour of the kitchen gardens, she was pleased with the selection of herbs.

"Mint, sage, chives, and chamomile," she recited. "Very nice, my lord. I see lavender and tansy. All effective repellents for pests. Ladies' bed-straw is also good. I shall send you some from my garden."

"Thank you, my lady," he said. "That is most generous of you."

"My pleasure, my lord. Excellent, quince," she murmured over the bush that was just beginning to leaf out.

"Walter's prescription for digestive ailments," Hugh said.

"Indeed, and when cooked down, a perfect addi-tion to fruits," Lady Emmalyn said. "I shall show him. In truth, we might be able to do something with quince and oranges."

"Would you like to see the roses?" Hugh was eager to avoid mention of that damnable fruit again.

"Yes," she said, following his lead. "Have you thought of keeping a garden journal, my lord? I started one some years ago. I find it most helpful in reminding myself where certain plants have come from and where they thrive best in my garden. And lest I forget—I am eager to see your pond. I have glimpsed it from my chamber window and it looks so inviting. I wonder how orange would taste on fish."

As the days passed, he found himself pointing out plants and shrubs and describing his plans for enlarging flowerbeds and expanding the orchards and extending the borders. He even told her of his desire to design a larger rose garden with a fountain like one he had seen in Rome. He hoped to obtain cuttings of the new rose from the East that bloomed twice in the summer. Sharing dreams, he realized later—small ones, but dreams still—he had not realized he had. She only smiled at him knowingly and urged him to continue. And he did, taking pleasure in sharing his strategies with her, pleasure he did not feel when he talked with Fulk.

She even worked along beside him, weeding a section of the herb garden as she went. She recommended the use of a trellis for grapevines where neither he nor his gardeners had thought of it before.

Every evening she appeared at supper dressed in a different creamy white-and-gold gown, her glorious hair uncovered, smelling of lavender and smiling as if she had looked forward all day to this meal with him. Unaccountably, the sight of her always pleased him. As had become their custom, they shared a trencher of some orange-flavored concoction and a goblet of wine, and they talked of a project he had begun to build—a new longer and larger quay so that bigger ships could come to Sully—and about the village tradesmen she was beginning to know from their business calls upon her at the castle. Though he did not like to admit it to himself, he was beginning to look forward to those evening meals. He was beginning to think of their experiment as an intriguing—if frustrating— game. In the game she fed him something tasty and smiled, and he pretended he cared little for the morsel and did his damnedest to keep his hands off her.

The weather remained fair, though it had not warmed up as much as he expected. The winter crops—the wheat, barley, rye, and oats—were greening the fields. The spring planting was going exceptionally well. He had sent his gardeners out to work in the fields to get in the last of the beans, peas, and hops.

He had spent that day dispensing justice as the lord of Sully with the aid of Father Paul on the steps of the church. They heard grievances and dispensed settlements once a month.

By supper at the end of their first week together, he was feeling satisfied with the affairs of Sully and pleased to have Lady Emmalyn's company at his table. He descended the stairs from his chamber to find that for the first time, she had preceded him and was waiting for him beside the fire. She turned and smiled at him when she heard him at the door. Flames leapt in the hearth behind her. The sunlight was fading and the wind had come up to chill the room.

She rose. So did the dogs that were as likely to follow her about the castle these days as they were him. How easily their allegiance had shifted to her. There was a deep pink blush to the lady's cheeks, and the firelight made a flickering gold halo of her hair. "My lord, Walter has fixed something special for us to ward off the cold turn."

Hugh waited in the doorway for his body's reaction to fade. Thankfully she had not questioned him about the effect of oranges on him since that first morning. So he had no need to tell her about his dream of the past night in which she fed him oranges—from her gleaming lips to his—as they lay in the grass by the fish pond. There had been more to the dream, having to do with smooth skin and wet heat, but he did his best to dismiss the memories now.

What would it be like to enter this hall each night knowing she would be there? Companionable, sweet, purposeful Emmalyn. And what if the night did not end with supper? That would be good, too, but that was lust. The lady deserved more from him than that. He ignored the desire in his loins and strode across the hall to the fireside. "What orange thing has Walter prepared for us this evening?"

"He has spiced our wine." She poured a goblet full and offered it to him with a coy smile that surprised him. He had learned over the past few days that she was not a flirtatious woman, just as she had told him. She was confident in her womanhood and in herself and fell back on no feminine wiles to get what she wanted when dealing with him or the servants. She could be diplomatic and had a good sense of humor. She could cajole, but she did not purposefully seduce. She was too honest for that.

"This is the Isle of Sully's wine mulled with spices and orange slices," she added.

He met her gaze over the cup. They had had the customary goblet of wine with supper every night. He had ordered Walter to decant their best French wines for the lady's benefit. Sully's wines were strong-flavored and more to a man's taste. However, it appeared Walter had taken things into his own hands tonight.

"Have you tasted Walter's brew?" he asked.

"No. I was waiting for you." She leaned closer and whispered conspiratorially, "My lord, we have enjoyed Walter's creations these last few evenings with varying degrees of pleasure. And he worked on this so hard and was so pleased with himself, we must speak well of it, no matter how it tastes."

Hugh nodded, taking the cup from her, allowing his fingers to linger on hers.

With a blink of surprise, she met his gaze again. A touchingly vulnerable smile blushed across her face. She removed her hand slowly, then turned away so quickly that he missed the pleasure of savoring that unguarded expression.

Did she find him attractive enough to blush at his advances? Odd, he had never contemplated that possibility. He had never felt at a loss for admiration from the ladies, but he had never been foolish enough to believe that every female should fall at his feet either. There was little in the world as enticing as a modest woman's blushes. And Emmalyn was a very modest woman.

He sipped the mulled wine, too distracted by this new thought to concentrate on the flavor.

"Umm, that is good," she said, nearly smacking her lips and attempting to peer into the goblet. "I do not know why you have insisted on the French wine, my lord."

"What? The wine," he said, endeavoring to bring his mind and his body back to the moment. "Yes, the spices and the orange flavor make it quite tolerable."

He offered her the customary shared cup again, and she took it, sipping deeply this time, and grinning at him when she finished. A drop of wine threatened to fall from her lower lip. She licked at it quickly, then laughed.

Hugh stared, a fraction of a second away from bending down to kiss her.

The sound of the silver bell Fulk rang each evening to signal the serving of the evening meal stopped him. Gratefully, Hugh offered his arm to Lady Emmalyn, and they walked to the high table with the other castle residents seated below—as chaperones.

* * *

He had nearly kissed her; Emmalyn was certain of it. She had seen the way Hugh's gaze lingered on her mouth, his eyes intent on her lips to the exclusion of all else in the room. She took a deep, calming breath. How long had it been since a man had looked at her that way? Even when her husband had, the feelings his gaze evoked were unlike the ones roiling in her now. Though her hand was steady when she put it on his arm, her insides quivered with anticipation. What would it be like to be kissed by this man?

"Tonight Walter has prepared for us roasted pork with an orange honey glaze," she said, taking her seat on the high table bench next to him. She sat the wine goblet down on the table between them and gazed expectantly upon the huge platter the page set before them.

"You and Walter have been most creative. A week has gone by and we have not had the same dish twice." Hugh sat next to her, a small smile on his lips.

It almost took her breath away.

"There, I knew you could do it," she said, touching his arm and laughing. For the past week she had watched him and wondered if he could smile. So many times, particularly in the garden, he would come close to allowing the beauty of the day or the growth of a plant to bring a smile to his lips, but it had never quite happened. He had resisted time after time. She wondered if he did not purposely resist other things as well. "You can smile," she said.

"Of course I can smile," he said, the smile vanishing. "What made you think I could not?"

"Oh, do not stop so soon," she said, dismayed.

"You never smile. Now I am sorry I said anything about it."

"It troubles me to learn that I have been such dour company," he said.

"Never that," she protested. "Just solemn. Here is the supper roast. Carve, my lord, and forget that I spoke of it."

Hugh carved the meat with a steady hand, generous and precise as always in his serving at table. She quickly turned the conversation to the day's work. The meal passed easily, as it always seemed to do when they shared thoughts about the gardens. It was not until she saw Fulk order more wood be put on the fire that she realized that the hall had grown cold and the wind's howling louder. Drafts made the wall torches flicker.

The hour was late. The other castle residents were leaving the room, and the dogs, satisfied with their supper scraps, had curled up before the fire to sleep.

"More spiced wine," Sir Hugh ordered, then turned to her at the table and offered his hand. "Shall we sit closer to the fire? The spring warmth seems to have forsaken us tonight."

She agreed, but when she settled in her chair, she shivered. He moved to the side of his large chair and gestured for her to join him. "Sit with me tonight," he invited. "Warmer for the both of us."

Though they sat close on the high bench table every night as they shared their trencher, he had never offered to share his fireside chair, though both chairs were huge enough to accommodate two people. Wondering why he had done so tonight, she hesitated.

"I promise to try to smile at least once more if you will join me," he said, with such solemnity, she feared she had offended him. Then, to her relief, he chuckled. A wonderful warm sound.

She laughed softly and rose to join him. She sat down in the corner of his chair. They sat thigh to thigh, their backs pressed against the solid wood of the high back of the chair that thwarted the drafts stirring in the hall.

"Warmer?"

"Yes, thank you," she said.

"This is better," he said, settling back so that he faced her.

"I have been wondering about something," Emmalyn said, feeling brave enough at last to ask what had been on her mind for some time.

"And what would that be?" he asked, sipping more of the spiced wine he had ordered.

"I was wondering why you do not display your Crusader's surcoat or the cross you won for taking the Crusader's vow," she said. "I have seen knights hang theirs in their great hall or their chapel. Yet I have seen yours nowhere in the castle."

Any hint of that smile that had dazzled her vanished. Harsh lines darkened his face. "I choose not to display them."

Emmalyn was immediately sorry that she had brought up the topic, but now that she had, she was not going to drop it until she knew more.

"Why not?" she asked, taking the silver wine goblet from him and sipping from it. "You have earned the admiration and respect that comes with being a Crusader."

"I earned nothing," Sir Hugh said, his sensuous mouth thin. "I would not deceive people into thinking that I had."

"I do not understand," she said. "To join the Crusades was your boyhood dream. Something you waited many years to do."

"I did not fulfill my vow." He gazed pensively into the fire. "I and the others never reached the Holy Land. We never prayed at the altar of the Holy Sepulchre."

Puzzled, she began, "But, my lord, you captured—"

"We sacked a Christian city," Sir Hugh said, his icy gaze holding hers. "Constantinople is a Christian city. We had no right to do what was done there. Fighting Christians and looting the churches for their holy relics in the name of a Crusade. To pretend we did anything heroic or honorable is dishonest and ignoble. I will be forever sorry that I had any part in it."

"I have little doubt that such an act was not of your choosing," she said in a small voice.

"It was not," he said, turning away, his voice full of disgust. "There were intrigues and contracts and secret meetings with the Venetians and agreements with the Franks. There seemed to be little to do but trust where I should not have trusted. To pledge my allegiance to men to whom I never should have been loyal."

"So you returned from Constantinople, your dreams turned to disillusionment." She nodded, understanding more now.

"Dust in the wind," he muttered. "My father died while I was away. Edward had ensconced himself, his wife, and their brood here in the castle in my rightful place as lord. It seems they had not expected me to return and were none too pleased when I did. He had the gall to suggest I go back to the Holy Land while he looked after Sully."

"Your very own brother?" Emmalyn swallowed a gasp of indignation. "What happened?"

"I threatened to appeal to the Church courts," he said, a smile—grim and thin-lipped—curved on his lips. "The Crusade may have destroyed my honor, but I was not going to allow it to rob me of my inheritance. Edward and his family left the isle. Since I had no son, he remains my heir, and I have allowed him to be my seneschal for the isle's few properties on the mainland."

"I see." She nodded again. "So now you have chosen to devote yourself to the gardens of Sully."

"The only good things that came from the Crusade were the cuttings and the orange trees that I brought home with me," he said with resignation and a strange bitterness. He stared into the shadows of the great hall beyond her.

Emmalyn watched him, her heart aching for the man who had lost his dreams. She understood at last why he rarely smiled.

Chapter Five

"So you brought those beautiful orange trees home with you," she said, lightly touching his knee, longing to change his mood, to bring him back from the brink of darkness that had descended upon him with the mention of the Crusades.

He started, staring at his leg where she had touched him. In the silence she could hear the wind still howling outside the great hall. Then she was surprised to find him studying her face intently as he had earlier, when she was certain he was thinking of kissing her.

"You are such a good man and a fine knight, my lord," she began shyly. "If I kiss you, would you think it was because of the oranges?"

"Emmalyn?" He leaned toward her. "Never."

"Then kiss me, my lord," she said, leaning toward him, yearning to know if kissing him would be as pleasant as she had speculated.

His mouth covered hers in a tender kiss. Emmalyn closed her eyes and yielded to the sweetness, glad of the feel of his hand on the side of her head, stroking her hair. She pressed her hands against his hard thigh. It was wonderful. He was wonderful.

"God's teeth!" He lifted his mouth from hers only long enough to speak. "I wish we had done this sooner."

"Did the oranges keep you from it?" she murmured, watching his lips and longing for them on hers again.

"I do not know what kept me from it," he said, breathless. "But whatever it was, I was a fool to heed it."

He kissed her again. This time he threaded his fingers through her hair, and she spread her hands against his chest. She could feel his heart beating rapidly beneath her palm. Above them the wind's howl became a whistle and raindrops began to beat against the shutters.

His mouth moved over hers, gently nipping at her lips and teasing the corner of her mouth with his tongue. She tasted him back, savoring the sweetness of the dark wine and the bittersweet aroma of the oranges steeped in it.

This was unlike any kiss she had experienced. The sensuality of it carried away her emotions, stealing away any doubts, any uncertainties about her ability to appeal to him. He wanted her. What stunned her, though, was how much she wanted him. The taste of him on her lips, the feel of him beneath her hands, the scent of him in her head brought a sweet sense of anticipation—not dread. It was such a wondrous shock.

When the kiss ended, she laid her head against his shoulder, too weak to hold it up a moment longer. She felt him kiss her brow. The tenderness of his gesture made her sigh and close her eyes. She had never known such pleasure in the arms of her husband. Was this what desire was like? Magical. Would it lead to true love? Was this what she could win for Julianna?

Or—dare she even hope—for herself?

She pushed herself away from Hugh and looked up into his face. "Are you certain that was not the power of the oranges speaking through you?"

"How can mere fruit from a tree inspire feelings like this?" he whispered against her ear.

She smiled, closed her eyes, and leaned her head against his jaw. It was as firm and strong as it looked. "How, indeed."

"Ahemm, my lord," Fulk said.

The sound made Emmalyn start, and she tried to pull away from Hugh. Neither of them had realized that the steward was even in the hall. But Hugh only allowed her to shift slightly.

"What is it, Fulk?" he asked, a note of irritation in his voice. "It is near Compline."

"My lord, I know it is late," Fulk stammered, embarrassed, impatient, and flustered. "My lord, I am so sorry to interrupt. I thought you would want to know. It is . . . my lord, it is snowing outside."

"Snowing!" Hugh hastily put her from him and sprang to his feet.

Emmalyn knew she was forgotten. The news was almost enough to make her forget their kiss, too. Snow would be harmful to many of the plants in the garden. It would freeze apple blossoms, diminish the wheat harvest, and kill back the newly sprouted herbs, making their growth slow.

But for the orange trees the snow and ice were deadly.

"It never snows on Sully," Hugh said.

"Only in the old men's tales," Fulk said, bewilderment on his face.

"I must see to the trees," Hugh said, turning to Emmalyn.

"Of course. I will come with you," she said, rising and speaking without a second thought. "I can help."

Large snowflakes dropped from the sky like wet white feathers against the darkness, already clinging to the trees and shrubs and covering the ground with a blanket of white. The angry wind gobbled at the flames of the three torches mounted on the garden wall and tore at the glossy leaves of the six unprotected orange trees.

Hugh followed Fulk from the hall straight to the garden and did not wait for his cloak. Emmalyn remained in the great hall only long enough to order his short cloak and hat and her own fur-lined wrap. As soon as they were brought she headed for the arbor. She was glad she spared the time to get the warm clothes when she stepped out the door and the brunt of the wind hit her. As soon as she reached the arbor, she insisted that Hugh put on the wraps. At first he resisted, too anxious about the orange trees to stop work, but she kept after him until he plopped the soft felt hat on his head and shrugged into the wool cloak.

Fulk and a gardener were already dragging out the sails and attempting to drape them over the ribs of the arbor to keep the icy wet flakes from the trees. The wind snatched at the canvas, flapping the corners upward into the gale. Hugh caught at the loose fabric. Seizing it at last, he began tying it down so the wind did not rip the covering away.

Emmalyn went to the sick tree first, brushing the freshly fallen snow from it as quickly as she could.

Using the corner of her cloak she worked with a light touch, flicking the sticky flakes from its leaves. The last thing the poor tree needed was to have its leaves withered by cold. When she had removed as much snow as she could from the little tree and the first covering was tied down sheltering it, she went to the next. It was a much taller tree. She flung the edges of her cloak as far upward as she could, aware of the men fighting desperately around her to get the next piece of canvas covering in place. She was rewarded with the sight of small clumps of snow falling to the ground. She worked as quickly as she could.

The wind clawed at her as she worked, its icy fingers stinging her cheeks, numbing her hands, and spearing through her fur-lined cloak to chill her to the bone. Yet she did not stop to warm herself. She understood the battle they fought. They dare not give up the fight for the sake of the precious orange trees. However, Emmalyn knew that they fought for more than that. They were fighting for the survival of the last fragment of Hugh's dream, to make something good come of his Crusader's vow.

More of his throng of gardeners appeared, lugging additional sections of canvas between them. Another carried a broom into the arbor and began sweeping the snow from the flagstones. Two gardeners began carrying in iron braziers and a supply of firewood.

When Emmalyn had done as much as she could do for the trees, she stepped back, making way for the men. The next step as soon as the canvas cover was secured would be to light the braziers. The arbor would be kept warm that night at all costs. The vigil would be a long, cold one. And she would share it with Hugh.

* * *

They never heard the Compline or the Matins bells over the rumbling of the canvas in the wind. Hugh had seen to it that the coverings were tied as tightly in place as could be managed, and the braziers burned brightly, their flames nearly futile against the cold at first. But little by little, the edge of the cold inside the covered arbor dulled. The smoke slipped out the opening left at two points. Snow on the upper branches Emmalyn had been unable to reach began to melt and drip from the larger trees. By the ringing of Lauds, the gale had died.

Still, the wind had brought with it an even deeper cold to creep across the isle. It moved along the ground and stole into the garden. It sneaked into the arbor below the edges of the covering.

"It is still a few hours until dawn and there is little more we can do," Hugh said, listening as the last of the chiming bells faded into the darkness. He felt the cold maliciously seeping into his feet as he sat in the arbor. "This is the truly dangerous time. The snow is over. What remains on the ground will protect most of our native plants. But what is not covered may freeze. It will deepen and kill the oranges if we cannot keep it at bay."

"We will have victory over the snow and cold, my lord," Emmalyn said with a confidence that he did not feel.

He had told her to go, to take herself to her bed and stay warm. This was his garden. She had no responsibility for it. Yet she was still here, pale but unruffled, sitting on the litter that Fulk had brought out for her when she had refused to leave. Hugh had forgotten about the thing his mother had used when she traveled around the isle. It still had the down pallet and the furs on it that she had used for comfort.

Emmalyn was sitting on the edge of it, feeding firewood to the flames of one of the braziers.

Fulk and the other servants were gone, dismissed for the night. They were alone.

"Do you want the oranges so badly that you would suffer this discomfort not to lose your chance for them?" he asked.

Her head came up and she stared at him, the firelight flickering on her face. Her mouth twisted in a look of annoyance.

"I am here because I want to see your orange trees survive, whatever the outcome of our experiment," she said, dropping another piece of wood on the fire. "Besides, I know that you have plenty of oranges in your storeroom. Walter showed them to me."

Sorry he had questioned her purpose, he said no more.

Still holding his gaze, she continued. "All gardeners fight the elements. It is a battle we understand. If we do not help each other, who will?"

Then she looked away and with her gaze on the brazier fire, added, "It is a noble thing you have done, my lord, to bring these trees back to England, to take the time, to spend your fortune, and put forth your efforts to bring something good out of a venture that was a regret for you. Such an act should not be lost to the errant whimsy of the winds. Truly, that is why I am here."

"You flatter me," he said. "I brought these trees back for my own satisfaction, not for England, not for posterity—and not for your plan to bring your daughter happiness."

"That is very honest of you," she said, concentrating on the fire again. "But not completely true.

You are not a selfish man. I know selfish men. My husband was one, and you are not like him in the least."

Surprised by her authoritative tone, Hugh glanced at her. "What am I like then, pray tell?"

"Above all you are a man who values honesty, and I admire that," she said, without looking at him. "And though you have suffered grief and a grave disappointment, you believe in the future. You may not admit it to yourself and certainly not to others. You play the part of a hermit and keep yourself apart from the affairs of the world. But the manner in which you care for your land and your people—and your gardens—tell a different tale. All true gardeners possess deep in them an incredible optimism and a belief in the future. We believe that what we do makes a difference in the world even if it is only with the life of a tree or the blossoming of a flower that would not have existed without our help.

"It is part of what makes us dig in the dirt and carry the water. It is what makes us ignore the stink of the manure we spread and force ourselves to pluck greedy insects off leaves—or even brave the icy cold of a blizzard."

"Fine sentiments." Hugh snorted softly. "You make a gardener sound as noble as a warrior."

"Gardeners are warriors with spades. Did you not know, sir knight, that you gave up one army for another?" She gestured in his direction. "The brazier behind you needs wood."

He realized he had let himself get caught up in her words and forgotten the task at hand. He turned to the fire, quickly feeding the hot coals with the wood the gardeners had left until the flames leaped again. He fed them more wood until he was satisfied the fire would burn for some time. He did the same with the other braziers.

Then he turned to Emmalyn once more. Was it possible this woman knew him better than he knew himself?

Crossing the length of the arbor, he sat down on the litter next to her.

"There is little we can do now but wait until dawn to see how much damage is done," he said. "Are you warm enough?" He pulled a cover up over her shoulders.

"Your hands are cold," she exclaimed when his fingers brushed her cheek. She grabbed his hands in hers, faced him, and pulled them inside the warmth of her cloak.

Heat flooded through him instantly, irresistibly. He freed his hands from her grip and placed them against her ribs. The feel of her life beneath his palms sent a surge of desire through him that he could not hide.

"Kiss me," she whispered, gazing up at him and covering his hands with her warm ones.

Briefly he considered saying no. He thought about how the time and place were not right, but that did nothing to cool the hunger flowing through him, nothing to keep the sweet memories of their first kiss from leaping to his mind. So he did as she bade and covered her mouth with his own.

Emmalyn wrapped her arms around his neck and twisted her fingers in his long hair. She held his head fast this time while she did the kissing using her tongue, exploring his lips. He moved his hands upward, filling his grasp with her breasts, kneading them gently. Was that her own whimper she heard?

He pulled his mouth free and fastened his lustful gaze on her face. They were both breathless.

"God's bones, I want you," he whispered, slipping his arms around her and pulling her closer.

"And I want you," she said, aware and astonished that for the first time in her life she truly wanted a man to touch her. She yearned for his lips on her neck, for his hands on her skin, for his caresses—personal and intimate—while she touched him. Her breasts were suddenly sensitive, and she longed, even ached, to have his manhood inside her.

They stared at each other for a long moment, her hands against his chest, his hands firm on her back, both apprehensive about what was about to happen.

"My laces," she whispered at last.

His hands moved up her back, his fingers tugging at the closing of her gown. Though the silk was too sheer to withstand the heat of his touch, it was still more between them than she could bear. She sighed when the garment loosened, and his fingers pulled it and her shift off her shoulders and down her arms. Then his hands were on her bare throat and his lips found hers again. He moved his tongue in and out of her mouth with deliberate leisure. She tipped her head back, savoring each nuance, the sleek texture and the sweet taste.

He tugged on her clothes again, baring her breasts. His lips moved from her mouth, kissing his way downward to the breasts he had captured in his hands. He bent to them. She closed her eyes and stroked his hair as he began to feast on her, his mouth stirring sensations in her that she had never known before but knew she never wanted to live without again.

He made small sounds of gratification as her breasts responded to his loving. She sobbed with pleasure. He devoted himself to increasing her delight.

"Hugh," she whispered his name involuntarily.

"I cannot have enough of you," he groaned, flinging his head back. He placed his hands on either side of her face and peered into her eyes. "I cannot have enough of you," he repeated before gently pushing her backward on the litter and rising over her to take her mouth again.

Locked together, he pulled the cover over them against the cold and any prying eyes. Inside their dark cocoon he kissed her again, his hands finding their way up her skirt. His callused fingers moved upward beneath her shift, above her hose and garters, caressing her thighs and onward toward the wedge of curls between her legs. His questing fingers found her most sensitive flesh, and the sudden intimacy made her suck in a breath. She knew he found her warm and moist.

"I want you, too," she said, feathering kisses across his jaw.

" 'Tis evident," he whispered, taking her hand and placing it on the hem of his tunic. "Then help me become yours."

Tugging urgently, she aided his struggle to remove the garment, listening to him curse softly before he was finally free of it. He flung the tunic away, then burrowed beneath the covers again. With his help, she found the belt at his waist, which fastened his drawers and hose. Even in her passionate eagerness, she was surprised at her own dexterity in the dark. She quickly unfastened the buckle and thrust the belt aside. To her surprise he took her hands and placed them on his aroused manhood.

"This is for you," he whispered against her mouth.

He was smooth, firm, and large already, needing no help from her.

Hugh slid his hands beneath her bottom and drew her against his thigh, rubbing his firm flesh against her wet heat. Emmalyn sucked in another breath. She had never known herself to be so sensitive *there*, but his blatantly erotic movement inspired unique sensations, a sweet burning that flared outward from her feminine core to flood throughout her body, building to some pinnacle she had never known. It was so new, so unexpected. It was happening so fast. Too fast. In a panic, she reached for Hugh's leg to stop him.

He grabbed her wrist and held it. "No, let it happen," he urged, the steady rhythmic pressure of his thigh against her never halting. "Let it happen."

She could not have resisted the peak if she had wanted to. The burning sweet soaring swept over and through her. She moaned.

She felt his arms tighten around her, and she knew he had expected her to shatter this way, knew he had intended it. And she knew it was right. Yet how could such a flight of pleasure be anything less than a sin? At the moment, she was too weak to care. She curled into his embrace, pressing her cheek against his chest and taking comfort in the sound of his thrumming heart.

"You are lovely and so full of passion," he murmured against the top of her head.

She smiled at the flattery, and then remembered what an honest man he was. She had never thought of herself as passionate. Slowly she moved the palm of her hand over his chest and downward between them, savoring the solidness of his belly. When her fingertips encountered a long, ragged welt across his ribs, she stopped and her smile faded.

"What is this?" she asked, running her finger along it.

"A battle scar," he murmured. "Not much for a Crusader. A cut and a cracked rib."

Emmalyn said nothing, but as lady of the castle she had nursed a few knights. She knew how painful cracked ribs were, and how long they took to heal. He was making light of his wound, like a proud man who did not wish to be pitied. She did not argue with him. Her palm moved downward again, along his side encountering another scar. "And this?" she asked.

"From a tournament," he said. "Long ago. Before I took the Crusader's vow. The festering was worse than the wound."

A fearful thought struck her. "Do you still fight in tournaments?"

"No," he said. "I have had enough of battles. They are follies for younger men with hotter blood than mine. I will not fight again unless it is in the defense of Sully."

His admission brought a sigh of relief to her lips.

"Your blood is hot enough for a lady, my lord," she said, trailing her fingers along his skin again, over the rise of his hip. "And you are a passionate and generous man. Yet you have not taken your own pleasu—"

"I will," he said, then hissed as her hand caressed him, boldly this time, stroking his full length.

She discovered a drop of moisture on the very tip and spread it around the cleft.

Hugh hissed again. Brushing her hand away, he rose up over her, pulled up her skirt around her waist, parted her thighs with his knee, and, little by little, buried himself inside her. With slow, patient strokes he became part of her, and with each thrust she felt the sweet burning of arousal flare inside her. Eager once more for completion, Emmalyn arched upward against him, her body grasping his with each stroke.

He uttered explicit words of praise that made her feel desirable and womanly. Again and again he sank into her body, each thrust becoming more powerful, the tempo increasing. Each time he almost withdrew, giving them the ultimate sensation when he sank back into her. Soon their rapid breathing matched.

When the flood of sensation was imminent again, she clung to him and he to her. They surrendered to each other and to the desire that neither had expected to find with the other.

Chapter Six

Emmalyn awoke to Hugh's kisses across her brow and his bare arms around her.

"Awaken, my sweet lady," he murmured. "We must lace you back into your dress."

The scent of him, his warmth, and his voice—all seemed so natural at first that she could not imagine what it was that he was concerned about.

Then she remembered their lovemaking and bolted upright. The arbor was lit by the glow of the coals in the braziers. Beyond the arbor, the false dawn had begun to light the garden and brighten the canvas.

"It is all right," he said, sitting up with her, pushing aside her hair and tugging at the back of her dress. "We have nothing to hide, but I would not have the gardeners see more than they have a right to see."

"Yes, of course." Emmalyn pulled at her shift and then the sleeves of her gown, dragging the neckline up into place.

At her back she could feel Hugh working with the laces.

"There, that will have to do for now," he said, kissing the side of her neck.

She crawled from under the covers and off the litter, working her bunched-up skirts down where they belonged and dragging something with her. When she caught at it, she discovered she had Hugh's belt entangled in hers.

She freed it, laughing softly. "I believe this is yours," she said, handing it to him.

Still sitting beneath the covers, he took the belt. "I think this is yours," he said, pulling her fillet from their cocoon.

They both began to laugh at the absurdity and the wonderfulness of it, of being so entangled, so linked. Laughing still, she found his tunic and tossed it in his direction. Struggling with his belt, he found her cloak and threw it out from beneath the covers.

"Here, put this on before you catch your death," he said, chuckling.

She laughed again, picked up his hat, and tossed it at his head.

He snagged the flying hat as he leaped off the litter. He seized her arm and swung her around. She was still laughing. It was impossible to stop.

"One last kiss," he said, taking her by the shoulders, "before we go about the business of seeing how bad the damage is."

He kissed her soundly, possessively, and with conviction.

Before either of them could say anything more they heard the voices of the gardeners approaching the arbor.

"We will talk tonight," he said, pulling away from her. Then he went to greet Fulk. Though she would have liked more time to explore their newfound intimacy, she understood. When he flipped back the canvas from the entrance to invite the steward in, she could see that a thick blanket of snow still lay on the ground. There was work to do. Daylight could not be wasted.

Pulling her cloak close around her for warmth— and to hide the wrinkles of her gown—she went to the orange trees, eager to see how they had fared.

In the first light of dawn she could see that black edged many of the once glossy leaves. Yet some were unaffected. The leaves closer to the trunk were still green and flat, she noted as she examined the trees more closely. She walked down the line, studying each in the growing light of day. All was not lost. Their efforts had been successful.

She smiled and turned to tell Hugh, but he was busy with the gardeners, clearing away the braziers and scooping away the snow outside. Most were gathered around him, their faces eager for his orders, warriors about to go into their own kind of battle. They had plants other than orange trees to concern them.

Emmalyn's maid arrived with a fresh cap and veil, and a kitchen boy arrived with hot cider and bread. Hugh paused in issuing orders only long enough to send them directly to Emmalyn. As he detailed a list of instructions to Fulk and the others, the sun broke over the horizon showing a clear sky. With its rays striking the arbor, Emmalyn heard the first drip, drip, drip of the melting snow. The cold would not last. That was good news.

When Hugh dismissed the gardeners to their duties, he turned to her. She had donned her veil and arranged her cloak in a decorous manner. She smiled at him, offering him a tankard of steaming cider.

"How do the trees look?" he asked.

"Good," she said, moving toward the last tree, the stunted one. She stopped in front of it and Hugh joined her.

Her heart sank at the sight. They stared at the poor thing in silent dismay.

Nearly half the leaves were shriveled or black, and around the trunk lay a dozen or so leaves that had fallen.

"Oh, no," she whispered.

"Love cannot win out over cold," he said, as if he had expected no less.

"Not always, I suppose," she said. "But I had hoped we could save this one, too. You and the gardeners worked so hard."

"And you, too," he said, putting a hand on her shoulder. "But sometimes hard work is not enough. Still, we saved the others."

She nodded. "I suppose."

"Get some rest." He took her arm and attempted to draw her away from the tree.

She resisted, so gloomy about the failure of their vigil that she could not bring herself to leave.

"Emmalyn," he whispered into her ear, "you were up all night. You need rest."

"No, I am all right," she said, allowing him to lead her away at last. "I will work in the kitchen garden. Walter will be anxious about the herbs. He and I will take stock of the damage. Promise me you will not do anything to the tree."

"No, of course I will not," he said.

"You will leave it there in the sun with the others," she said, afraid that he or one of the gardeners would find a use for the large terra-cotta pot and throw the tree out. "We will not give up yet."

"I will leave it," he said, placing a hand on his heart, smiling—patronizing her, she realized.

She did not care. The tree had become important to her. She was unsure why; she just knew that it was.

"I promise," he added when she refused to budge.

She nodded and left the arbor, seeking out the herb garden, where Walter was already directing a gardener in uncovering the plants. The sun was melting the snow quickly. She suspected that by the time it set there would be little evidence of the blizzard on Sully—other than the destruction wrought on the poor little orange tree.

Hugh threw himself into the work of assessing damage and of rescuing what could be saved. Though concentration was rarely a problem for him, his mind wandered every time he looked up to see Emmalyn directing a gardener or conferring with Walter. And he found himself looking up often, as if he needed proof of the pleasure he had known the night before. Needed to reassure himself that she was truly there—a real woman, not some amorous fantasy he had conjured. Yes, by the saints, she was real.

The pleasure they had shared during the night had been more than merely physical. Lord knew, that part had been extraordinary, but he wanted more. He hoped she did as well.

They had shared something in the arbor that he had not shared with a woman before—a nearness, an intimacy, a true union. He was unsure of what to make of it, and this was not the time to consider it. Yet he could not help but wonder if she felt for him what he felt for her.

Or did she believe that what had happened between them was part of the game they played over the oranges?

Hugh worked the day through with the gardeners, Fulk, and even Emmalyn to salvage what they could. He was pleased to find as he moved from one part of the garden to the next that the devastation was not as severe as it might have been. Some fruit tree blossoms were lost, but not all. The vegetables that were just sprouting were wilted, but during the course of the sunny day, they renewed themselves. In the kitchen garden, Emmalyn and Walter reported that they had found the herbs, cooking and medicinal, had not suffered greatly.

No, not enough destruction had been done to endanger their food supply for the winter to come, provided no other whimsy of nature descended on them.

The cook was elated with the condition of the kitchen garden, but Emmalyn's smile was clearly distracted. Hugh knew that she was worried about that bloody tree. He should have left the bloody thing on the ship. For all the trouble, it had yielded nothing. And for some odd reason her concern for the stunted, barren thing annoyed him.

As the sunlight began to fade, Emmalyn excused herself to dress for supper. Vaguely aware of the delicious smells escaping from the kitchen, Hugh watched her walk toward the castle, mesmerized by the sway of her skirts.

"Well, my lord." Walter braced his hands on his hips and stared at him expectantly. "We have another fine supper for you this evening. Mayhap you would best be about doing some washing up yourself and thinking about offering the lady something better than a litter in the arbor."

Hugh frowned at the cook, none too pleased

with the thought that the whole castle was probably talking about how he and Emmalyn had spent the night together. The interesting thing was, though, Hugh realized his relationship with Emmalyn seemed to please his people. Gardeners, kitchen staff, maids, grooms, clerks, pages, and carters, too, smiled when they spied them together, and their smiles were of genuine pleasure. Thinking about it further, he recalled that even Father Paul had only smiled and waved when he had seen Hugh and Emmalyn at mass; he never asked why he had not been invited back to the castle for another supper.

On any other day Hugh would have scoffed at Walter's pointed suggestion that he prepare himself for the evening meal and continued to work along with the gardeners until the light was hardly sufficient to tell a weed from a plant. Today, however, he decided that Walter was right. He smelled of sweat and smoke. If he wanted to lure Emmalyn to his bed again, he needed a bath.

Leaving the others to their work, he strode into the castle. He called out orders for a bath to be sent to his chamber. And as he took the stairs, two at a time, he was whistling.

"We must congratulate Walter on another fine meal," Emmalyn suggested as they finished supper in the great hall. "A hearty appetite you had, my lord, after a day of work. Did you like the bread flavored with orange rind and drizzled with honey?"

"Well enough," Hugh said, annoyed to find that they were once again talking about oranges. She looked lovelier than earlier tonight, a blush in her cheeks that had not been there before and a smile that seemed to put a special glow in her eyes for him—at least he liked to believe so.

"I thought it quite inspired on Walter's part," she said, shoving the trencher toward the serving boy who removed it immediately. "Tell Cook to send in the special pot we have prepared," she instructed the boy.

"What is this?" He watched her nervously smooth the tablecloth before her.

"I have a surprise for you," she said, without looking up at him.

Her uneasiness troubled him. Strange—seeing his gardeners wince and cringe did not trouble him. That she had any reason to be uneasy in his presence made him frown.

"What more could surprise me after last night?" He forced a smile.

"As I recall, my lord, you did not think it proper to use oranges for any vanity," she said. The boy returned from the kitchen with a small pot similar to the one that contained the orange honey.

So that was it, Hugh thought, his smile becoming genuine. Women could not resist, could they? They must have their beauty enhancers—their eyelash darkeners, their cheek rouges, and their perfumes. Why not indulge her? "What is it you have thought of, my sweet lady?"

"A lotion," she said, eyeing him hopefully.

"Orange-scented, of course, and for what purpose, my lady? To whiten the skin? Yours is lovely, fair, and smooth."

"No, it is not a face cream," she said, chuckling. "I was thinking of work-roughened hands and itchy, dry skin."

Hugh immediately held up his hands to examine them. "Were they so rough?" he asked in a whisper. "I heard no complaint last night."

She stared at his hands for a moment, apparently shocked. Then she began to laugh and took his hands in hers. "No, my lord, I was not thinking of that. Well, maybe a little. But I meant that all of us who dig in the dirt every day would use this lotion to sooth the skin. And I think it might have other benefits as well." She blushed, the rosiness staining her face from the roots of her hair to the neckline of her gown.

Her blush charmed him—stirred him.

"Shall we try some?" she said, still holding one of his hands and reaching for the pot the kitchen boy had brought.

"By all means." He was glad of the excuse to touch her without appearing too possessive.

She removed the cover and dipped her fingers into a thick pale orange liquid and began to smear it on the back of his hand. The first touch of it was cool, yet smooth. As Emmalyn spread the lotion across his knuckles, her warmth warmed the lotion and heightened the silkiness of her touch. She worked the lotion into his skin with her fingertips in a circular motion that recalled her touch as she had explored his body the night before. Then she began to rub the lotion into each of his fingers, drawing each digit through the small fist of her hand, stroking them—several times each. His mouth went dry.

"How do you like it?" she asked, gazing up at him innocently. "You would probably use it on your hands at the end of the day's work."

At the moment nothing about the lotion seemed remotely connected to work.

"Umm, you must try it," he said, pulling his hand from her grasp and taking her hand. He reached for the lotion, scooped up a generous portion, and began to apply it to the back of her hand. He pressed lightly, allowing the slippery lotion to take his fingertips across her skin.

"Smell the citrus," she said, smiling at him. "I think this might be as inspired as any of the food Walter and I have made."

Hugh could smell only her. And she was all that he wanted. Gently he turned her hand and began to smooth the lotion into her palm. In a slow, teasing circular motion he stroked her open hand.

She gave a little gasp, but neither of them looked at the other.

Patiently he worked the lotion toward her wrist, nudging the snug sleeve of her gown back and exposing her delicate white skin. Beneath his fingers he could feel her pulse, light and rapid.

She watched him, her smile fading, and released a shaky breath. "My lord, does the lotion please you?"

"Yes, very much," he choked out. "Emmalyn, will you stay with me tonight? Or was last night just a diversion?"

She studied him in silence, her eyes dark and her expression sober. "In your bed?"

"After last night," he murmured, holding her gaze, "there is nowhere else that you belong. Nowhere else that I want you to be."

"Nor any place else that I want to be." Her lips curved upward at the corners. "And we can try more of the lotion?"

"We can try anything that pleases you," he said, surprised at how relieved he was at her response.

When the fire in the hearth of the great hall had burned down and the others were leaving to find their beds, Hugh led Emmalyn upstairs to his chamber. There by candlelight he undressed her, slowly, taking the time to enjoy the sight of her soft skin and her gentle womanly curves.

Her shoulders were delicate; her breasts, barely, visible through the golden strands of her long hair, were generous enough to fill his large hands, a fact he had discovered by touch the night before but that aroused him even more when confirmed by sight. Her waist was narrow. Her legs were as long and shapely as he had imagined, and the hair of her mons was as golden as the hair of her head. When all her clothes lay on the floor and he had gazed his fill, he gave her a steady hand to help her climb the steps to his curtained bed. She turned to sit on the edge, all gold and ivory.

"Now you undress," she said, her gaze bright and unabashedly curious.

Hugh's gaze never left her as he pulled off his tunic, unbuckled his belt, and stepped out of his drawers and hose. He heard her breath catch as she studied the length of him. He let her look her fill. He had nothing to hide and there was no hiding that he wanted her.

"Do I pass inspection, my lady?" he asked, unable to keep a smile from his lips.

"Indeed, you do, my lord," she said, returning his smile with a beguiling one of her own. Then she turned and crawled farther into the shadows.

Hugh needed no invitation to join her and found her holding the pot of lotion.

"What now?" he asked.

"Your neck is red from too much sun," she said, though her gaze was traveling across his chest and downward. "I think the lotion might relieve the burn."

He could not imagine anything he was less concerned about at that moment than sunburn. "If you wish, you may rub lotion on it—later," he said, taking the pot from her hand and setting it on the bedside table.

"Later?" she asked.

"Later." Gently, he pulled her back against the pillows.

She reached for him eagerly, chuckling. Her lips tasted sweet, not of orange but of wine and woman. He could not get enough of her mouth—of her. He trailed kisses downward, along her neck, her fragile collarbone, and her throat, allowing his hair to trail along her fair skin.

She tugged on his hair. "You torture me," she murmured.

"This is only the beginning of it," he said.

Beneath his palm her nipples were tight buds. When he took one into his mouth, she sucked in a gasp of pleasure and arched her back. As he suckled her, his hands stroked lower, over her navel and lower still. Her skin was so smooth and warm. He found her mons gratifyingly downy and damp as he searched for her most sensitive place, gently parting her. He knew he had found her center when she moaned and tossed her head back and forth against the pillow.

The sound was, oh, so sweet. He longed to hear more. Stroking the inside of her thigh, he encouraged her to open further for him, and when she did, he kissed her intimately. With passion he assaulted the center of her pleasure. Twisting her fingers in his hair, she rewarded him with more sweet, urgent moans until he could bear no more.

Rising over her, he parted her thighs with his own and entered her.

She accepted him into her wet snugness and his groan joined her long heartfelt sighs.

Bracing himself on his elbow, he looked down into her flushed face. He gazed into her eyes, half closed in passion, as he pushed deeper. She whimpered softly.

Buried inside her, he pressed his forehead against hers. "The only magic in this is ours," he whispered. "No potion's. No aphrodisiac's. Ours. Yours and mine."

"Ours," she murmured, slipping her hands down over his buttocks, tormenting him with her fingertips. "Ours."

Only then did he begin to move again. She raised her hips to meet his thrusts, her breath catching with each one. He could not deny the overwhelming sensations her movement—and her sighs—stirred in him.

Still, he waited for her. And when he knew she had found the peak of her pleasure, he sank his fingers into her hair and kissed her as intimately as his body possessed hers. Her climax was long, and the strong, rhythmic clasping of her flesh around his pushed him over the edge. He released her mouth and, burying his face in her hair, he found his release.

Then all was quiet. When he did move again, it was only enough to roll onto his side and gather Emmalyn in his arms. He sank into a dreamless sleep, vanquishing from his mind any thoughts of her departure at the week's end.

Chapter Seven

In the days—and nights—that followed, Emmalyn was astonished and pleased to find Hugh speaking kindly to his gardeners, humming songs, walking with a lighter step, and seeking out her company at all times of the day with a smile on his face.

She was nearly as astonished at how much differently she herself was seeing the world. Each morning the sunshine seemed warmer. The flowers bloomed brighter. At night the stars seemed more dazzling. Wine tasted sweeter. The dark hours of pleasure in Hugh's bed were the most satisfying she had ever known—and she could only wish that they were longer and that there were more of them. She had always tried to see the best in life as it was, with its dark whimsy and cruel turns. But these days, life had never seemed quite so wonderful. She was in love and love was wonderful.

The weather since the blizzard had warmed, the nights becoming mild and the days bright and balmy. The healthy orange trees had recovered, their fruit continuing to ripen, and more white blossoms burst open. The little tree was not doing quite so well, but it had stopped dropping leaves and the remaining ones had regained their dark green color. She was pleased to see it clinging so valiantly to life.

"I wish I could stay and nurse you through the hot days of summer," she said to the tree, touching a particularly glossy leaf. "Alas, the fortnight of my stay has drawn too rapidly to an end. The boat from the mainland comes tomorrow. Julianna's betrothal ceremony is only a few weeks away. I must be there."

And she wanted badly to take a good supply of oranges with her. Which meant she would have to once again bring up the subject of the experiment with Hugh—a subject they had carefully avoided all week.

"How do I go about reminding Hugh of our bargain without seeming to gloat?" she murmured.

Doubtless the oranges had brought them together. What else could it have been? What else could have induced her of all people, and after all this time—years of loathing the very idea of a man's touch—to such heights of passion? With passion, deep and enduring love had followed—after all, Hugh was a handsome, honorable, and gentle man who she would have come to care for as a friend. Without that spark of hot, consuming desire to kindle the fires of passion then love, they would certainly be parting as nothing more than fellow gardeners.

Yes, it was the orange, that unrivaled fruit, that had ignited that all-important spark.

Of course Hugh would be reluctant to admit that his ardor was the result of eating fruit. No one really wanted to think they did not have control over their feelings.

"A man especially will dislike the notion of being so manipulated," she said to the tree as she recalled his husky vows that the oranges had nothing to do with the passion they shared.

Nothing had changed her desire to give love-inspiring oranges to her daughter. In truth, Emmalyn was more determined than ever that Julianna should know the joy of sharing her heart and her body with a man who shared his in return. The experience was beyond measure—beyond expression. It brought a smile to her lips every time she thought of Hugh's lovemaking. Perhaps Julianna and Stephen would find such love on their own. It was not unheard of. But it did not happen often, and Emmalyn was unwilling to take the chance.

That Julianna might be condemned to a cold, loveless married life, as she herself had been, was unacceptable. She would do whatever was within her power to ensure that did not happen. And that meant collecting from Hugh the prize she had won in their wager: the oranges.

Emmalyn dressed carefully for supper that night, wearing her finest linen shift beneath her best blue gown and the gold silk braid belt. She bade her maid to brush her hair until it shone its brightest. She smoothed her dry hands with the orange lotion and pinched her cheeks to add a bit of color to her face. Satisfied after a look in the small polished metal mirror she had brought with her, she took a deep breath and went down to the great hall for supper.

Hugh was waiting for her by the fire, as he had

been other nights over the past week—except this evening his frown had returned.

"My lord," she said in greeting as she swept into the room with her head held high. "Has Walter sent word of what he is going to serve us this night?"

"No, he has not," Hugh said, staring at her, his hands clasped behind him. "But I asked that there be no oranges in our food this evening."

Doing her best to hide her surprise and concern, she asked, "And why is that?"

"It is your last night, is it not?" he said. "Our experiment is at an end. The boat leaves on the tide tomorrow."

"Yes, so I understand," she said, mentally racing through all the things she might say to lighten the mood. Parting from him was going to be difficult regardless of how short their time apart might be. She would be occupied with the betrothal ceremony and wedding preparations for the next few months. But once Julianna was wed . . . she would be free to build her own life.

"We have serious things to discuss tonight, Emmalyn." He turned from the fire and folded his arms across his chest.

"Yes, we do," she agreed, wondering—hoping— that their purposes were the same. She did not want to leave with things between them unsettled. She believed he loved her as she loved him, yet he had not said so. Surely that was the *serious* subject he wanted to discuss. Yet he seemed so distant . . . so unyielding. As he had been when she first arrived on Sully.

"My daughter's betrothal date nears and I must depart." She forced a smile to her lips. "But let us not speak of serious things on an empty stomach, my lord. There is the bell. I believe supper is served."

As they shared their trencher, she prayed Walter's excellent food would mellow Hugh's mood. But through the courses, his frame of mind did not improve. Though he was a civil enough supper partner, he hardly touched her and seldom met her gaze.

She did most of the talking, chattering on about the herbs that she planned to send to him for the kitchen garden. She divided up the food and poured the wine. Yet none of it, not even her wittiest charm or her winningest smile, shook the grimness of his thinned mouth. Moment by moment he seemed to be returning to the gruff, taciturn man who had greeted her upon her arrival on Sully.

When they left the table and went to the chairs by the fire, thankfully most of the others who supped in the great hall had left for the night. She knew that the moment had come that would determine their future. She settled into the corner of his huge chair as she had for the past week.

To her surprise, Hugh stepped away from his chair and sat down in hers. Suddenly a huge breach seemed to stretch between them.

"I have enjoyed my stay," she said, sitting back and deciding to build slowly to her request. "In truth, to be here with you has been one of the most wonderful experiences of my life."

"For me as well," he said, gazing into the fire.

Then why did he not sit next to her? she wondered.

"I understand about your daughter's betrothal," he continued without looking up, "but I wish that we did not have to part."

Her heart leapt when she heard his words. Of course, that was why he was so dour. He did not want her to leave. Still, his solemnity troubled her.

"Come with me," she said, moving to the edge of her chair. Why had she not thought of this before? "I do not want to be parted from you either. Come to Trentworth, my lord. I know his grace would be pleased to see you. And I would have you meet my daughter and see the gardens. But, most important, we would be together."

"My place is here," he said without hesitation.

"Of course." She sank back into the chair. Disappointment—and a niggle of fear—grew inside her. "I will miss you, Hugh."

"What will I do without you?" he asked, gazing at her for the first time, a sad smile on his lips.

"The wedding will be in June, so I need not be gone for long," she said, feeling brave enough to smile at him. "I could not bear it. The last week with you has been too wonderful. I feel like a new person with a new life. I know you have your doubts, but do you honestly believe that this would have happened to us without the oranges?"

His smile vanished and a glimmer of pain darkened his eyes. "Is that what you believe?"

"You cannot deny—"

"I cannot deny the oranges have medicinal power," he said, steepling his fingers beneath his stubborn chin. "However, I do deny their power over lust. I cannot in good conscience approve of the use of aphrodisiacs to encourage lust or love where none would have grown otherwise. It is false."

"False?" she asked, lurching forward in her chair again. Her heart was beating rapidly, not just because the promise of getting the oranges seemed to be fading but because she could feel something important might be slipping away from her. "But I love you. You love me. Do you believe what we have is false?"

"If you believe you would not have loved me without the aid of some bloody fruit, yes, it is false," he stated in slow, precise words that she knew belied anger and pain. He rose from the chair, his features becoming as harsh as those of a stranger. "How can it be anything more?"

The glimpse of his emotions made Emmalyn wince. She yearned to deny the truth of what he said, but she could not. She remained on the edge of her chair. Their future, her heart was at risk. "Hugh, in truth, I do not know where our love came from. I do not care. But I have no doubt that the love I feel for you is real and deep and true. It comes from my heart! What does it matter that I sipped orange-flavored wine or spread orange honey on my bread and yours? We love each other."

"No, *you* love a man who happened to be available when you ate an exotic fruit," he said, his voice low and fierce. He paced away from her, then turned on his heel and paced back. "I knew I loved you when you entered the great hall with your hair uncovered. You did not love me until after eating orange-flavored food. You do not love me. That is false! I cannot accept a false love."

"What?" Emmalyn stared at him in disbelief. She stifled the sudden sob that threatened. A sense of panic overtook her as she searched her memory for the moment when she knew she loved Hugh, but she could not find it. She did not care. What did it matter? She loved him. Slowly she rose from her chair. "You deny my love?"

"I deny what is untrue," he said, his voice cold and flat.

A cold hollowness swept through her, leaving her bereft. Lost. Unloved.

She studied his face, hoping to see some hint of

indecision, of some doubt, but found none. Knees so weak she could barely stand and hands trembling, she turned from him. The hall was dark and the fire had burned low on the hearth.

"I see there is no altering your decision," she said, staring at the floor without seeing it. "Then I will say my farewell and be gone in the morning. No need to see me off. I know you have work to do."

"As you will," he said, standing aside to allow her to pass. "I wish you a safe journey."

"Thank you for your hospitality," she managed to mumble as she started toward the door, desperate to quit the scene before her tears began to fall. But when she reached the door, she knew that she had one more thing to say. She turned to find that he was watching her intently.

"I can only speak for myself, my lord," she began, striving to keep her voice steady. "But I have come to love you. Maybe it happened because of our experiment or maybe it would have happened anyway. But I do know that I love you and always will. Because I love you, I wish you happiness, and I am sorry that I will not be part of it. Good-bye, Sir Hugh."

He watched her leave the great hall, unhurried, her head held high and her tears unshed. He had seen them well up in her eyes, but they had never fallen. If they had, his resolve would have been lost.

When her gracefully swaying form was gone, he paced to the fire, her words of love echoing in his head. The image of her face, the pain and shock in it when he told her that her love was false and untrue, lingered clearly in his mind. His gut twisted. Even then, she had had the daring to speak those pretty words of love to him. Fine words from a woman who thought a man's body could be ruled by an orange.

With disgust, he kicked at the andirons. Tomorrow life at Castle Sully would return to what it should be—the safe and satisfying routine he had established before she came to invade his garden and disrupt his life. He would sleep alone, rise early, go to mass, break his fast, then go to work in the garden. He would let the sun warm his back and the soil nurture his soul as he dug in the ground and his garden grew.

The once gratifying role made him frown. The prospect—the only thing he had sought for himself since the Crusades—suddenly seemed to hold only emptiness.

With a heavy heart Emmalyn distractedly watched the last of her traveling trunks carried aboard the homeward bound cog. The horses had been loaded and secured belowdeck for the day-long voyage. Her maid and steward were arranging a pleasant place for her on the deck. The weather was fair and the winds adequate. The passage should be timely and agreeable enough. By evening she would be sleeping in an inn on the road toward Trentworth.

That knowledge brought little pleasure.

She was leaving Hugh behind and her quest had been a failure. In the face of Hugh's denial, everything but their love had lost importance. She had come away without the oranges.

Of course, she was looking forward to seeing Julianna, who would be untroubled by the fact that her mother had failed since Emmalyn had not spoken to her daughter of her quest. Even if she had, Julianna was too sweet and unselfish to berate her for failing. Thank heaven the girl had inherited only her father's good looks, not his petty nature.

Still, even the prospect of seeing Julianna could not erase the pain in Emmalyn's heart. She hated leaving Hugh—and with such animosity between them where there had been nothing but love. She had lost him, but what was worse, she could not overcome the guilty feeling that she had hurt him. That had never been her intention. Never.

She glanced upward toward Castle Sully, perched on the cliff above the bay. Hugh had lost his dreams. He was a wounded, angry man. Though his bodily wounds had healed, the wounds in his heart were still raw. A boar under the same circumstances was incredibly dangerous. What could one expect from a man in a similar state?

Yet she could not help feeling that she had failed him as well as Julianna. She should have been able to make him believe in her love. She had not. Tears sprang to her eyes once again, and she fought them back.

Around and above her she heard the cry of the gulls and the sailors shouting directions to the men below on the quay. The gangplank was being pulled aboard, lines were being loosened, and the oars were being shipped and readied. From the mast above, the sails were prepared for unfurling. She could feel the movement of the ship beneath her feet. They would be pushing off soon.

Soon the love of her life would be left behind.

She was about to turn away from the railing when she caught the sound of her name being called from shore. The voice was faint. For a moment, hope burned through her. Could it be Hugh?

She whirled back to the railing, clasping the salt-water-worn wood and leaning over it to search the crowded quay for his familiar face. There it was again, her name being called. Who? At last a waving arm caught her eye. She found the face. Walter.

"My lady, Sir Hugh sends you a parting gift," the cook shouted over the noise of the cog's imminent departure. Behind him stood two pages bearing baskets of shiny ripe oranges.

"Sweet heaven, he sent them anyway," she murmured to herself.

Without delay Emmalyn went to the ship's captain. The gangplank was lowered again, and Walter lumbered up it as fast as his bulk would allow him. The pages followed.

"My lady," he huffed, breathless and red-faced from his exertions.

"Walter, what . . ." she trailed off, eyeing the oranges in wonder.

"Sir Hugh wished you to have these as a parting gift," the cook said, putting a hand on the railing to steady himself.

"That is very generous of him," Emmalyn said, glancing at the baskets. Two large baskets. He had been generous, indeed. Her heart lightened a bit. And she had doubted him. She had won their challenge and vowed her love. He had honored his word. She wished Hugh had brought them himself, but she knew that was too much to expect.

She gestured to her steward to find a place for the baskets. "Did his lordship send a message?"

"Yes, there is a message," Walter said, touching his forefinger to his head and looking upward. "Now let me see. I want to get it right. He said to tell you the oranges are for you as a friend to use as you wish. And Godspeed. There, that was it. Godspeed, my lady."

No mention of love, she noted with a sinking heart. No invitation to return to Sully.

"And what would you have me tell his lordship, my lady?" Walter asked, peering at her expectantly.

She sighed as she gestured to her steward to tip Walter and the pages for their efforts. How she loved Hugh. Her heart was full to bursting with it. And she had told him so. He knew the truth, if he would not believe it.

"Tell him, thank you," she instructed, painfully aware that there was nothing more she could say.

Hugh stood on the castle ramparts, his hands clasped behind him and the wind pulling at his hair. His anger had faded into a sense of gloom. He watched the cog sail out of the bay, taking his happiness with it. He was glad that he had sent her the oranges.

He knew they would not help her daughter, but he also knew that she believed they could. It would be petty of him to withhold something from her that she considered so important. And what were a few bloody oranges compared to the love he had been prepared to give her—if only she had believed in it. If only she had been able to accept that it was real and true and not some . . . some fruit-induced fever.

When the cog was out of sight, he turned away and walked down the steps into the garden to resume his life. He went around to the arbor where the gardeners were moving the larger orange trees from beneath the grapevine's shade into the sun. They had moved three of the trees already. Two trees and the ailing one remained in the shade of the arbor.

He examined the sickly tree, noting that despite the new, healthy leaves Emmalyn had told him of, many yellow ones dangled from its stunted branches. He debated silently what to do with the thing. He had promised her that he would keep it and give it a chance to grow, but she was gone. What need did he have of a dying tree?

Chapter Eight

The first thing Emmalyn did upon reaching Trentworth—after greeting Julianna— was to select the
plants that she wanted to send to Hugh. Within a
few days she had set aside the specific varieties that
she would forward to him. Then she had the plants
packed up and sent on their way.

Most of her time, though, was occupied with last-
minute arrangements for the betrothal ceremony.
As she dealt with menu plans and the preparation
of guest chambers, Hugh was never far from her
thoughts, but the only time she had to dwell on
her pain and regret for what might have been was
at night, when she lay alone in her bed.

Before the betrothal, she arranged for the young
couple and her new in-laws to sup at her table.
Julianna and Stephen seemed to like each other.
They laughed, each eyeing the other with innocent
but distinctly lusty gleams in their eyes. Their youthful playfulness brought a smile to her lips. Stephen's parents were nice people, and they seemed

delighted with the king's choice. They were kind to Julianna and generous to their son. Emmalyn was pleased.

The betrothal ceremony went off very well. The wine was plentiful and tasty and the food fresh and rich with spices. Her gift of oranges was appreciated. Over the weeks leading up to the wedding, Emmalyn told the young people of first tasting the fruit in the bishop's court and of its medicinal benefits—as well as its alleged amorous blessings. They laughed and blushed. She even told them about the night the blizzard had descended on the Isle of Sully, about how the canvas and the braziers had been brought out to save the delicate trees from the cold and snow. Well, she did not tell them quite everything about that night.

Weeks slipped by into months as the wedding ceremony and celebrations were planned. Invitations were sent out. A wedding dress and trousseau was decided on and the seamstresses set to work. Menus were planned. Gardens were weeded and trimmed. Stores of candles and firewood for the guests were laid in. Hay for their horses was stacked behind the stable. Sleeping accommodations were arranged, chambers cleaned and aired. Troubadours, jugglers, and animal acts were summoned. A list of prisoners to be freed in the name of goodwill was assembled and submitted to the bishop for his approval.

When the June wedding day came, all was in order. Emmalyn was harried and exhausted, but that did not keep the happiness she felt for Julianna from shining on her face.

"I wish you were here," she murmured to Hugh as she took her place in church. She longed to know how he was faring. Did he miss her? Did he even think of her? Or had he thrust her completely from his mind and returned to the self-sufficient existence in which she had first found him. She had sent a letter with the plants, informally inviting him to the wedding, but she had received no response. Though disappointed, she had been unsurprised. He had been clear about rejecting her love. She was certain he considered any liaison with her over.

Devoting herself to being the happy mother of the bride was all that was left for her. As she sat in the Trentworth chapel, which had been festooned with flowers, ribbons, and greenery, she concentrated on the lovely ceremony with a radiant bride and an ecstatic bridegroom.

Kneeling at the altar beside her bridegroom, Julianna was beautiful. She had eyes only for Stephen. His gaze never left her face. Though their hands trembled as Stephen placed the ring on Julianna's finger, Emmalyn recognized the tremor as pleasure and excitement—not apprehension or dread. She smiled through her tears of sorrow for losing a daughter and joy to see her wed.

They would fall into bed on their wedding night with eagerness and passion. Anyone could see it coming. And then they would fall in love. Emmalyn was certain of it. The seeds of their joy had been in their eyes *before* the betrothal—she had seen it there when they supped with her. Julianna would find her happiness with Stephen. The oranges would have nothing to do with it. Their love would come from their pure willing, well-intentioned hearts—and from God.

A sob of surprise and elation escaped Emmalyn. Why had she not been able to see that before?

She pressed her fingertips to her lips to keep from emitting another.

You were right, Hugh! she silently told herself. *The oranges had nothing to do with our passion or love.*

She had not tasted anything orange for months. She still loved him as much as she had the day she left Sully.

How could she have been so blind to the truth?

The celebration was no less successful than the ceremony. The colorful processional wound through the streets of the village. The dancing, food, and drink that followed were enjoyed by all, as were the jugglers, acrobats, musicians, bards, and dancing bears. The church bells tolled for joy, and white doves of peace fluttered into the blue summer sky. The residents, high and low, along with the guests of Trentworth, enjoyed themselves for three days and nights. The Bishop of Somerfield declared it the best wedding he could remember attending ever.

When it was over, Emmalyn sent Julianna off to her new home with the last basket of oranges and the recipes. However, from the gleam in her new son-in-law's eye and the sweet way he treated Julianna, Emmalyn had no fear for her daughter's happiness. Aching with weariness and wishing that Hugh had been there to see the blissful smiles on the newlyweds' faces, Emmalyn climbed into bed. Knowing that she had done all she could for her daughter, she pulled the covers over her head and slept for an entire day.

Midafternoon, just after the ringing None, Hugh stood outside the arbor staring at the little orange tree. He had not given the sickly thing a close look since the day three months earlier when Emmalyn had left. That day he had decided to keep it, as he had promised her he would, instead of having the gardeners chop it for the mulch pile. He had avoided the bloody thing ever since. It reminded him too much of those mornings when he had found her fussing over it and insisting that love would make it grow. He would not be standing here now but for Fulk's insistence.

Hugh was aware of the steward watching him as he studied the stunted tree.

It still sat at the end of the line of tall, thriving orange trees, closest to the arbor.

"Do you see it, my lord?" the steward asked, pointing to that which he wished to direct his master's gaze. "There and there."

Hugh nodded. "Of course I see it. I am not blind."

Unfazed, the steward gave a short laugh. "Who would have thought?"

"Indeed," Hugh murmured.

Before either could say more, the trumpeting of a herald's horn shattered the silence. At the same moment a young page burst out of the castle door and ran pell-mell into the garden, babbling something about a lady and bowling straight into Fulk, who managed, just, not to fall over.

"Sir, the lady has returned," the page cried, skidding to a halt on the flagstones and regaining his balance. "She is here. Lady Emmalyn is outside the gate, as beautiful as ever on her white palfrey. She came back. My lord, she came back!"

"Contain yourself, boy," Fulk admonished with a frown. "A page delivers tidings, whether they be good or ill, with calm dignity."

The youth hung his head. "Yes, sir."

Hugh said nothing. Inside, though, his head was filled with questions, and a knot had formed in his stomach. Why was she here? What more could she want of him? Though he had avoided admitting it to himself, he had been miserable without her. Sweet *Jesu*, he had only last week begun falling asleep again without hours of sick longing in his heart. What right did she have, coming back here to disturb his peace of mind?

He had been glad to receive the plants she had sent, as she had promised, and he had thrown her invitation to her daughter's wedding into the fire. She knew how he felt. Did she think she could change his mind, to accept her on her terms?

Fulk's face was full of apprehension when turned toward Hugh. "Do you wish to grant entrance, my lord? Will you receive her?"

A moment ago, before Hugh had examined the tree, he would have sent her away without seeing her—at least he would have tried to do it. Whether or not he could have resisted the sight of her, he did not know. And it was beside the point. Scowling at the little orange tree, he grudgingly admitted that he could not turn her away without showing it to her. It would be unfair.

"Yes," he said to Fulk. "Admit her." He turned away, trying to think of some excuse, something he must do, that would take him to the other side of the island. "Show her to the chamber where she stayed before," he called over his shoulder, heading for the pear orchard. It was not the other side of Sully, but it would do for now. "I will receive her in the great hall when I am ready."

Sir Hugh would receive her, Fulk had informed her with a frown. She had been relieved when the steward had returned with that message after a long delay at the gate. She had feared he might not. She had no letter from the bishop to force his hand this time. She had only his goodwill and hospitality to depend on. He granted her admittance, though not graciously.

Anxiety tight in her belly, Emmalyn stared at the empty dark great hall. So Hugh had closed it up after she left.

The hearth was clean and cold. The tables had been cleared away and the shutters were just being flung open upon Fulk's orders. Fresh air and sunlight drifted into the lofty hall. She had left her maid and one of the castle chambermaids hastening to open and air her chamber for her stay that night.

When she looked down at the fireside chairs, she found them covered in a layer of dust.

"His lordship spends most of his time in the garden or at his writing desk, making notes about the garden, as you advised," Walter said as he arrived with a tray of food. When he saw her looking at the dusty chairs, he gestured to one of the servants. A maid quickly wiped down the chairs and the small table between. Walter set down a tray of bread, cheese, and orange honey. "Please sit, Lady Emmalyn. We are pleased to have you back."

"Thank you, Walter," Emmalyn said, looking over the food. She was so eager to see Hugh that she had no appetite, but she did not want to offend the cook. "This looks wonderful, but no orange honey for me, please." She picked up the honey pot and handed it to the cook.

He stared at it in surprise. "Yes, my lady. Is it not to your liking?"

"Oh, no, Walter," she said. "I am just abstaining from orange things right now."

Clearly puzzled, but too respectful to question her decision, Walter bowed and left the hall. Emmalyn settled into her chair. She was exhausted after the passage and getting her things and the seedlings unloaded from the cog and up the hill to Castle Sully. She was eager to see Hugh. Nearly an hour passed before he put in his appearance.

Her heart sank when Hugh strode into the great hall. He was frowning, a deep furrow between his brows, his eyes narrow, the corners of his mouth turned down. Otherwise, he looked well; clean shaven, his hair pulled back and tied with a leather strip, as was his habit when working. Her heart fluttered at the sight of him. But if she had held out any hope that his long absence was unrelated to her arrival, that hope died at the sight of him. It was obvious that he was highly displeased to see her.

"My lord," she began, covering her disappointment as best she could. "Thank you for receiving me, Sir Hugh. I have brought more seedlings that I have promised."

"There was no need for that," he said. "You could have sent them."

"I know, but I thought I would bring them myself, along with my personal thanks for the oranges and the news of Julianna's wedding," she said, ignoring his abruptness.

"And what do you want?" he asked, standing before her, his expression guarded.

She put her hand to her chest in a futile attempt to ease the tightness growing there with the knowledge that she had brought this wariness to his face. Life had disappointed him. She had disappointed him. So he had cut himself off from the world again. How would he welcome her declaration of her new understanding of love?

"As I said, I came to thank you. And I came to share some seedlings with a fellow gardener. If that is too much of an imposition, I will go."

"The boat will not return to Sully for a fort-night," he said. "You know that."

"I can find lodgings in the village," she said, clasping her hands before her. "You have been generous, my lord. I would not inconvenience you."

"No, that is unnecessary," he said, turning to signal a page. "You are welcome here. Boy, tell Cook we will sup now."

By everyone but you, Emmalyn almost added aloud.

The high table was soon set up, covered in a snowy white cloth, and laid for supper.

"There you are," Walter said, appearing with his pudgy fists braced on his hips. "Supper is ready to serve, my lord and lady. The lady ordered no dishes with oranges," the cook added, as if warning them of something they should know. It was enough to make her wonder if the cook had understood more about their experiment during her previous stay than he had admitted to her or Hugh.

Hugh cast her a curious look. "As the lady wishes."

What had he expected of her? she wondered.

They passed a quiet meal of flounder poached in an herb sauce served on white bread, buttered peas and crisp lettuce fresh from the garden, and cinnamon and honey cakes for a sweet. They sat side by side on the bench without touching knees or elbows. In truth, she felt that Hugh was taking care not to touch her. Their discussion of the garden continued, halting and awkward—as if they were strangers who had no real liking for each other.

At one point during the meal, Hugh had taken aside Walter, to speak about meal arrangements, she assumed. She did not hear what was said.

If Hugh had possessed any passion for her, it

had faded, she decided as they talked. She had been foolish to think of anything else.

"Truly, why have you come?" he asked at last, when the torches had burned low, the other benches were empty, and most of the great hall had fallen into shadows.

She hesitated. Should she tell him what she had come to understand about her love for him as she watched her daughter wed? Did he still care enough about her to want to know? From the coolness of his welcome, she doubted it. "As I said before, to express my gratitude. I do not come to ask anything more of you, honestly, my lord."

"No more oranges?" he asked, giving her a sidelong glance.

She shook her head.

"Tell me about your daughter's wedding."

His request surprised her. She always loved talking of her daughter; she began, speaking slowly at first, afraid that she was rattling on about details that he would have little interest in. Yet as she talked, he listened and even asked an occasional question.

"I believe he really likes her," Emmalyn said, leaning forward to speak of her new son-in-law.

"How could he not?" Hugh said, studying her, the hint of a bemused smile tugging at his lips. "She is your daughter."

The suggestion of a smile was such a pleasure to see and the compliment was so unexpected, Emmalyn was left momentarily speechless.

"That is kind of you to say, my lord," she finally managed.

"I have something to show you." He reached for her hand and drew her from the table. "Come with me."

Surprised and puzzled, she followed him out of

the great hall and down the familiar passage to the garden. After his obvious reluctance to see her, his haste to show her something in the garden was confusing. His grip on her was firm and unrelenting as he led her out the door into the fresh air and toward the arbor. Only a peachy glow of the summer sun lingered on the horizon, and a cool breeze blew in off the sea.

"The garden looks well, my lord," she said, admiring the arbor as they passed through it. All of the trees and plants seemed to be flourishing under Hugh's direction.

They stopped at the row of orange trees. The fruit trees had grown taller in her absence. She smiled at the sight of every branch heavy with fruit.

"And the little tree?" she asked, moving to the end of the row to find it sitting in the shadow of the others, as it always had.

"Look for yourself." Hugh took a torch from a wall sconce and brought it closer, the flames chasing away the shadows.

Emmalyn gasped the moment she saw the first one, a glowing white blossom. In the light of the torch she spied at least a dozen blossoms gleaming against the dark, glossy leaves. Though still smaller than the other trees, the branches were full of leaves and dotted with pristine blooms. Their fragrance, heavy and sweet, tickled her nose. "It survived!"

"I thought you would want to know," he said, watching her. "I would have given up on it but for my promise to you."

"So, my lord, are you not glad that I coaxed that promise from you?" she said, laughing at him in her delight. "This tree, too, will repay your efforts and bear you fruit."

"Indeed, I have you to thank," he said.

He shocked her by seizing her hand. And for a moment she thought he was going to raise it to his lips and kiss her fingers.

Their gazes met, her fingers still gripped by his. She felt a blush flood into her cheeks, and her heart fluttered with hope. Maybe he did still care for her. Perhaps there was still a possibility of love between them.

Chapter Nine

Guardedness came into his expression, shadowing his eyes. His smile faded. Gazing at her hand as if he did not know how it came to be in his, Hugh released her and stepped away. The halting awkwardness that had troubled them at supper returned.

Emmalyn's soaring heart faltered. Her spirits plunged. "I am pleased that you are happy about the orange tree, my lord," she mumbled, tucking her hand into her sleeve.

"Would you like to see how the plants you sent are doing?" he asked, avoiding her direct gaze, his tone polite, nothing more.

"Yes, I would." Once more hiding her disappointment as best she could, she inspected the new additions to the garden that had been made with the first shipment of plants she had sent. She admired his work and made suggestions about where the new seedlings might be planted.

"I look forward to planting them tomorrow," he said with courtesy.

"I would like to help," she said, suddenly overwhelmed with disappointment and an aching heart. "If you will excuse me, my lord, I wish to retire for the evening."

"Of course." He carried the torch into the castle and upstairs, where he bid her a chaste and proper good night in the hallway, just as he had the first week of her earlier visit.

When she closed her chamber door behind her, she sighed. Yes, she had been a fool to think that she could rekindle anything with him. He was lost to her, if he had ever been hers. Perhaps they could remain friends, but she was not sure she could accept that. For those few days after the blizzard, they had shared so much more, and she yearned for that intimacy of mind and body again.

She pulled off her cap and veil as she crossed the chamber to the bedside table, where her maid had left a candle burning. Laying aside the cap and veil, she turned toward the candlelight to untie her belt. She had pulled off her dress and rolled her stockings down when her eye caught the sight of something unusual on the pillow. She paused, squinting into the shadows to get a better look at whatever it was.

There on the white linen lay an orange, round, shiny, and promising. She sucked in a breath of surprise. Of bewilderment.

She snatched up the fruit and whirled around to her maid's pallet in the corner of the chamber. "Margery? Wake up, Margery. What is this doing here?"

Sleepily, the girl raised herself up on one elbow. "What is that, my lady?"

"The orange on my pillow," Emmalyn said,

impatiently standing over the girl. She did not usually trouble Margery if she was sleeping, but this was important. "How did it get here?"

"The cook brought it, my lady," Margery mumbled through a yawn.

"Was there a message?"

"Yes; let me remember," Margery said, blinking at the candlelight. "Something about his lordship would be glad to give you an orange a day if it makes you happy."

Emmalyn stared at the orange in her hand, trying to understand what the message meant. He had spent the afternoon with her, had shared a supper trencher with her, remaining painfully polite, even guarded the entire time. Now he offered to share an orange with her—*now* he offered an amorous invitation.

Orange in hand, she was out the door scurrying down the passage barefoot without thinking to take the candle. She knew the way to Hugh's chamber.

Hugh sat in the dark at his writing table, watching the moonlight move across his chamber floor. His garden log lay open before him. Soon after Emmalyn had left the isle he had begun to do as she suggested: make notes on the progress of the garden, just like a ship's captain entering weather conditions and garden events in a log. He had noted the date of the blizzard as the first entry. He wrote nothing about how he and Emmalyn had spent the night in the arbor, but he would never be able to look at that entry in the log without remembering their passion, their pleasure, and the sweet realization that there might be real joy in life as well as pain. And that Emmalyn was the one who could help him find it.

However, he had entered nothing for this day—the day of her return. The day he had stood beneath the pear trees in the orchard and realized what a fool he had been. Now his future hinged on one orange placed on a pillow. He did not know what to write.

The door to his chamber burst open. Hugh leaped to his feet. He knew who it was, but he had not expected her to make such a dramatic entrance.

"What is the meaning of this?" she demanded, marching into his chamber with her hair loose and nothing more than her linen shift covering her. He knew well enough what was under that shift. How her breasts filled and warmed his hands. The sweet smoothness of the inside of her thighs against his.

She held the orange out toward him. "Tell me, my lord."

Hugh cleared his throat. "You told me you had not had an orange for some time. I thought perhaps you would like one."

"I have not partaken of an orange because I knew you are distrustful of its influence." She gave an angry shake of her head. "You rejected my avowal of love because of oranges."

"Because of your belief in the *power* of oranges," he said, studying her. "I have never believed in them."

"Nor do I now," she said, advancing on him like a stalking lioness. "That is why I returned to Sully. To tell you that you are right. The oranges had nothing to do with what happened between us. I sat in the church and watched my daughter and her betrothed pledge themselves to each other, and I realized that love had nothing to do with what anyone eats. My love for you comes from the heart and from God. You were right. And I wanted you to know it. Then I returned to find you frowning and rude.''

"I have been miserable," he said. She said she loved him, he silently rejoiced. He reached for her hands. "And I have had time to reconsider my thoughts on the love you offered. Come sit with me by the window.''

She hesitated, glaring at him.

He was thankful when she put the orange on the writing table and accepted his hand, allowing him to lead them to the window bench in the moonlight.

"I, too, have given much thought to us," he began, admiring the silvery light glittering on her golden hair and limning her bare shoulders. "Emmalyn, you mean more to me than anything else in my life. The pain of living without you made me ask myself some questions. What if you came to me for the oranges? What if you professed your love under the influence of an aphrodisiac? What does it matter? I have six orange trees bearing fruit now. Emmalyn, I love you. You can have an orange every day if it pleases you. Just stay here on Sully with me. As my wife.''

She put a hand on his arm, clutching his sleeve and staring at him, her lips parted and without breathing. "But do you not see? It was my fear of unhappiness that kept me from believing in you and trusting our love. You do not need to feed me oranges to make me stay.''

"Emmalyn," Hugh said, covering her hand with his, "will you marry me?''

"Do you mean what you say, my lord?" she asked in a whisper. "Truly? Because to be loved by you is all that I ask.''

"Oh, yes, my lady," he said, gripping both of

her shoulders now. "I mean every word of it and will swear it on my sword before Father Paul if you like."

"No need of that." She slipped her arms around his neck. "Just kiss me."

Hugh kissed her, pulling her close, savoring the feel of her breasts pressed against his chest. He ravaged her mouth. Without releasing her lips, he scooped her up into his arms and carried her to his bed. And so they began their lovemaking in the moonlight. She was as passionate and responsive as he remembered. He gladly returned her passion.

The magic scent of oranges filled the air, and the warm smooth skin of their beloved moved beneath their hands. They found pleasure and joy in each other.

Two weeks later, with permission of the king and the approval of the bishop, Father Paul married them in a simple ceremony in the chapel of Castle Sully. Emmalyn wore an orange blossom chaplet on her brow, and Hugh wore his golden knight's chain for the first time since he had returned from the Crusades. It was time to put away the regrets and grudges of the past. He knew now such things did not matter. Surviving and loving was all that was important.

In his garden log, he wrote that day "Sir Hugh of the Isle of Sully wed Lady Emmalyn of Trentworth. Skies were fair, the breeze light and southerly, and prospects for the future bright."